retro retro

....

fictional flashbacks

retro retro

fictional flashbacks

edited by
Amy Prior

First published in 2000
by Serpent's Tail,
4 Blackstock Mews, London N4 2BT

website: www.serpentstail.com

Set in Plantin by Intype London Ltd.
Printed in Great Britain by Mackays of Chatham plc

10 9 8 7 6 5 4 3 2 1

contents

acknowledgements

....

Special thanks to Laurence O'Toole and Pete Ayrton at Serpent's Tail, my free email providers, and all those who helped in the search for contributors – Victoria Hobbs, Susan Corrigan, Cris Mazza, Nicholas Royle, Lucy Woollett, Joan Curtis, and Anne O'Daly.

'Let's Go' is extracted from the book *Not Her Real Name* by Emily Perkins, © 1996 Emily Perkins, reprinted by permission of Doubleday, a division of Random House, Inc. and Macmillan.

'The Love of Watches' by Tobias Hill was first published in *W – The Waterstone's Magazine*, no. 13, Spring 1998.

introduction

There's a place where the teddy boys hang out, all immaculate slicked-back quiffs and chewing gum. In the pub a few doors away the cider drinkers sit, comparing pan-sticked faces and back-combed black hair. The cinema on the corner is showing a revival of an old silent classic and in the diner close by people sip milkshakes on bar stools designed just as they would have been back then. Over the road there's the shop that sells the original bakelite kitchen dishes you once admired at your grandma's, except they cost more than you could ever afford and you wonder if your grandma still has hers. Pasted over the large advertisement on the board are fluorescent-coloured posters for some club on Saturday. You see illustrations of bell-bottomed dancers and recognise some of the bands from the days when you watched 'Top of the Pops' with excitement. A suited man passes by, tired from the office. He pauses briefly outside Woolworths to gaze at a plastic replica of the Millennium Falcon, the spaceship he is planning to buy, a toy that was his favourite when he was ten years old; one he used to fly in his bedroom, imagining he was Hans Solo.

Our pick 'n' mix attitude to retrospective culture is found in lots of streets in any city. In *Retro Retro* writers draw on our preoccupation with retrospective culture to develop sixteen original short stories.

According to US cultural critic Marshall McLuhan, the nostalgia of retro culture is a form of escapism from uncertainty: 'When faced with a totally new situation, we tend always to attach ourselves to the flavour of the most recent past. We look at the present through a rear view mirror.' This view of retro culture is a common theme in those stories that take place in one time, but have an aspect of a previous era, such as a character or an object. In Pagan Kennedy's 'Glitter', an art student in a transitional life-stage seeks refuge in a thrift store. In Brett Ellen Block's 'Future Tense', a frail old man living in a violent neighbourhood gains strength from his obsession with *Butch Cassidy and the Sundance Kid*.

Travel, always bound up with the uncertainty of new situations, provides a backdrop for a few of these stories. In my story, 'Miss Shima', a lonely Chinese woman, newly arrived in Britain, becomes preoccupied with the glamour of Hollywood musicals. Travel is also a form of escapism: it acts as a kind of cocoon, allowing characters more freedom to play with possibilities of time. In Eleanor Knight's 'Rosa', a touring Canadian music student has an encounter in contemporary Budapest involving '50s film star Jane Russell.

Other stories in the collection are simply set in the past, and these draw heavily on the writers' unique experiences and interests. In Emily Hammond's 'Doko Ni Iki Mas Ka', we observe life in an alternative US college in the '70s. Joyce Carol Oates provides us with an insight into '50s college girl New York in 'Strand Used Books 1956'. Cris Mazza takes us to '70s suburbia in 'His Helpmate'. Some stories flirt with 'metanostalgia'. In Susan Corrigan's 'Mr Pharmacist', set in the '80s at an original drugstore soda fountain, we become nostalgic about the '80s' preoccupation with the '50s.

Retro Retro brings together some of the best new and

established literary talent from Britain and the United States, who use their varied cultural knowledge to create a diverse fiction collection.

Amy Prior, January, 2000

brett ellen block

....

future tense

I was in the lavatory at a bus station washing my hands
when the man next to me began to cry. It was a frigid
evening in the dead of winter, 1978, and he and I were
the only people in the room. The man was dirty and
dressed in layers of ill-fitting clothes, clearly homeless,
but he didn't look quite as shabby and run-down as the
other men I'd seen sleeping on the snow-covered steam
grates outside the station. He took a rag from the pocket
of his frayed coat and wiped his face with it. I could tell
that he was young, probably not over thirty, maybe even
my age at the time – twenty-five.

We were standing in front of a long mirror over the
sinks, and he was staring at me as he wept, trying to
force me to acknowledge him. I couldn't remember ever
having seen a man cry like that, such unabashed and
earnest tears, and the honest truth was that I was almost
afraid to meet his gaze. When I finally did, he whimpered, 'There's a guy outside and he's dying.'

The man waited for my response. I didn't have one.
Though I wasn't shocked by what he'd said. As far as I
could tell, that was the sort of thing that happened in
bus stations at night. A buddy and I were traveling down

from Boston to Baltimore for the holidays, me to see my parents, him for his wife and son, and because of a snow storm we'd missed our connection in Newark, stranding us and another dozen or so people until the next bus arrived. Since we'd gotten to there, we'd already seen one woman vomit, two men fist-fighting over candy from a vending machine, and a handful of drunken bums stumbling through the station singing a rousing chorus of 'Oh Holy Night'.

'And I thought Moscow bus stations were bad,' my friend, Yuri, had said.

Yuri was Russian and he didn't speak much English, which meant he didn't speak much at all. Back then, that was just the kind of friend I needed. I'd met him at the heating and air-conditioning repair school I'd just dropped out of. The classes were short and easy enough, but a box of cheap tools upon graduation wasn't worth the effort. Those days, nothing was.

Something inside of me, just beneath the skin, had gone numb without reason or justification. Everything that had interested and concerned me ceased to be important. It was as if my brain had been pumped full of air, causing the world to go mute, then life was reduced to a matter of going through the motions. So having a homeless man tell me that some guy outside was dying had about as much effect on me as the water I'd dried off my hands did.

'You look like a doctor,' the man said hopefully. 'I bet you could help him.'

The fact that he thought I looked like a doctor told me a lot about the sort of person I was dealing with. The reflection that met me in the mirror above the sink was haggard and unshaven, in dire need of a shower, a bed. I looked as careless and grim as I felt. I'd been on a bus for the past six hours, sweating in my heavy clothes, which were wrinkled and not even clean to begin with. I figured that of all the people stuck in the station that night, he hadn't sought me out specifically. My guess, I was the first person he'd stumbled upon and he was desperate, willing to stoop to flattery. Still, I liked the idea that I could be mistaken for a doctor.

'A water-heater is about the only thing I'd be able to fix,' I confessed.

'Good enough,' he said, with the nervous optimism of someone who was either truly scared or truly crazy. He told me his name was Ben, then he broke for the door, expecting me to follow him. And to my surprise, I did.

Yuri was sitting on a bench waiting for me, his feet resting on his suitcase. He had his cassette-player out and he was listening to these 'Teach Yourself English' tapes with an ear-piece. We'd barely spoken on the bus ride down from Boston, but I'd heard him whispering his lessons, his thick accent turning the phrases into a kind of chant: 'I went to the store. I am going to the store. I am going to go to the store.'

When I rushed past in pursuit of Ben, Yuri called to me, his English choppy but distinct, 'James, where are you going?'

Most of the other passengers had fallen asleep, sprawled out on the rows of benches, and like Yuri, none had noticed Ben, who was sprinting toward the other side of the station. 'Come on,' I shouted to Yuri and kept going.

When Yuri caught up to me, he was panting from carrying both of our bags. He passed me mine gratefully. He was a small but sturdy man in his forties with the hard hands of a farmer, the life he had left behind for a better one, fixing refrigerators in America. He had been forced to leave his wife and their young son in Baltimore with her relatives in order to move to Boston. A cousin of his had offered to let him, but only him, live there rent-free and to help pay for him to learn a trade. It was an opportunity he couldn't pass up.

Yuri kept a miniature calendar in his wallet to keep track of how long it would be until he could see his family again. 'I am thinking of tomorrow, not of this day,' he would announce, crossing out each date. 'I am keeping my head there so this day will go more fast. But sometimes I am worrying tomorrow will not be better. That tomorrow is other word for not so soon.'

As we jogged through the station, both of us already out of breath, Yuri asked, 'Why we are running, James?' I didn't have a good answer. Chasing after Ben had been more of a reflex than a conscious decision.

'If I tell you, Yuri, you'll stop,' I said and guided him into the corridor that I'd seen Ben turn down.

The sound of our shoes hitting the floor filled the deserted hallway and ricocheted off the red, tiled walls. With the bright, fluorescent lights and the smell of cleaning fluid, it was as if we were running through an empty swimming pool. Ben was standing in a corner at the end of the secluded corridor, near the back entrance to the station, and someone was lying on the ground below him.

'Hurry up,' Ben hollered. 'I think it's too late.'

I wasn't prepared for what I saw. Ben's statement earlier in the washroom appeared to be accurate. Slumped on the floor was a man in his late fifties, blood drying in his silvery beard, one side of his face beaten black. One of his eyes was swollen shut, and from the way he was holding his arm, it must have been broken, maybe some ribs too. His leg was propped up on his blood-stained jacket, no doubt hurt as well. Yuri put his hand to his mouth, appalled.

'See,' Ben said to me, sniffling. He bent to comfort the man on the floor. 'It's going to be okay, Marvin. I found somebody who can help.'

'Pardon me,' Yuri began, resting his suitcase on the floor, 'but please to be telling me what is happening?'

Marvin lifted his head when he heard Yuri's voice. He opened his good eye and squinted at him.

'Butch?' Marvin said. 'Butch, is that you?' He tried to smile, but his lips pinched into a wince.

'Sorry,' Ben said. 'Marvin can get a little confused. He has this thing about *Butch Cassidy and the Sundance Kid.*'

Marvin groaned, and Ben pulled a bottle of Coke from his pocket to give him a drink. This was some sight, I thought. Me, a flakey kid, some delirious old man who'd been beaten to a pulp, and a Russian immigrant who probably thought we were all nuts. It seemed like the opening to a bad joke, and I was part of it. It had yet to dawn on me exactly what that implied.

Once Marvin started sputtering on the soda, Ben capped it and stood. 'So can you help him, right?'

Yuri knelt to examine Marvin's injuries. Gravely, he pronounced, 'We need to be calling police or hospital or . . . what is word?'

'An ambulance? No way.' Ben was shaking his head vehemently. 'Marvin won't let those emergency people near him. He's afraid of them. Said he saw them electrocute somebody once.'

'Electrocute?' Yuri didn't understand. 'But his leg, I can tell it is broke.'

Ben stood his ground. Yuri turned to me, bewildered. I knew I should have had a plan, but nothing would come to me. Marvin was a mess and what he needed was a doctor, a real one, pronto. But since he wouldn't let us get help, there was little more I could do other than ask Ben, 'Who did this to him?'

'These two jerks who deal dope around here. They're always cruising up and down this street. But they're not big time. They're just bullies with a car. All Marvin did was give one of them the finger.'

'They kicked me when I was down, Butch,' Marvin wheezed. 'They fought dirty. I needed you, Butch. Where were you?' His question was cut short by a fit of coughing that sounded like nails rattling in a paper bag. When he caught his breath, he went on. 'I woke up outside in the snow. I couldn't feel a thing. Not my fingers or my toes. I licked my lips and they felt like cold rubber.'

This description was apparently for my benefit. Marvin probably thought he was helping me with my diagnosis. From what he'd said, all I could tell him was that I sympathized. I knew exactly how he felt. I'd been walking around for the past few weeks without feeling my legs move or my feet touch the ground.

I had stopped going to school, let all of my bills go, and was about to be evicted. Why bother, I thought. I could no longer see anything on the horizon. The future wasn't bleak, it was blank. Returning home to my parents, to their inevitable disappointment and disapproval, only promised to make matters worse. But I had no other choice. I'd been bounced out of every college in the greater Boston area for screwing around and skipping classes, and my parents had stopped sending money. They were fed up with second chances. For them, this would be the last straw. Worse yet, I wouldn't be able to explain my behavior to them. I couldn't even explain it to myself. All I knew was that somewhere, somehow, a switch had been flipped, one that I sensed I wouldn't simply be able to talk myself into flicking back to normal.

'I just wanted to die with my boots on,' Marvin declared, then resumed coughing.

Yuri pulled me aside. 'Back at my village, I have seen men like this, hurt in accidents with tractor or kicked by mule. This man, Marvin, he has boot-print on side of his head. We cannot let him be falling to sleep.'

'I'll take your word for it,' I said.

Marvin had stopped hacking and was now dozing, so Yuri clapped loudly. 'Do not fall to sleep, Marvin. You have to stay awake.'

The wind, which was howling outside, was blowing so hard that it made the back doors tremble, sending cold gusts seeping inside. Marvin mumbled something, then nodded off again. Ben was wringing his hands. 'Oh God, man. This is bad,' he kept saying. 'This is really bad.'

Yuri and I exchanged glances, then he went and crouched down beside Marvin. 'Sundance,' he said, his accent dulling the word. 'It is me. It is Butch.'

Marvin opened his eyes. 'Butch?' he whispered. 'Butch, where are we?'

'Sundance, you have to be staying awake. We are making last stand.'

'Okay, Butch,' Marvin said with effort. 'I won't fall asleep on you. I'll be right here at your side.'

Yuri shrugged at me. He was as surprised by what he'd said as I was.

Ben's face brightened. Yuri nodded to him to get out the bottle of Coke for Marvin, then Yuri started rummaging through his suitcase and handing me clothes, all of his clean socks and shirts.

'I have seen this movie *Butch Cassidy and the Sundance Kid*. It is good movie,' Yuri told me. 'Cowboys and outlaws. I wanted to be cowboy when I was young. Did you want to be cowboy, James?'

'Sure,' I said, suddenly remembering. Growing up, I'd had recurring dreams in which I was a different cowboy every night: Billy the Kid, Roy Rogers, Jesse James. They were the most vivid dreams I'd ever had, technicolor visions of yellow prairies and wide, blue, cloud-dotted skies, galloping horses and fearsome shoot-outs. Each morning I woke up a hero. I hadn't thought of those dreams in years.

'Sometimes, when I was child,' Yuri said, 'I was taking rope and making . . . How do you call it?'

Ben glanced up from tending Marvin. 'A lasso?'

'Yes, a lasso. And I would say, "Yee-ha", like I was American cowboy.'

'Yeah, I used to do that too,' Ben said eagerly. 'But I could never get the lasso to work.'

'Oh, it is simple,' Yuri claimed proudly, closing his suitcase. 'I could show you sometime. No problem.'

'Really?' A grin spread across Ben's face.

Yuri took a shirt from my hand and began ripping it into strips.

'What are you doing?' Ben asked him.

'Socks to clean blood. The shirt for his leg.'

'I can make it, Butch.' Marvin made an attempt to sit up, but fell back in pain and closed his eyes.

'No way, man. You've got to do something, man,' Ben pleaded.

'Stay awake, Sundance,' Yuri ordered, snapping his fingers, then he tossed me another one of his shirts, indicating for me to do as he was. In confidence, he said, 'Quickly, James. We have not much time.'

I began tearing up the shirt without even considering that, most likely, it was one of the only ones he owned.

'As a boy, my father gave me book on cowboys,' Yuri said as he gingerly threaded the strips of cloth underneath Marvin's leg. 'He bought it on black market for my birthday. I cannot guess how much it cost. The book was having pictures of cowboys on horses and cowboys with guns, every kind of cowboy. It also tells how to make lasso. That is where I learned.'

Yuri laid a folded sweater on each side of Marvin's leg to brace it, then carefully tied the strips to immobilize it. Marvin was holding his breath to bear the pain.

'But one day, a boy from my village, Vassily Ubussakov – his name I remember – this boy stole my cowboy book. When I go to get it back, he says to me, "If I cannot have it, you cannot." Then he throws my book in fire.'

We all held a stunned silence until Ben protested, his lip quivering, 'That's not right, man. That was your book, man.' He began pacing the hallway, biting his lip. 'That was your book.'

Marvin seemed to have come out of his stupor. 'I'm real sorry about your book, Butch,' he said, lowering his eyes in deference.

Yuri finished binding Marvin's leg without another word. I had stopped shredding his shirt and was holding the pieces limply in my hand. 'Thank you, James,' he said, taking what was left of his shirt.

It seemed to me that I had never been less worthy of thanks in all my life. I had dragged Yuri into this situation and now he was bailing me out, a man whose last name I had never asked. At that moment, I was glad he didn't really know me, didn't even really know the language. Because if he had, he might have truly perceived how low I had let myself go. The feeling of debt overwhelmed me, as staggering and unbearable as the raw draft that was shuddering through the seams of the back doors, raising chills on all of our skin. I deserved to be cold, I thought, a lot colder than I was. It would have served me right for the way I had been acting. I owed Yuri and I needed to pay him back.

'Oh no,' I heard Ben murmur.

A set of headlights had swung across the dark, snowy street outside the rear entrance. Ben rushed over and pressed his face to the glass. He stood there for a minute, then motioned me over. In a low voice, he said, 'That's them, Derek and his stupid sidekick. That's who knocked Marvin around. I can tell by the car.'

'They have nothing better to do than drive around in a snow storm?' I asked.

'No,' Ben replied.

The battered, old Lincoln Continental was cruising up the street. Whoever was driving must have seen us because the car slowed down, then pulled over in front of the entrance, just feet away. I hoped the glass doors were locked, but there was no way to be sure unless I pushed one, and by then, the man behind the wheel was staring right at me. His head was shaved bald and he had a brutal face, the kind that made me want to look away, but at the same time told me not to let him out of my sight.

Ben edged back from the doors, eyes frantic. Derek, the driver, cranked down his window.

'Long time no see, Benny boy,' he shouted. 'How's that friend of yours?'

Ben's mouth fell open, but he didn't respond.

'He's fine,' I answered. 'Thanks for asking.'

Derek raised a doubtful eyebrow. 'Oh yeah?'

'Sure. He's out roping some doggies right now.'

I heard Yuri say my name, cautioning me, but I waved him off.

'Who are you, asshole?' Derek demanded. He sounded drunk.

'The name's James,' I said. 'Jesse James, in fact. Ever heard of me? I'm one of the toughest outlaws who ever lived. So I'd watch my step if I were you, kemosabe.'

'This kid's mental,' Derek said, elbowing the man in the passenger seat who I couldn't make out. 'Did you see what I did to that old-timer?' he asked me.

'Yup.'

'And?' he sneered.

Yuri was patting Marvin's cheeks to keep him awake. He was fading fast. 'James,' Yuri urged, 'I do not think . . .'

'Well, now that we've met,' I said, hooking my thumbs into my belt loops, 'I just want to know one thing. Do you wax that head of yours or pull the hairs out one by one?'

Derek's eyes narrowed. There was less than three feet of sidewalk between us, and he appeared to be gauging how long it would take for him to get to me.

I crossed my arms, cocky, cavalier, egging him on. The adrenaline racing through me made my bones feel like wire. The cold wind pouring in from outside was buffeting my face, reminding me of its shape and contours, something I'd lost track of along with the rest of my body. The hum of the fluorescent lights was as loud as an alarm. I lodged myself squarely in Derek's glare and said, 'You ought to get a hat, partner. How can you even see yourself in a mirror with that high-beam shine?'

'James,' Yuri repeated, his voice now brittle with tension.

I couldn't make up for what had happened to Marvin

earlier, the beating he had braved, or for what had happened years ago to Yuri, the burning of his beloved book. The bad guys had not lost and the good guys hadn't won. The world was not right, it was not fair, and it was not clear. But I believed that, for an instant, I could make it so.

Derek said something to the passenger, then opened the car door slowly, letting it rock on its hinges. He was wearing heavy boots, and his leather jacket had been worn gray in places, as if by his muscles from the inside out. Snow was whipping through the air, pelting him, but he did not seem to notice. It took two steps before we were toe to toe with only the door between us. Derek stood close enough to fog the glass with his breath.

'You think you're funny, kid?'

'No, I think you are, partner. A big guy who beats up old men, that's as yellow as they come.'

Derek motioned for his buddy to get out of the car. A barrel-chested man clad all in black, who was equally as big and doubly as frightening as Derek, joined him at the door. His silent, hulking presence personified every dark, shadowy menace that I had ever dreamt of or thought I could dream up. And now I was face to face with him.

It was a showdown, and I was out-numbered and out-sized. My heart was stomping in my chest, my pulse thundering in my ears. Yet I felt better than I had in weeks. But then the fear really kicked in, meaningful, comprehensible. I realized what I had gotten myself into and my knees literally shook.

'You were saying, partner?' Derek snarled.

Then, in the reflection on the glass door, I saw Yuri step up to my side. Ben appeared on the other, forming a wall. We were smaller, skinnier, and far less intimidating, but there were three of us and two of them. Derek gave us the once-over and snickered, unimpressed.

I put my hands out by my hips as though ready to draw two imaginary guns and said, 'What I was going to say was that you shouldn't polish that head of yours, partner. Because I've got to tell you, the glare is blinding me.'

The force with which Derek hit the door was enough to send the three of us back a couple of steps, but the door didn't budge. It was locked. Derek shook it and kicked it and, finally, put his fist on the pane, contemplating what to do next. The other man remained still, ready to back Derek up; he was unnervingly calm, with lifeless, unreadable eyes, and that terrified me.

All of a sudden a police car rounded the corner at the far end of the street. It was heading toward the bus station. Derek backed off, cursing.

'It's the cavalry,' Ben uttered, amazed.

'You're one lucky lunatic, Jesse James,' Derek spat, jabbing his finger in front of my face, then he bolted for the car. But the other man waited, staring me down. In his hollow eyes I saw my fate, diverted, the punishment for all I had and had not done avoided. And those eyes told me that I had been lucky, this time and so far, but that someday my luck might run out.

'Let's go. It's the cops,' Derek commanded and the man returned to the car, then Derek peeled out, sending a flurry of snow from the car's roof into the air. The tail lights made the snow glow red until the car was out of sight.

Yuri gave an audible sigh of relief. Then Ben began whooping and cheering, 'Chickens. Yellowbellys. Yee-ha.'

Yuri wiped the glass clear of condensation and tried

to flag down the police car. 'They see us,' he exclaimed, smiling. 'They are coming.'

'Butch,' Marvin whispered, his breath burbling. 'Butch, did we win?'

I watched as Yuri and Ben rushed to Marvin's side. We all had to hope it was not already too late.

To this day I can remember Marvin's face as it was right then, the strange, swollen mask of a man who had missed out on the stand-off of a lifetime, yet who was happy, in spite of his pain, to know that the fight was being fought. Even after the police had come and questioned us and the emergency medics were wheeling him out on a gurney through the snow, Marvin's expression never wavered.

A crowd of the other stranded passengers had gathered around to watch the scene. Somebody said that the next bus was pulling in and that we would be departing soon. The snow storm was dying down. Yuri and I would get on the bus and make it to Baltimore by morning. He would get to see his family and I would go home.

I never saw him again, nor Marvin or Ben. I do not know what became of any of them, and for that, I am partly glad. Because in my mind I had created futures for them, whole lives, and they were doing well. Things had changed and gotten better. I never returned to Boston, not even to collect the things I had left. After Christmas, I did, however, send a package back there, to Yuri care of the school where we had met. In the package were new shirts, some sweaters and socks, and a book about cowboys.

I am a professor now, teaching classes of my own in Engineering, and spending most of my days on the kind of campus I'd ducked and ditched for so many years. At times, I catch myself studying my students while I lecture, noting whether they slouch or yawn and checking their eyes for any sign of that old sensation. I do not think of that night in the bus station often, but occasionally the memory comes involuntarily, out of the blue, an unconscious reminder when I am losing faith in the world or myself. Then the thought returns as vivid as the dreams from my youth, and I feel honored to see the faces of those three men.

Once Marvin and Ben had gone in the ambulance and the police had cleared the crowd, Yuri and I were left to gather what remained of his things. I picked up his clothes while Yuri folded them as neatly as he could and re-packed them. When I leaned over to get the last scrap of his clothing, something poked me in the back of the leg and I jumped, my nerves still keen and frazzled from all that had happened. But then I realized that it was only the lid of his suitcase, touching me in a place where I could finally feel it.

pagan kennedy

glitter

It was 1980 and I'd come out of sleazy suburban Camaro-filled Maryland to save myself in art school. My first years in Baltimore, I wore paint-splattered jeans and constructed a video installation, just like everyone else. But then I began to think the whole art-school thing was pretentious. Sophomore year, I found myself blowing off classes and wandering around Fell's Point, Baltimore's own heaven of strip joints and junk shops. When summer came, I moved into a loft down there, which I shared with a girl who made giant bugs for some John Waters film.

And then I discovered Miss Patty's store. Her place was a few blocks from where I lived, hidden on one of the side streets. From the first moment I pushed open the door, I knew I belonged in that cavern of clothing racks and piles of scarves and old drugstore displays and gothic lamps with glass thingies on them. I started going every few days. I'd try on a pair of Carmen Miranda heels and a satin slip then teeter over to the mirror to look at myself – a glitter rock tramp, a Frank N. Furter sexpot – and think 'This is it.' What I'd found at Miss Patty's was what I thought I'd find in art school, a place where people might love me for my own freaky, sex-obsessed, shy self.

At first, I was scared of Miss Patty, who ran the place. She had the face of an old-maid teacher, seemed stuck up, and was always leaning on the counter gabbing with this or that friend. When I bought something, she would ring it up without looking at me. But even then, she was someone I wanted to know.

One day, walking past the store, I saw a 'Help Wanted' sign taped up. I peered through the dusty window. Miss Patty was alone in there, talking on the phone. So I went right in and waited until she hung up.

'I want to apply,' I said, and then, when she didn't react, I added, 'you know, for the job.'

'Do you have any experience? Because this is a high-class establishment, as you can see.' She gestured toward a mannequin covered in glitter, which sat under a poster for *Faster Pussycat, Kill, Kill*.

'I worked for an ice cream store. In high school.'

'I meant experience in the world of couture. I insist that all my girls train in Paris.' She lifted one lazy hand to her lips and pretended to take a drag on a cigarette.

I did my best to play along. 'Oh, but I did train in Paris. House of Baskin and Robbins.'

'Well then, that's different,' she touched her hair. 'I am quite familiar with Mademoiselle Robbins. She does wonderful work. I'm so glad she sent you to me.' Miss Patty held out her hand limply and we shook over the counter.

'Thank you,' I said, confused. Miss Patty hadn't so much as cracked a smile; she almost had me believing that I'd flown in from Paris.

'There's just one other thing. What sign are you?'

'Scorpio.'

'Oh dear,' she said. But then she patted the tight curls on top of her head, as if pushing some idea back in place. 'Well, we'll just make do. We'll just have to, because I'm Aquarius and Scorpios are like poison for me. You can look it up for yourself in Linda Goodman's *Love Signs*,' she waved at a worn book on the shelf behind her. 'Not that we're going to be lovers,' she laughed. 'The book has other applications, you know.' She reached over and patted its spine. 'It tells you how you're going to get along with anyone, if you read between the lines.'

So I became Miss Patty's girl. She called me either Miss Julie or Mistress Julie. 'When you are Miss Julie, you're a timid little shop girl who scurries around helping customers. But when you are Mistress Julie, you are one of those dominatrix saleswomen who always screech, "You break it, you buy it." Is that understood?' she said to me the first day, and I nodded.

But as it turned out in the following weeks, she didn't much care how I acted. Mostly, we gabbed with the people hanging out in the store, or went for coffee, or sorted the clothes. On trash days, we'd cruise around in Miss Patty's Impala, stop whenever we saw a truly fabulous pile of fabric and jump right in. The truth was, most of the clothes in our store came out of the garbage.

We tried to clean the stuff and sew it up, but usually we couldn't do much. You just had to use your imagination with our clothes. You had to picture what they must have looked like before the rips and stains, or maybe how they might gleam in the dark cave of a club at three in the morning. It was that kind of imagination we used all the time, everyone I knew back then, especially Miss Patty. Because, underneath the satin dress and blonde wig and pink scarf, underneath the silk stockings, she kept her dick crammed into a halter-type device so it hardly showed. I know this because she used to complain about how much it hurt to the other transvestites. Sometimes I couldn't help from imagining her dick inside that thing, packed as tight as a snake in one of those fake cans of peanuts you buy at a joke shop.

So school kind of got lost in the shuffle. Basically, I just stopped going. I didn't miss it. In art school they handed you five popsicle sticks and told you to make a statement. But at Miss Patty's store, we were the statement – our bodies decked out in boas and turbans, our insane lives.

At least, I think my life was insane, but maybe it only seemed like it at the time. I slept around a bunch, but now I wish I'd been even more of a slut, while I had the chance. We took it for granted then, casual sex. You could go home with any skinny guy wearing a leopard-skin jacket over his hairless chest. In fact, that kind of Iggy Pop clone was our ideal man back then. We lusted after guys with bad posture, sickly skin and eyeliner, never suspecting how – in just a few years – sleeping with an obvious junkie or bisexual would seem suicidal.

Anyway, about eight or nine months after I started at Glad Rags, I met this guy in a band that was a copy of the Knack or something. The Dead Beats, that's what they were called. They were playing in the living-room at a party, using effects boxes and patch cords all covered with duct tape, so feedback kept screaming out of the speakers. Between the noises from their equipment and their music, they pretty much cleared the room.

Later, after the hostess put on a tape and people began moving back in to dance, I turned around and this guy from the band was standing beside me. I knew he was one of the Dead Beats because he was wearing their uniform – black jeans, white shirt, skinny tie.

He says, 'She shouldn't be playing the Ramones,' referring to the tape that was on.

And I'm like, 'What's wrong with the Ramones?'

'There's no purity there.' He took a swig out a bottle of Scotch – not a normal-sized one, a tiny one like they give you on an airplane. Everyone else was holding beers, dangling bottles from limp hands. You hooked the bottle under its lip with two fingers, so it swayed and sloshed beside your leg. This was the standard 1980-punk-rocker drinking pose. The Dead Beat guy was trying to hold his drink that way too, only his bottle was so small he had to pinch it between his thumb and forefinger. He thought he was so cool but really he looked like he was carrying around a bottle of beer that came from a dollhouse.

'Purity? That's what you want?' I said. 'Your music didn't sound very pure.'

'We have shitty equipment.'

'So what bands are pure? Tell me.' Why was I even talking to this guy? Because despite his obvious jerkdom, his lips pouted just right and I guessed that he had a smooth, sinewy chest underneath that button-down shirt.

'Kraftwerk is pure,' he said, taking another nip from the bottle.

'How about the Pretenders?' For maybe a half-hour or so I quizzed him on bands – pure or not pure – but I never figured out what the hell he was talking about. Which led to me climbing into his wasted Nova and going home with him. The whole way, I had to sit wedged behind his guitar case and listen to him rant about sine waves, the mathematics of music, stuff like that. It was worth it, because he turned out to be great in bed. I still remember a moment from that night like a bleached-out Polaroid: his slick, white body sliding across my stomach while his eyes tunneled into mine. He never stopped staring into my eyes. It was like he was after something beyond an orgasm, some way – besides the obvious one – into my body. 'Oh Jesus,' he groaned and then curled around me and fell asleep.

Next morning, he was back in asshole mode again. I woke up because he was shaking my shoulder and saying, 'You've got to leave.' No kiss, no nothing – he was all business now, holding a Fender bass by its waist. 'I need to practice.'

'Geez,' I said, getting up slowly, feeling bruised.

'We have a gig, our first real gig, in a few days. I have a lot of work to do.'

'Okay, okay. Cool your jets. I'm just trying to find my dress.'

He sat down next to me. 'Listen, um,' he struggled for my name, 'Julie. It's just that it's not great timing, you know? Maybe later. Why don't you give me your number?' He searched around for some paper. It was only then that I noticed how bare the room was, just a folding chair in the corner and some metal shelves for his clothes.

As I walked out of the apartment, I saw all the depressing details I'd missed the night before. In the kitchen, a card table and some more folding chairs, a black-and-white poster of The Specials – and no food on the shelf except for a jar of peanut butter. 'Rick,' I said to myself because I'd just remembered his name. I opened the door and blinked in the late-morning light of a Charles Village street, row houses lined up along the sidewalk. The view from his porch reminded me of those pictures they used in high school to teach us about vanishing points and perspective, one of those pictures where the buildings are nothing but a bunch of lines converging on a horizon.

'Rick,' I said to myself again, and for a moment I thought maybe I understood his thing about purity. Maybe the barren black-and-whiteness of his apartment had something to do with his music. Maybe he imagined that, with all the frills stripped away, he could get to the truth.

'Well, look what the cat dragged in,' Miss Patty said.

'I'm sorry. Am I late?'

Miss Patty was sitting in the back room, fiddling with the vintage sewing machine. 'I was referring to your general air of *déshabillé*. What is that trashy little thing you're wearing? I love it.'

'I went to this party last night and never made it home. I'm kind of hung over.'

'That, my dear, is the secret of glamorous people everywhere. Hangovers. So anyway, who was he?'

I sat down on a pile of clothes, resting my head against the wall and told her about the jerk.

'Is he an Aries?'

'Are you kidding? I don't know his sign. I don't even know his last name,' I said. 'Anyway, it was just a one-night thing.'

But I was fooling myself about that, because when Rick called two days later, I jumped at the chance to see him – even though it involved going to a club to hear his crappy band play. I'm telling you, I was desperate to get laid again by this guy. I didn't care how lame he was as a person, he had this sexual intensity that I had never properly experienced before. I was used to art-school guys with their apologetic fucks.

The night of our date I had the worst clothing crisis of my life; I must have tried on every dress in my closet. Back then, clothes were my drug. Most people drank or got high; me, I tried on clothes. I used to think the right outfit could protect me from anything. In a ratty tulle dress or a faux-cheetah coat, I became queen of the night, all hard eyes and junkie glamour, untouchable, able to seduce any guy. I believed the best clothes lingered even after I took them off, like ghosts on my naked body.

I finally found just the costume to make Rick adore and fear me – antique beaded shirt, toreador pants, see-through high heels and globby earrings. I looked and felt like an extra from a 1950s movie about drug-crazed beatniks. In my clunky high heels, I walked around on top of the clothes on the floor, trying to pick up. I especially concentrated on clearing the bed, because we might come back here. If we did, I wanted Rick to see how beautiful my bed was. I'd found this amazing brass headboard on the street and hung antique Christmas ornaments all over its metal curlicues. It looked like something out of Dr Suess.

Anyway, because of my clothing crisis and the subsequent cleanup, I was late, which turned out to be a good thing. I showed up at the end of the Dead Beats' set and didn't have to wait long before Rick jumped down from the stage, sweat shining on his face.

'Hey,' I said when he found me at the bar, 'I've never seen this place so crowded.'

'Oh, they're all here for the ska band.' He wiped his forehead on his sleeve, sat down. 'Anyway, at least you made it.'

'Yeah, though I'm kind of wondering why I bothered, considering the way you kicked me out the other day. After I left your apartment, I thought "He has to practice his bass right now? It can't wait a few minutes?" Geez, what kind of excuse was that?'

In the reddish twilight of the club, his eyes looked like two holes in his head. He was staring me down, refusing to glance away. 'That was the truth, though,' he said. 'When I woke up, all I could think about was practicing. I'm trying to get this sound when I play, like a broken power tool or something.'

I found that really depressing, the way Rick took himself so seriously and yet was so bad.

'Still,' I said, 'if you sleep with someone, you should say something nice to them in the morning, even if you don't mean it.'

'I never say anything I don't mean.' He kept his eyes locked on mine.

'Never? Well, that's got to be an exaggeration. What about when we were making out in your room and you said you'd never been so turned on in your life?'

'I meant that. I really clicked with you,' he said flatly.

'But if you liked me so much, why'd you act like I was dirt the next morning?'

'I didn't. I just told you I wanted to practice.'

'Oh, you just told me you wanted to practice,' I said sarcastically. 'Well, I could just tell you some things that would make you feel pretty shitty. It's like, you can't go around saying whatever you want to people.'

'You can with me,' he said, downing the shot that had appeared beside him on the bar. 'It would make me really mad if you lied to me.'

'It's not that I lie to anyone. It's just that I censor stuff out, you know.'

'Well don't,' he said. 'For instance, right now, tell me whatever you're thinking.'

I was annoyed by this for one second, and then the next second I thought, 'Why not?' 'Okay,' I said. 'That jacket you're wearing? You probably think it's really New Wave – really retro Buddy Holly – but it obviously came from J.C. Penney's or something and was made two years ago. It's acetate. Listen, we've got these antique prom jackets at the store where I work; I'll get you one of those.'

'Okay, that's interesting to hear,' he said. His voice went up an octave, he was so upset.

So I changed the subject. 'Hey, what do you do? I mean, where do you work?'

'I don't,' he said. 'I'm in grad school at Hopkins. Physics.' He stared at me like he was challenging me to say how uncool that was.

'Hmmm. Well that explains a lot.'

'Like what?'

'Oh,' I say, 'like your whole thing about purity, which I still don't understand.'

His jaw tightened. 'It's very simple. Have you ever seen an oscilloscope? When I play, I have a picture in my head of how all the sound waves would look if they were mapped out on an oscilloscope. You know our music isn't just a barrage of sound. It's an intricate design.'

'But, I don't know, is that really the point? What about the feelings behind?' I said timidly.

And he stared off, then snapped his head back toward me. 'Yeah, well . . . so, where do you work again?'

I told him about Miss Patty's, how I'd ended up there and stuff. I could feel myself getting happy, just talking about the place.

He listened with his eyes narrowed. Then he's like, 'Julie, you shouldn't have quit art school. You're too smart to be working at some store.'

'Well, for your information,' I said, stirring my whiskey sour, 'art school didn't exactly require any brains – just the capacity to swallow a lot of bullshit.'

'Hey,' he held up one hand, 'cool it. I was only telling you what I thought. Has it ever occurred to you that you quit art school because you were afraid?'

'Oh,' I said, cocking my head, 'well as long as we're talking about what we think, has it ever occurred to you that your band sucks?' Then I winced. 'Ouch. I didn't really mean that. I'm sorry. You just made me so mad I had to think up the meanest thing I could say.'

'No,' he said. 'It's fine. I knew from the beginning how you felt.' He started blinking fast and then looked down. 'I have to admit, I really wish you liked what I'm doing. You're the most interesting girl I've met in a long time.'

'Well, look, I've never been into that assaultive kind of music. It's just not my taste, okay? What do I know? You all could be the next big thing.' I leaned close to him. 'But it doesn't matter how your band does. Because you know what? You're really, really good at something else besides playing the bass. You're the best I've ever had.' Then I kissed him, twisting my tongue down deep. He opened up his mouth to me, tilting his head back and letting me in like so few boys know how.

Which led to us going to my place. We huffed and puffed on the Dr Suess bed as the Christmas ornaments jingle-jangled and the mattress farted under us. Wedged against Rick's body, I felt like some kind of crazy snake, curling and hissing.

Only in the morning–after he left and I woke up with my beaded top and toreador pants crumpled underneath me – did I remember the identity I had concocted the evening before, the hard-eyed beatnik chick. With any other guy but Rick, my clothes would have set the tone for the whole date: I probably would have ended up doing the Watusi on the dance floor or saying 'Man' a lot. But with Rick, the clothes didn't matter. I was always naked around him.

So he became my boyfriend though there were some annoying aspects to it. One day, he noticed some collages I'd taped up in a corner, stuff left over from art school. He'd never even given my Dr Suess bed a second glance, but he went apeshit when he saw these stupid pieces of paper with colored squares and triangles and ink smudges all over them. 'Julie, these are brilliant. Why don't you do stuff like this anymore?'

'Oh please,' I said. 'I did those for a class, but they just didn't mean anything to me.'

'Well, you should keep it up.'

Right then, I realized something about Rick: He wanted desperately to be an artistic type, but he didn't have the faintest clue how to do it. Which is why, I guess, he came up with scientific theories about punk music. His heart never told him what was good and what was bad.

Oh, but at Miss Patty's we ate it, we wore it, we dreamed it – though we would never have used a word like 'art' to describe that thing, the only thing we could always trust to make us happy.

In the store, we had a shelf full of paperweights made by a friend of Miss Patty's. These plastic globes were filled with water and had glitter that spun around when you shook them. Inside each paperweight there was a little gay guy wearing chaps and a leather jacket; his lumpy feet were attached to bright-green Astroturf-type stuff, and a plastic rainbow arched above him. The outside of each paperweight said, 'Greetings from Over The Rainbow'.

I always thought of the store as being like that – a garish, beautiful bubble inside of the straight world, a place where you could be whatever you wanted and no one would bat an eye. But maybe it was too much like a plastic bubble for Miss Patty. She lived in the back, her room partitioned off by a velvet curtain. She almost never left the neighborhood around the store. Everyone in those few blocks knew her; she was – amid the drunks and whores and old sailors who inexplicably always seemed to be missing an arm or leg – an upstanding citizen, a pillar of the community.

Of course, she did get hassled, even in our magic circle. Once these jocks came into our store and started laughing at the rubber brays and other sexy stuff we kept up front. Then one of them suddenly notices Miss Patty: 'Jesus Christ,' he says to his friends, 'that's not a lady.'

'And you, sir, are not a gentleman,' Miss Patty called out in her shrillest voice. I thought there was going to be trouble, but somehow the frat boys just slunk out. Miss Patty had this power over people.

Maybe that's why she had so many groupies. Well, not groupies, but people who hung out in the store just to be around her, or maybe for the free heat. There was Leo, with wild hair and a crooked smile; and Angie, a sixteen-year-old piece of jailbait; and Eddie, an old biker who'd had to sell his bike; and Rod; and a bunch of others. They annoyed me sometimes – milling around, getting in my way – but they also felt something like family.

So of course I dragged Rick into the store to meet everyone, and of course it was a disaster – which wasn't Miss Patty's fault. She beamed when she saw him, 'Rick – Ricardo! Welcome to the glamorous world of slightly used fashions.' She held out her hand to shake, but Rick kept his own hands in his pockets, so she ended up adjusting her hair.

'Hi Rick,' Leo called from the broken-down chair where he'd been camped out all day, chain-smoking. He wore a flowered jacket, black jeans and long red fingernails. He looked pretty filthy because he was residing in a men's shelter, but I have to say for him that his nails were always done perfectly, not a chip.

'Did you know,' he announced to no one in particular, 'that the Dalai Lama is coming to America next week? I really want to get tickets, because I met him once and he was just a fascinating man.' When Leo said 'fascinating' he opened his mouth wide and put one hand on his chest to show how emphatic he was.

I started laughing. 'Leo, come off it. You didn't meet the Dalai Lama.'

'Why yesssssss, I did, Miss Julie. Back when I lived in India.'

I thought Rick might appreciate how ridiculous this whole scene was, but he just grabbed my hand and said, 'We have to go.'

When we were on the street, I wriggled my hand away from him. 'Why are you being so obnoxious?'

'Those people are a bunch of lunatics. You're the only sane one in there.'

'They're my friends, okay? I just wanted you to meet my friends.' My voice got loud. 'You are so closed-minded.' I went on and on like that, yelling at him right there in the street and it turned into another one of our frightening fights.

Whey did I stay with Rick? Because he introduced me to hysteria and eventually I got hooked on it just like junk. Our sex, so scary in its intensity, was what first got me started. But later, the sex hardly mattered. It was the fights I got horny for, the screaming and screaming until I felt drunk with hatred.

I've never been that way with anyone except Rick. In general, I'm a reasonable person. I compromise. I keep my cool. But because we started out telling each other the so-called truth, later on this translated into a particular kind of cruel and lawless fighting.

'You are a fucking college boy,' I'd spit. 'You are just a visitor in my world. In five years, you're going to be sitting in an office somewhere making a pile of money.'

'Oh, your world, huh? You call hanging out with a bunch of transvestites your world? Do you think Miss Patty really cares about you?'

I'd narrow my eyes. 'You're pathetic. You just don't have a clue.'

And so it would go.

Maybe after all Rick said I wanted proof that Miss Patty loved me, or maybe I was just high-strung during this terrible period. Anyway, I'd be hanging clothes or something and then just suddenly burst into tears and drop to the floor, all hunched up, hugging my knees.

'Oh dear, what is it?' Miss Patty would call. 'Oh you poor thing.' I wanted her to come over, touch my back, stroke my hair, but she never did.

'Goddamn,' I'd weep, 'my life is so horrible.'

'Oh please don't cry,' she'd say. 'Why don't you take a break. Give Rick a call.'

She didn't want to see my pain and she didn't want me to see hers – though I always tried to pry.

'Are you going out with anyone,' I'd ask.

'Well, I went dancing with my crazy beau from Buenos Aires last night,' she'd say. 'My dear, Argentina is a country in which fascism flourishes. Need I say more? The man had to have everything his way.'

'I don't get it, Miss Patty,' I'd say, ultra-serious. 'What does that mean? Did you sleep with him?'

'Sleep with him?' she'd howl. 'What are you suggesting, my dear? Do you think a man like that would let me sleep?' And then she'd laugh at her own naughtiness.

I knew that underneath the crushed velvet and orange fringe of all her stories, she was hiding some secret pain. She kept it all trussed up, like a dick in a halter, never showing it to anyone. And since I'd gotten so addicted to truth-telling with Rick, this seemed like a pitiful way to be and I think I wrote her off at that point.

Well, things got worse and worse, until finally after about six months, I managed to break up with Rick. Though of course when I say 'break up' it wasn't like that, a clean break. I backslid a lot. But the day finally came when he showed up at my loft, apologetic as always, and I just had no stomach for it. 'I still love you, you know that,' I said, crying. 'But I'm going to close this door and you're going to leave.'

After I got him out of my life, I had a lot more energy for other things. That summer, a friend of mine was acting in a Shakespeare-in-the-park play and she convinced me to volunteer to build the set. I constructed huge trees with purple leaves and ladders hidden behind them so Puck and the fairies could climb into the branches. The play bombed, but *The City Paper* said my set was brilliant, and from there on in I started getting a lot of free-lance jobs – sets, props, wardrobe – enough finally to quit the store.

When I told Miss Patty, I hugged her, feeling the skinniness of her back beneath my hands and smelling her incense-y perfume.

'Oh dear, Miss Julie. How am I going to manage without you?' she said, and finally stroked my hair like I'd always wanted.

'I'm still going to hang out here, okay?' I said, but even then had an inkling that things would change. Fell's Point was starting to look awfully clean – yuppies had been buying up buildings in our neighborhood and stripping away the form stone, the painted screens and the concrete steps. Suddenly, we had all these brick houses to contend with, not to mention brass door knockers, and worse, the business people walking to their cars in the morning while we were coming home from clubs.

Sure enough, Miss Patty's landlord sold out to The Ski Shop and she had to leave. But she seemed to take it okay. 'Wait until you see the new place I'm renting,' she raved to me. 'It's so glamorously seedy, you won't believe it. It's right beside a bar with one of those flashing neon signs.'

Her new store did better than ever, partly because it was near a sort-of-rich neighborhood and also because antique clothes had suddenly become trendy, even in the straight world. She painted the floors white and got the smell of piss out of her stuff. But she always seemed sadder in the new store. It was a more official kind of place where you couldn't have a bunch of street people hanging out.

I stopped in every few weeks, and at first it was a girls-having-lunch kind of thing with us. We'd gossip for a while; we'd even do a little business if I was looking for costumes. And then at some point in the next few years, things changed between us – I started showing up at the store to check on her because I was worried.

'Forgive me if I'm not very chipper today,' she said once. 'I just can't keep up my Suzie Sunshine act these days.'

'You don't have to put on an act for me,' I said.

The thing was, people had begun getting sick. Some of them I knew from the store; most I didn't know, but Miss Patty told me about them. She'd framed all their pictures and hung them on one wall of her room and she kept a votive candle lit underneath. She took me in back one day and showed me that wall. And there was Leo, his cheeks hallowed out, holding a balloon and smiling. And Rod in a wheelchair, also smiling, just before he went back to Minnesota to die.

The candle flickered and sent up a smell of church, and the doomed men watched me from inside their frames, and Miss Patty said, 'We were so naive back in the old days, weren't we? I just adored being naive.'

Rick used to say I wasn't really part of Miss Patty's world, and he was right, because it was only a matter of time before I left it. Eventually, I got a set-design job, health insurance, a sane boyfriend. And standing beside Miss Patty that day, it was like I was on the outside and she was on the inside with the glitter falling down all around her.

cris mazza

....

his helpmate

1978

Instead of wedding presents, Dale's parents had loaned Loralee and Dale $350 so they could get the apartment they wanted. The deal was: the money would become a gift in nine months when Loralee proved she wasn't pregnant.

The place was a pretty nice one-bedroom set-up with a garage downstairs. That's why Dale wanted it – a place for his band to rehearse. The group he'd played with in high school could've continued to get gigs at school dances the first year they were married, but Dale said this wasn't the band that was going to make it – big brass sections like Chicago and Blood Sweat & Tears were already old news – so he might have to fish around for a while. He only used the garage to jam once before the band broke up. The other guys went off to college.

'To become *band teachers*,' Dale said, bashing around the kitchen, getting a glass of milk. Dale's high school band director had been an old fart who drank in his office and let the students use the practice rooms to make out.

'Did you hear me?' he said.

'Yeah, along with a million things crashing – I'm not *deaf*.'

'Well, you didn't answer.'

'I didn't think I always had to answer everything.'

'Well, sometimes you act like this's just where you stay until you're allowed to go back to wherever it is you go.'

Where she went was a trade school for glorified nurse-aides who would make minimum wage when they graduated and got jobs. The school had been a wedding present from her mother.

1979

Even though the band hadn't been good for much more than pocket money, it was hard to make the rent each month after the guys broke up. Loralee got food stamps and only paid half the gas and electric bill at a time, letting it increase so much that it took a big chunk of her first three or four paychecks from her new job driving a school bus – which she got in January after quitting the medical-assistant school – to finally pay it off in April, a few months before their first anniversary.

Dale couldn't convince the unemployment office that his old band was a job. Once a week he went to a local music store and gave a drum lesson to one student, but the kid quit to join a baseball league sometime in March. Dale came home and jumped on the bed like a trampoline, hitting the ceiling with his palms.

'Happy?' Loralee asked.

'You wouldn't believe the relief to be rid of that snotty little dickhead.' Then when Loralee didn't answer he said, 'You're not going to start arguing about money, are you?'

'When have I *ever*?'

'This's just the time I can see you starting.'

'Lay off, will you?'

'How about if I lay *on*?' He'd stopped jumping and was beside her on the bed, squeezing her breasts, then began to pant and pushed her to her back. She opened her legs and winced because she wasn't quite ready, but by the time he finished it didn't hurt so much anymore, just felt a little numb.

'Hey,' he said, 'we don't want to be having babies right away. Shouldn't we start using rubbers?'

'You think I haven't taken care of that already?'

'So what'd you do – get *fixed*?'

'Har-de-har.' It itched lying next to him when they were sweaty. He had quite a lot of hair on his body, but they could both tell it was thinning on his head. He said it might be because he wore a ponytail in high school, so he got a haircut and wore it halfway to his shoulders. He grew a beard too and had it for almost a month. The next time he told Loralee her tits were too small, she said he didn't have to worry about going bald because he could just turn his head upside down.

When he shaved he said he was doing it because the beard would be too hot in the summer. Then he said he was shaving because he had an important audition coming up. An established club band had advertised that they needed a new drummer. Loralee went along with him to where the band was rehearsing in a nightclub. The tables were all shoved into a corner and a Mexican boy was polishing the floor with an electric buffer, but the band leader shouted at him to get out of there. It took longer for Dale to set up his drums than it took for the band to decide not to hire him, so while Dale put his set away again, Loralee asked the leader why they didn't want him.

'We need more than a disco beat, sweetheart,' the leader said. 'Can you sing?'

'Fuck you.' But she was smiling.

The first day of school in the fall Loralee wore leather jeans and a navy flight jacket with a pair of cowboy pistols in holsters. At the first bus stop, after the kids got on, she stood at the front of the bus facing them, her hands on the pistol butts, feet spread, and said, 'Now don't nobody give me no trouble.' Then she realized they were all kindergartners and first graders who'd probably never been on a bus before, staring at her like a movie. She stopped wearing the guns, and the leather pants were too hot anyway. She put an ad in a singles newspaper and sold the pants for $35. Dale said whenever they sold something, that could be their grass money. He bought it from one of the guys in his old band who was selling for a living.

Up until Christmas a lot of the mothers met the bus with their kids, and at least once a week one of them had something to complain about: someone stole their kid's lunch, someone was spitting, someone had a water pistol and was squirting everyone, someone was pulling hair. Loralee looked back at the mothers – standing on the sidewalk below the driver's side window – the same way the kids usually stared at her. One day she said, 'These kids just sit here, they don't *do* anything.' She usually didn't think about the kids or pay any attention to them while she drove. She drove the same bus every day, the kind with ripped dark green vinyl seats that stick to bare legs, a horizontal sticky black plastic steering wheel, gum on the stainless steel frames of the seats and in the ledges of smeary windows, ribbed rubber runner down the center aisle which she was supposed to sweep every day but the sand could never be completely brushed away from the grooves.

During Christmas vacation, Dale agreed to go dancing, but they ended up staying at their table all evening, hardly talking, as Dale listened to the band. One of the trumpet players was a guy from his old band who'd gone to college. Dale rested his chin on his hands on the tabletop. At the first break, Loralee asked him if he was going to go talk to his old friend.

'I don't have anything in common with future band teachers,' Dale said.

Loralee went to the restroom, then on her way back stopped by the back of the stage where some of the band members were smoking cigarettes. The trumpet player, Mick, remembered her. 'Dale is here too,' she said.

'You two still married?'

'He's right out there.' Loralee pointed through the microphones and wires.

'Getting bald, isn't he?'

'He's been trying to get a gig, Mickey. Know of anything?'

'There're just too many drummers around, Loralee. Guys with a lot more experience. Hell, Dale can't even read music.'

'He can't?' Loralee looked out at Dale. It seemed like he was asleep on the tabletop, but then she saw his hand moving. He was drawing something. He picked up the salt shaker, poured some on the table, then resumed drawing.

'Just tell him to keep trying, that's all I can say,' Mick said.

'Okay.'

'So what've you been up to? Have any kids yet?'

'Hell no!'

'Well, tell Dale to keep trying!' Mick laughed.

'Bastard.' She grinned, then looked at Dale again.

The band had to go back on stage, so Loralee went back to the table. She swept up the salt which Dale had finished drawing in. 'Wanna go home?'

'Naw, let's stay and hear how terrible the second set is.'

'They're not so bad. We could dance or something.'

'Naw.' Dale leaned back in his chair and stared at the ceiling.

'Mick says your chances would be better if you could read music.'

'That's 'cause he *has* to or he'll flunk outta school.'

Loralee ordered a drink. Dale took out a half-used joint, lit it, took a few tokes, then snuffed it out again. 'How the hell am I gonna learn to read music?'

'Let's get a book. You can learn at home.'

'Who gives a damn what *he* thinks. Drummers don't need to know any notes.' The band started a tune, the lights dimmed and a flashing colored strobe began rotating over the dance floor. Loralee moved her chair a little closer to his. He lit the joint again, cupping it in his hands to hide it, then put it out after they'd taken some tokes and put the rest in his shirt pocket. 'What a goddamn crock of shit.' It looked like he was scratching his chest, but he was feeling the joint through his shirt pocket. 'I guess I'll hafta learn to read music.'

Loralee found two beginning music books, one for piano, one for drums, and brought them home to Dale, which didn't leave any money for grass for a while. He was watching television, sitting on the couch with his snare drum in front of him, tapping it with a drumstick.

So Dale memorized the names of all the keys on his electric keyboard and learned how rhythms were written.

He tapped out all the patterns in the drumming book while he watched afternoon reruns of *The Honeymooners*, *I Love Lucy*, and *The Andy Griffith Show*. Loralee listened from the kitchen or bedroom. When there were long stretches of laughter without dialogue, she rushed into the living-room to see what Lucy was doing.

When Dale wanted more grass he said they could sell the electric keyboard, a wedding present from the old band members.

1980

They gave her a junior high route in January, so Loralee did finally sell the keyboard to one of the kids. Then Dale went to see one of the other guys from his old band – the one who sold them their grass. The guy set Dale up in business.

'The trouble is,' Dale said, 'I've got to know people who want to buy, and I don't know too many people anymore.'

'That's true,' she said. The brown paper sack on the kitchen counter held four sandwich bags of grass.

'So maybe you could help?' Dale said.

'Who do *I* know?'

'What about the kids on your bus?'

'Come off it, Dale, they're in junior high!'

'That never stopped me from smoking grass.'

'God, that's a little different than *selling* it to them.'

She did manage to sell one of the bags to a fifteen-year-old who hung around the junior high but didn't go to school there.

'What about some of the teachers at school?' Dale said. 'Are they all geezers?'

'Some of them aren't too bad,' she said. 'There's the one who looks pretty cool, I think he teaches something good like art, but I don't *know* him . . . and I'm not going to call anyone *mister* while I offer to sell him grass.'

By that time, Dale had smoked almost all of one of the remaining two bags.

She found an ad in the newspaper saying that Mick's band was playing Fridays and Saturdays at one of the beach motels. That wasn't the name of the band, but that's what she called it when she told Dale.

'Let's go hear Mick's band again,' she said. 'Maybe they've improved.'

'Nowhere to go but up,' Dale said. Usually he wore a baseball cap with a beer emblem on the front, but he was holding it, resetting the plastic snaps. She noticed how bald he was getting, touched his head with her palm, smoothing the hairs back.

'Careful you don't wear any more of it away,' he smiled weakly.

She made him dinner on his twentieth birthday. She'd already turned twenty-six weeks earlier, so they made it a double birthday. He said he wanted to make love. They lay down with him on top, his eyes looked dull and lifeless, sort of glazed over, but he seemed to be smiling. Then nothing else happened. He dozed and drooled on her shoulder.

The next Friday, Loralee told Dale she had to bus some kids to school for a night choir program and wait there to bus them home. She went to hear the band by herself. She did a lot of dancing in the first set, but hardly looked at her partners. She watched Mick pump his pelvis while he played his trumpet. As soon as the first set was over, she made her way to the stage. Mick was emptying spit from his valves.

She touched his arm. 'Hey, Mickey, can we go some-where and talk?'

He didn't answer for a moment, but his eyes dropped below her face. She'd worn a mid-length skirt, loose tank top and boots. 'Sure.'

'Where?' she said. 'Not outside, if that's okay.'

'Sure, wanna sit at a table?'

'No. Are there any secret places?'

'How would I know?' Then he smiled. 'Let's look.'

The band had been playing in the motel disco, near the bar and restaurant. After searching around the employee lounge and supply rooms, they found a closet-sized room with a lot of light switches, meters and gadgets that looked like thermostats.

'So what's the big secret?'

'Not a secret,' she said. 'A favor – I need a big favor. A *real* big favor.'

Mick took a flask from his pocket and drank. 'Want some?'

'Thanks.' She swallowed, then sighed. 'You think you could get Dale into your band?'

'You two *still* married? We've got a drummer, we don't need another.'

'He's learning to read music, he needs something, I hate the sound of this, listen to me, I'm begging, aren't I?' She giggled and reached for the flask again. 'I just mean, it would just be something to do . . . to help an old friend.'

'But what the hell are we going to *do* with him?'

'Let him shake the maracas, sing a song or two, *any-thing*.' One of the straps of her tank top was hanging off her shoulder. She put it back up, but it fell again. Mick drank from the flask, looking at her shoulder. She'd tied her hair back with a piece of yarn, but it had loosened while dancing, so she pulled it off the rest of the way and combed her hair with her fingers. Mick reached over his head to the hanging light-bulb and hit it, making the light swing. The shadows flipped across their faces.

'I always wanted to do that,' he said. She smiled – they were acting like two middle-aged people at a class reunion, but he still had a full head of hair and she wasn't fat. Then Mick put his hand on her bare shoulder. He drank again, holding the flask with his free hand, handed it to her and she drank the remaining few mouthfuls. He had his other hand on her other shoulder and her stomach felt like hot oil. With both hands he pushed her top down to her waist. The flask made an echo-y sound when she dropped it. He was moving closer, his hands on her tits, thumbs flicking her nipples. She leaned against the wall; the plaster was clammy and made her shiver harder, but she wasn't cold. Whatever was in the flask had made her throat burn all the way down. Mick seemed to suck on her mouth instead of kiss. Then with one hand he unbuttoned her skirt and let it drop around her feet. Loralee kicked it away, and Mick stepped back. 'Leave the boots,' he said.

They both giggled and shushed each other. He kneeled on the floor beside her feet, ran his hands up her legs, then pulled her underwear down. 'C'mon.' He took her hand and tugged until she kneeled then sat, and he pushed her backwards until her shoulders hit the cold concrete floor.

'You're not gonna tell me you're doing *this* for Dale's sake, are you?' he asked. 'Or do *you* wanna sing in the band too?'

'Yuckity-yuk.' She raised and bent her knees which made it considerably easier for him to penetrate.

He kept moaning, 'Oh my god, oh my god,' over and

over, then, 'you're not going to get pregnant, are you?'
She didn't answer and he didn't ask again. His body
slapped against hers as he made each thrust. Her breath
was pushed out of her and she sucked in another.

When he finally finished, he grabbed her butt and bit
her shoulder. 'Oh my god,' he said again. Abruptly he
jumped up and pulled up his pants. 'What time is it?
Can you hear the band?'

'I don't know. Mickey, will you call Dale?'

He was tucking in his shirt, stopped and looked at her.
She stretched, lifted a foot, barely touched his leg with
the toe of that boot. 'I'll come listen if you do.'

'I'll see,' he said. 'I don't make the decisions.'

Smiling, she dropped her foot to the floor again, knees
bent, legs parted, just slightly.

'Yeah, okay, I'll call him.' He picked up the flask and
left.

After she brushed away as much dirt as she could
reach on her back, shoulders, bottom and legs, Loralee
put her skirt and top back on. She found her underwear
thrown into a spiderweb in a corner.

Dale was having headaches and wouldn't allow the radio
to be turned on. He watched television, sometimes
without any sound, but usually with the sound on very
low. The only station they could get clearly was an independent, no news, no sports, no prime-time shows, just
reruns. Dale breathed with his mouth open.

'Your drums are rotting in their cases,' Loralee said.

'Let 'em rot.'

'You don't mean that. What if someone called you for
a gig tomorrow?'

He looked up at her, then turned back to the television
screen. He stared at Andy Griffith without smiling, then

looked at his hands. He looked at the palms, then the backs. The backs of his hands were freckled. Loralee sat on the arm of the couch and looked at the top of Dale's head. He couldn't wear his baseball cap when he had headaches. Without turning toward her, he groped for her and put his arm around her waist.

She wasn't home when the call came from Mick, but Dale told her about it. 'He says they need me as an auxiliary percussionist.'

'That's great!' Loralee squealed. 'When's the first gig?' It sounded a little unreal to gush like that, but he didn't seem to notice anything weird.

'I told him I'd think about it.'

She stared at him. His eyes seemed to be retreating into his head. 'Why?'

'It's second fiddle. And the rest of the band hasn't even agreed yet. It's like they feel *sorry* for me. Shit. He said to come to their next gig. He said to be sure to bring you too.' Dale was filling a glass with water at the kitchen sink. When he returned he asked, 'Do I look pale?'

'No more than usual.'

'So I told him we'd be there – it's tonight, okay? If I feel well enough, that is.'

She wore tight faded jeans she'd found at a yard sale and a T-shirt with a picture of a rock star (she wasn't sure who it was) on the front. Dale wore his baseball hat. He'd showered but was sweating again already. 'I think something's wrong with me,' he said.

They met Mick behind the band's stage and he offered them his flask. Loralee took several big swallows, but when she offered it to Dale, he shook his head. 'Just listen at first and see what you think, then come on up and sit in,' Mick said to Dale. 'We're thinking of adding

a lot of extra percussion effects and need a guy to do it.'
He sort of poked Loralee in the back after she turned
around to go back out to her table.

The last tunes in the first set had no brass, and before
the band even banged the first note, Mick was pulling
her out of her chair to dance. 'I arranged the set this
way,' he said, smiling. He danced her to the other side
of the floor, then led her back to the dusty closet while
Dale jangled a tambourine and the band hacked out
'Sister Golden Hair' followed by 'Mr Bojangles'. Mick
said, 'We're letting Dale do a *long* improv solo on that
one.'

'Har-de-har. You think I'm putting out again just
'cause you're letting him air-fuck a tambourine?'

'Think of it as his job security.'

An expert squeeze to his balls and he finished halfway
through 'Sister Golden Hair' so Loralee was out dancing
to 'Mr Bojangles' by herself right in front of the stage
while Mick was still gasping pop-eyed on hands and
knees in the closet. Dale winked at her.

tobias hill

....

a love of watches

She has been observing him for some time when the noon muezzin begins. The sound shimmers like a heat haze over the Istanbul Grand Bazaar. She crosses Fur Merchant Street towards the watchmender's stall. Only his worn cap and face are visible behind cluttered shelves. The woman goes closer, noticing his hands, their steadiness. Watchworks are spread out on the worktop in a shining mess of brass and jewels.

He opens a watch in a single movement and holds the curved halves in the crooks of his thumbs. The call to prayer echoes down from the Pigeon Mosque. It has been years since the watchmender stopped work to hear muezzin, and longer since he has prayed. He is Turkish, and his religion is a private matter. He can hear Misha the Russian eight stalls away, chopping the heads off river bream, but the woman makes no sound. The watchmender extracts the mechanism and lays it out. Gems and flywheels glitter like fishguts.

'How much to clean a watch?'

He looks up when she speaks, his eyes lidded but sharp. The woman is holding a grey watch case. She has the skin of a north European; rich, white, verging on blue. It makes the watchmender cold to look at her.

She holds out the box. 'The arms are broken.'

'Hands,' he says. 'A watch has hands. No arms.' English is not her first language, he thinks. The accent forms low in her throat, sentences rising into questions.

'Can you fix them?'

'Of course.' He takes the box, still considering the woman. Under her linen clothes she is all height and bone, as if she ate more nourishment in childhood than she will ever need again. The watchmender feels an urge to feed her market food; mutton broth with eggs, or *borek* pastries with clotted cream.

He looks down. The grey box is surprisingly heavy in his hands. 'It will take days. If you are a tourist, maybe you don't have time.'

'I have time.'

'Ah. But you are German, no? *Sprechen sie Deutsch?*'

'Yes. No. I am from Austria.' The watchmender nods, dropping his head. He is making conversation; the woman's nationality is of no interest to him. He opens the grey box. Inside a watch is laid out flat, snug as a gun in its velvet cavity. Carefully, he takes it out and holds it by the thick, dark strap. His hand doesn't shake. His eyes close as he listens to its sleek tick.

It is a man's watch, very simple, and also very beautiful. The numerals are black Arabic, and the leather of the strap is darker than oxblood. An evening timepiece, the man thinks; the gold is a little heavy for daylight. Under the twelfth numeral is the maker's name, Patek Philippe of Geneva. There is a smoky odour on the metal, from the strap's old leather or the woman's skin. The watchmender knows he will remember it for the rest of his life as the smell of perfect things.

'It is a good watch.' Her voice is defensive. A wave of dizziness sweeps over the man. He puts the watch down gently on the worktop, not letting the gold click, not looking up at the woman.

'I cannot mend this watch. I am afraid – ' His smile is thin and unhappy. 'It is too good for me. Too old. The gold is very pure. I am afraid I will damage it. But the people who made this will mend it for you – if you send it to Geneva, they will even tell you about it. Where it was bought and sold – '

'No.' He glances up, surprised again. Her voice has become hard as bone. 'I brought it to you. How long will it take?'

He doesn't answer. Already the woman is getting out her diary, writing a name in blue ink, *Eva Kaltenbrunner*. Tearing off the page. I will never see a watch like this again, he thinks. She holds out the paper to him and he takes it.

'Okay, okay. Five days. I will write a receipt – '

'No. I will be here in five days.' The Austrian turns to go, caught up in the crowd of lunchtime shoppers. The watchmender sits quite still while she leaves, the box in his hands. Istanbul moves around him with its smells of Bosporus fish and new cardamon, the pods still on their long stalks, the flowers white with thin blue veins.

His name is Ismet, and he is a careful man. For three days he leaves the watch alone, cautious of obsession. At night he dreams of the Austrian woman as a child. Her father is reading her a poem in English. He is losing his hair young; black strands are combed flat across his gaunt temples. He wears a black suit as if it were a uniform. His lips move slowly over the words.

A was an Area Arch,
Where washerwomen sat;
They made a lot of lovely starch
To starch Papa's cravat.

On the man's wrist is the watch, bright as an oil spill. Ismet cannot hear any more over the tick of the watch.

By Tuesday the market is too hot for work. He closes the stall at lunchtime and takes the bus home to the Pera district, climbing the concrete stairs to his ninth floor room. The windows are open, and the apartment is filled with sunlight, the smell of kebabs and the sound of distant radio music. Ismet takes off his shirt and fetches the watch from his cashbox. There is a chipped plastic table in the window-light and he goes to it and sits down, a lean, tanned old man, the curtains blowing in around him as he works.

He opens the watch and peers inside. It is older than he expected, a 1920s manual movement. The balance wheel rests motionless between its pierced rubies. Only the hairspring moves, shivering in its nest of jewels. Ismet holds on to the gold back, keeping it where he can feel it.

He winds the rotor and the watchworks spring into life. He times them, counting off minutes against a stopwatch. For once, the naked movement disturbs him. It reminds him of fish out of water in the morning market, gills working the air. The gold watch-back is warm inside his fist and he opens his hand, turns it in his fingers and stops.

There is writing on the inside of the disc, clear incisions in the soft gold. The words are German and Ismet works through them, frowning. *To my friend Ernst Kaltenbrunner, Chief of the Security Service. Linz, May 1942. With gratitude, H.H.*

He sits back. For the first time in years he thinks of the war, the fear of waiting for invasion. The ugliness of swastikas, their broken legs and arms. Tangled with light, the curtains blow into Ismet's face. He swears and pushes them away, stumbling upright, the chair falling over itself behind him. The watch is still in his hands and he puts it back in its box. It is darker now and the air is cold, as if he has lost hours.

Ismet puts his shirt back on and goes out to eat. It is still early and he walks for forty minutes, killing time. At the Pera Glassware Factory he catches a group taxi into the city centre. The restaurants are just opening, and he buys food and drink to stop his thoughts; cracked-wheat bread and yoghurt, stuffed marrows and meats, raki alcohol diluted to the whiteness of milk. It is the small hours before he stumbles home.

He dreams of the Austrian. Her father is reading to her again. It is a lesson, Ismet sees; the father is teaching her English through children's poems. His eyes are hollow and intense in his thin face.

> *B was a Bottle blue,*
> *Which was not very small;*
> *Papa he filled it full of beer,*
> *And then he drank it all.*

The child is half asleep as he reads. He strokes her fair hair.

A telephone begins in a distant room, and a woman's voice cries out in accented German. The child opens her smiling eyes as Ismet wakes.

Sun comes through the apartment windows. It is late afternoon, and Ismet has slept through a whole working day. He dresses quickly. There are four ten-dollar bills in the cashbox. He puts them and the watch in his jacket pocket and goes down the unlit stairs. The bus back into town takes more than an hour, the rush-hour traffic grinding around it. At Teksim Square Ismet gets out. Between highrise banks and hotels is a Watches of Switzerland shopfront. Ismet goes inside and stands, catching his breath.

There are no customers. The shop air smells of raki alcohol. In front of the marble counter a man in a green suit is sweeping up broken glass. Ismet calls out and the man swears.

'Ismet. What are you doing here?'

'Selim.' He is stung by the younger man's rudeness. He points at the broken glass. 'May your soul be safe from harm.'

'Forget it. You smell like you sleep on the streets, not just work there.' Selim glances behind him. 'The manager locks up soon – '

'I won't be here to embarrass you. Selim, I need a favour.' He brings out the Austrian's watch. Selim whistles.

'You want to sell this? I'll buy it myself – '

'No – I just want to know where it was sold. The makers will have details, and you know people in Switzerland. You could telephone them. I would pay you.'

Selim is frowning, his thick eyebrows bunched together like muscle. 'Dollars? How much?'

Ismet takes out the notes. 'Please, Selim. Then I will leave.'

The younger man grunts an acceptance. Picking up the dollars and watch, he disappears into the back of the shop. There are leather armchairs in the showroom and Ismet sits down, but their softness is uncomfortable and after ten minutes he goes to the window. Outside, the Istanbul sky is already darkening to a sulphurous yellow.

'Ismet.'

He turns round. Selim is at the counter, fax paper coiled between his hands. He reads to Ismet in his loud, bored voice. 'Patek Philippe, gold rotor, twenty-seven jewels. The case is 1940s, but the movement is 1929. A marriage of parts. Marriages are less valuable than the original. Me, I never married.'

'Where was it sold?'

'It wasn't.' Selim flattens the fax, pointing out lines. 'This was the watch seller—Maxim Aron Singer. He received this movement in 1930. This was his shop—' Ismet reads. *78 Mozartstrasse, Linz, Austria.* 'An Austrian Jew, you see? But there is no record of the movement being sold. Only the writing in the watch. You know what I think about this watch?'

He leans closer to Ismet, breathing the aniseed reek of raki. 'I'm surprised they didn't put a swastika on its back.' He pushes the watch across the counter. 'Goodbye, Ismet. May your soul be safe from harm.'

He waits eight days for the Austrian woman. It is a hot summer, and the bazaar stinks of uncured leather and split kavun melons. At nights Ismet dreams of the watch, the smooth loveliness of its tick, and the Austrian child. This time the girl and the father are on a train at night. The girl is reading to her father. Bars of light and darkness flash over them as she recites. He looks down at his wrist, checking the time of arrival or departure.

> *H was Papa's new Hat;*
> *He wore it on his head;*
> *Outside it was completely black,*
> *But inside it was red.*

> *S was Papa's new stick,*
> *Papa's new thumping stick,*
> *To thump extremely wicked girls*
> *Because it was so thick.*

The thin man smacks his own knee. They laugh together, the sound lost in the rattling rhythm of the train.

> *W was a Watch of Gold,*
> *It told the time of day,*
> *So that Papa knew when to come,*
> *And when to go away.*

The man runs his hand across the child's hair. His eyes stare out of the train window. The watch is smooth and cool against her ear. She laughs again as the train pulls into an underlit station. Men pass the window in procession as the train slows; tall men in grey coats and grey helmets. There is a clattering near the carriage. Boots, and the machinery of guns.

In the evenings Ismet eats little. He sits by the apartment window, watching neon come up over the city, thinking of the watch. The metropolis outside is Istanbul, Constantinople, and Byzantium; each built over the other, roof tiles broken down into foundations, subways falling through into bomb shelters, burial chambers, glittering caves of mosaics.

He drinks raki with ice and water and considers the question of evil acts. Some nights he thinks that there have been moments in his life when the line between good and evil was thin as skin. Sometimes, it seems to him that good is a life's work, and that evil takes only one decision. He wonders whether he could steal the watch, or take it if it were offered. Turkish pop music drifts in through his rooms with the groan of traffic and the hoot of ferryboats off the Golden Horn.

It is Thursday in the bazaar. Ismet is doing no work and no business. He looks up and there is a woman coming down Fur Merchant's Street towards him. The low street trees hide her face, and as she walks closer the face remains hidden, the walker becoming taller, until at a certain point the trick of vanishing points is overcome and he sees that it is the Austrian and he stands, only realising that he has been holding his breath as he cries out softly.

She takes off her sunglasses and nods to him. 'I have come for my watch.' The Austrian's eyes are arterial blue. Not made for sunlight. Ismet turns away from them. The cashbox is locked and he struggles with it, pulling out the watch case. He lays it on the counter between them.

'Is it mended?'

'Yes. You are late. You said—'

'How much is it worth?'

He shrugs, still not meeting her eyes. 'Three thousand dollars. Maybe more. It is a marriage, so it is worth less.'

The woman pauses, then leans towards the watch-mender. 'If you like it, I will sell it.'

He looks up at her now. 'I don't have that kind of money.'

'I also have no money. And I owe you. I will sell it for five hundred dollars.'

He realises the grey box is still under his hands. He opens the lid, to see it one more time. The hour and minute hands gleam, black as wasps' feet.

'No.' His voice is still soft, barely audible in the roar of the bazaar. Ismet picks up the box and holds it out.

The Austrian makes no move for it. Her voice rises, gaining edge.

'It is my father's watch.'

'Yes.'

'He was a good father. There is writing inside, isn't there? I remember that. I always wondered what was written.'

'It says that it is your father's. As you said.' He tries to hand her the box again but she flinches away.

'No! I don't want it.'

He lowers his voice again. Shaking his head, as if he is talking to himself. 'How often do people get what they want? I think it is more often than they realise.'

'That is a cruel thought.'

'It is – ' he nods at the box, at her – 'your father's watch.' And he shrugs, as if to say, what can you do?

The woman considers him, not speaking. Then she turns and walks away. Ismet sees her re-enter the crowd. When he is certain she has gone, he takes the watch out of its case.

He holds it up to his ear. The gold is warm and smooth as skin. Inside he can hear the jewels and brass, meshing together. Above him the muezzin begins and he looks up, surprised, the watch held up in his hand like an offering.

joyce carol oates

....

strand used books 1956

In Strand Used Books on Broadway and Twelfth one
snowy March early-evening in 1956 when the street
lights on Broadway glimmered with a strange sepia glow
and we were two NYU girl-poets drifting through that
warehouse of treasures as through an enchanted forest.
Just past 6 p.m. Above the light-riddled city of New
York, opaque night. Snowing, and the sidewalks
encrusted with ice so there were fewer customers in the
Strand than usual but there we were! Among other
cranky, brooding regulars. In our army-surplus jackets,
our wool trousers and zip-up rubber boots. In our
matching knitted wool caps (knitted by you) pulled down
low over our pale foreheads. Enchanted by books.
Enchanted by the Strand. No bookstore of 'new' books
with pristine displays and neatly shelved books and
heated interiors drew us like the drafty Strand, those
bins of books untidy as merchants' bins on Fourteenth
Street, NEW THIS WEEK, BEST BARGAINS, WORLD CLASSICS,
ART BOOKS 50% OFF, REVIEWERS COPIES, HIGHEST PRICE
$1.98, REMAINDERS 25c–$1. Hardcover and paperback,
spotless and battered, beautiful books and cheaply
printed books, crude paper-bound galleys with pages

scribbled in mysterious annotations. And to the rear and sides in that vast echoing space massive shelves of books rising to a hammered-tin ceiling fifteen feet above! Stacked shelves so high they required sliding ladders to negotiate and a monkey-agility (like yours) to climb and the courage to reach up for a book risking light-headed-ness (if like me you had low blood pressure). We were enchanted with the Strand and with each other in the Strand overseen by surly young clerks all of whom were poets like us, or playwrights, actors, artists. In an agony of young-love I watched you as always these romantic evenings at the Strand prowling the aisles sneering at books unworthy of your attention, too-easy books, too-popular books, books too American and middle-class, books lacking strangeness, books without esoteric repu-tations. We were girl-poets deeply enamoured of T.S. Eliot but scornful of Robert Frost whom we'd been made to revere and memorize in high school, slyly we con-versed in code phrases from Eliot in front of obtuse others in our dining hall and dormitory, we were admiring of but confused by the verse of Yeats, we were yet more confused by the lauded worth of Pound, more enthusiastically drawn to the bold metaphors of Kafka (that cockroach!) and Dostoyevsky (Raskolnikov and the man 'beneath the floorboards' were our rebel-heroes) and Jean-Paul Sartre ('Hell is other people') and had reason to believe we were of their lineage though American middle-class, and white, and female. (For didn't we, as females, share male contempt for 'the female'? Surely this would make a difference?) Brooding above a tumbled bin of hardcover books contemplating Freud's *Civilization and Its Discontents*, Crane Brinton's *The Age of Reason*, Margaret Meade's *Coming of Age in Samoa*, D.H. Lawrence's *The Rainbow*, Kierkegaard's

Fear and Trembling, Mann's *Magic Mountain* and there suddenly you glided up behind me to touch my wrist almost shyly and whisper, 'Come here!' in a way that thrilled me for it meant *I have something wonderful to show you*; as often in those days we surprised each other with found-gifts, sunlight pouring through a leaded window in our lecture room in Bobst Hall, a graceful dark-skinned child skipping rope in Washington Square, on West Broadway a mounted policeman's sleek, sculpted-looking bay horse whinnying and shaking his magnificent mane. Found-gifts! Like poems these were, fleeting and magical and unexpected. And eagerly I turned to follow you though frowning, 'Yes? What?' because you were not to be trusted, your mercurial moods, your sulky silences, your resentment over my high grades, your weakness for showy superficial people, yes you were childish and self-absorbed and I adored and feared you, knowing you'd break my heart, so eagerly and yet with dread I followed you through that labyrinthine maze of book-bins, free-standing bookshelves, and stacks to the ceiling ANTHRO-POLOGY, ART/ANCIENT, ART/RENAISSANCE, ART/MODERN, ART/ASIAN, ART/WESTERN, TRAVEL, PHILOSOPHY, COOKERY, POETRY/MODERN where the way was treacherous, lighted only by bare sixty-watt light-bulbs and customers as cranky as we two stood in the aisles reading books, or sat hunched on footstools glancing up annoyed at our passage, and unquestioning I followed you until at POETRY/MODERN you halted, and pushed me ahead, and around a corner, and I stood puzzled staring not knowing what I was supposed to be seeing until impatiently you poked me in the ribs and pointed and now I perceived an individual in the aisle pulling down books from shelves, peering at them, clearly absorbed by what she read, a woman nearly my height (I was tall for a girl, in 1956) in a man's navy coat to her ankles and sleeves past her wrists, a man's beige fedora hat on her head, scrunched low as we wore our knitted caps, and most of her hair hidden by the hat except for a six-inch blonde plait at the nape of her neck; and she wore black corduroy trousers tucked into what looked like salt-stained cowhide boots. Was this someone we knew? An older student from one of our classes? *A girl-poet like ourselves, in disguise*? I was about to hiss at you, 'What's this? Who is—' when the blonde woman turned to take down another book (always I would remember this slender volume of poetry though I'd glimpsed it for but a fraction of a second: e.e. cummings' *Tulips and Chimneys*), and I saw that she was Marilyn Monroe.

Marilyn Monroe! In the Strand. Like us. And she seemed to be alone.

Marilyn Monroe, alone!

In Strand Used Books, a snowy weekday evening in March 1956.

The blonde actress was wholly absorbed in browsing, oblivious of us and oblivious of her surroundings. You could see she was a *reader*. She was one of those who *reads*. With concentration, with passion. Oh, with her very soul! It was poetry she was reading, so her lips moved silently. She frowned, she grimaced, she smiled, she nodded, she sniffed and wiped her nose absent-mindedly on the edge of a hand, so intense was her concentration; for when you truly read poetry, the poetry reads *you*.

Still, this woman was Marilyn Monroe! Despite ourselves, our repudiation of the sorry clichés of romance, still we half-expected a man to join her, Clark Gable, Robert Taylor, Marlon Brando (we adored, for a man); in fact, we'd read that Brando was in New York, might be rejecting Hollywood for New York and returning to the stage.

But no man joined Marilyn Monroe in the Strand.

No tall handsome leading-man. No dark prince.

For which, thank God!

How differently this story would end.

For what seemed like a very long time, but was probably not much more than a half-hour, Marilyn Monroe browsed in the POETRY/MODERN shelves as, from a discreet distance, two girl-poets watched covertly. The 'Marilyn Monroe' we'd have said we knew was a garish blonde showgirl, a Hollywood-glamor 'sexpot' of no interest to us except maybe to denounce, if we'd troubled to think about her, which we had not; this 'Marilyn Monroe' was as unlike that woman as (almost!) we were unlike her. We were dying of curiosity, what were the books she was examining, who were the poets? *Amy Lowell, Wallace Stevens, Harry Crosby, Louise Bogan, H.D., Marianne Moore, Elizabeth Bishop, Denise Levertov, Robert Lowell, Muriel Rukeyser*... A few of these Marilyn Monroe made a decision to buy, closing a book with that satisfied expression that means *I'll be reading this soon, in private*. She'd chosen maybe six books of poetry. Then she moved on, a leather bag slung over her shoulder and her fedora tilted on her head. We couldn't resist, we followed her! Careful not to whisper together like excited schoolgirls, still less to giggle wildly as we were tempted, a ticklish sensation like feathers in my nose, you poked me in the ribs to sober me, gave me a glare meaning *Don't be rude! Don't ruin this for us both*. In fact, I acknowledge: I was the clumsier of the two of us, a tall gawky Rima the Bird Girl with my springy red hair like an exotic bird's crest while you were petite and dark-haired, wavy dark hair smooth and shiny as varnish, and your long-lashed sloe eyes, you the wily gymnast and I the aggressive basketball player, our contrary talents bred in our bones.

Which of us would marry, bear children (three strapping sons!) like our fore-mothers, and which of us would persevere into young middle-age before blossoming into a poet's true career, could anyone have predicted, that snowy March evening in 1956?

As Marilyn Monroe drifted on through the maze of books and we followed in her wake. As through a maze of dreams. Past SPORTS, past MILITARY, past WAR, past HISTORY/ANCIENT, past a muttering bewhiskered old man we'd often seen in the Strand prowling the stacks like an obstreperous ghost, past several surly yawning bearded clerks who took no more notice of the blonde actress than they ever did of us, and so to NATURAL HISTORY where she halted, which surprised us, and there again for unhurried minutes (the Strand was open till 9 p.m.) Marilyn Monroe in her mannish disguise browsed and brooded pulling down books, seeking what?, at last crouched leafing through an over-sized illustrated book (curiosity overcame me! I shoved away your restraining hand, politely I eased past Marilyn Monroe murmuring 'Excuse me' without so much as brushing against her and without being noticed), Charles Darwin's *Origin of Species* in a deluxe edition. Darwin! *Origin of Species*! We were poet-despisers of science, or believed we were, or must be, to be true poets in the exalted mode of T.S. Eliot and William Butler Yeats; such a choice, for Marilyn Monroe, seemed perverse to us. But this book was one Marilyn quickly decided to purchase, hoisting it into her arms and moving on.

That rakish fedora we'd come to covet, and that single chunky blonde braid. (Afterward we would wonder: Marilyn Monroe's hair in a braid? Never had we seen

Marilyn Monroe with her hair braided in any movie or photo. What did this mean? Did it mean anything? *Had she quit films, and embarked upon a new, anonymous life in our midst?*)

Suddenly Marilyn Monroe glanced back at us frowning as a child might frown (had we spoken aloud? had she heard our thoughts?) and there came into her face a look of puzzlement, not alarm or annoyance but a childlike puzzlement: *Who are you? You two? Are you watching me?* Quickly we looked away. We were engaged in a whispering dispute over a book one of us had fumbled from a shelf, *A History of Botanical Gardens in England.* So we were undetected. We hoped!

But wary now, and sobered. For what if Marilyn Monroe had caught us, and knew that we knew?

She might have abandoned her books and fled the Strand. What a loss for her, and for the books! For us, too.

Oh, we worried at Marilyn Monroe's recklessness! We dreaded her being recognized by a (male) customer or (male) clerk. A girl or woman would have kept her secret (so we thought) but no man could resist staring openly at her, following her and at last speaking to her. Of course, the blonde actress in Strand Used Books wasn't herself, not at all glamorous, or 'sexy', or especially blonde, in her inconspicuous man's clothing, and those salt-stained boots, she might've been anyone, female or male, hardly a Hollywood celebrity, a movie 'goddess'. Yet if you stared, you'd recognize her. If you tried, with any imagination you'd see MARILYN MONROE. It was like a child's game in which you stare at foliage, grass, clouds in the sky, and suddenly you see a face or a figure, and after that recognition you can't not see the hidden shape, it's staring you in the face. So too with Marilyn Monroe.

Once we saw her, it seemed to us she must be seen –
recognized – by anyone. She might've been naked,
moving languorously along the aisles. If any man saw!
We worried she'd be endangered. She'd quickly become
surrounded and mobbed. It was such poor judgement
on her part to come to Strand Used Books alone. Maybe
she could shop at Tiffany's, maybe she could walk
through the lobby of the Plaza, maybe she'd be safe from
unwanted admirers in certain oases of privilege on the
upper East Side, but not here. Almost, we were angry at
the woman. She was an adult woman, not a girl, wouldn't
you expect an adult woman to have more *common sense*?
Perplexed, you stared after her and gripped my wrist
with talon fingers as sometimes you did, thrilled with
discovery.

'Y'know? She's like *us*.'

You meant: a human being like us. A female like
us. Amid the browsing customers (who were mainly
male) of the Strand, like us.

But it wasn't true, and I think you must have known
it. Even then. In the excitement and confusion of that
hour. For after our deaths, I mean the three of us, the
three of us in the Strand that evening, yet 'Marilyn
Monroe' would remain. She'd entered history, at least
American history. Twentieth-century history. Who
knows why! As if an actual bolt of lightning had struck,
of the Strand's customers that evening, *her*. And only
her. You could argue that such a destiny is unfair, unjust,
undeserved, and maybe that's so, but such an argument
is irrelevant. Maybe T.S. Eliot wasn't the great poet
we'd thought him, either. Yet 'Monroe' and 'Eliot' were
American history. In this very bookstore (next time, we
would check!) in the stacks marked FILMS/HOLLYWOOD
there were books containing 'Marilyn Monroe', books

about Hollywood movies and Hollywood 'stars'. For all we knew, 'Marilyn Monroe' would turn up in other books, in other stacks. And of course in her films. In such archives, well into the twenty-first century she would endure. She would never die. *Even if she should wish to die, Marilyn Monroe could not.*

By this time she was carrying an armload of books. We thought (we almost hoped) she was finished and would be leaving the store, but she surprised us by leading us over to JUDAICA. (Even the word was exotic to us!) In that formidable aisle there were books in Hebrew, German, Russian, French. Some of these looked centuries old. There were complete sets of the Talmud and cryptically printed tomes on the Cabalah. The titles Marilyn Monroe sought were all in English: *Jews of Eastern Europe*, *The Chosen People*, *A Concise History of the Jews*. She set her books and handbag on the floor and sat on a footstool and turned pages frowningly, as if searching for something; in this uncomfortable posture she remained for at least twenty minutes, often wetting her fingers to turn pages that stuck, and frowning more deeply, yet smiling too; we drew near enough to observe her moist parted lips, and her flushed, feverish cheeks. We worried the reckless woman was seated too near a main aisle, bright overhead light fell on part of her face, her plaited hair. Customers and clerks were continuously milling past.

At one point a clerk called out angrily, 'Hey you!' – and the three of us started.

(It had nothing to do with us of course. He'd caught someone trying to slip a book into an overcoat pocket.)

After this jarring interruption, Marilyn Monroe began to glance over at us. She met our eyes, and she knew. But stubbornly turning back to the hefty book on her knees with an actress's serenity, as if, aware of a camera trained upon her, she would take no heed. What poise, we were thinking. What professional control. And what beauty. Marilyn Monroe's skin was naturally luminous and her eyes a clear washed blue. (In that instant we'd seen. We'd never forget!) She was beautiful without makeup, her mouth was a beautiful mouth without lipstick. Does beauty matter? Why does beauty matter? Is beauty a kind of immortality, of the body? In images, at least? (I ask only out of intellectual curiosity. Rima the Bird Girl was no beauty as a girl, nor would she be, as a mature woman!) Her hair in a stubby braid. And that navy surplus coat, and corduroy trousers, and cowhide boots. Beauty was a flame you wanted sometimes to hide, or even to smother. It wasn't for us to understand, yet we understood.

For some time she ignored us, leafing eagerly through *A Pictorial History of Jewish Culture*. Then she began to glance at us sidelong, seeing that, yes, we were still there, in the aisle, without much pretense any longer of looking at books; and she smiled, a fleeting smile to indicate *I see you seeing me. Thank you for not speaking my name.*

As if it was a game. A girl's game. Maybe it was?

Never would we two have betrayed Marilyn Monroe's identity in the Strand that evening. Yet it's conceivable we might have spoken her name. But we did not.

I'm proud of us. We were so young.

We were young, headstrong, arrogant and pretty smart. Though we didn't think of ourselves as young. You were nineteen, I was twenty. You were the more mature of the two of us (maybe); unless it's more accurate to say, I was the less mature of the two of us. We were patient watching over Marilyn Monroe amid the JUDAICA stacks until at last she shut the unwieldy book with that decisive look that meant she'd be buying it, and gathered up her things and headed for the front counter to make her purchases, while we followed at a respectful distance. Marilyn Monroe understood we were her escorts. If anyone dared to approach her, we intended to crowd him out. We intended to step between him and her. Yet how oblivious were other Strand customers! It's a symptom of used-book lovers, we're oblivious of one another, usually; even Marilyn Monroe in her disguise which was in fact a kind of sexy-boy disguise, passed by unnoticed. At the front of the store, though, clerks were more alert. The store manager was more alert. Were they looking at her? Awaiting her? As she neared the cashier's counter and the bright fluorescent lights overhead, Marilyn Monroe began to lose courage. Out of her shoulder bag she extracted a pair of amber-tinted horn-rimmed glasses, and fumbled to put them on. She turned up the collar of her navy coat. She lowered her hat brim. It was then I stepped forward and said quietly, 'Excuse me? Why don't I buy your books for you? That way you wouldn't have to talk to anyone.'

The blonde actress stared at me through her oversized, slightly crooked horn-rimmed glasses, and blinked once or twice, and smiled. 'Oh gosh. Would you?' Almost I couldn't hear, her voice was so soft.

Which is just what I did. Marilyn Monroe's purchases that night at the Strand, of sixteen books, mixed hardcover and paperback, came to a staggeringly high total for me – $55.85. Rarely did I hand over more than a few dollars to the bristly-bearded cashier. This time, I may have trembled as I pushed twenty-dollar bills at him, in dread of the man glaring at me and saying suddenly, 'Who are you?' and glaring at Marilyn Monroe standing inconspicuously a few yards away. 'And who are *you*?'

But as usual the cashier didn't give me a second glance. Already another customer was pushing to take my place.

At the door, which opened out onto the intersection of Broadway and Twelfth, Marilyn Monroe said to us both in her whispery voice, 'You're so sweet, you two. Here.' She pushed into our surprised hands *The Selected Poems of Marianne Moore* (Marianne Moore! we'd hardly been aware of her but would come to love her poetry, in time) and stammered thanks but already she was headed south on Broadway on the ice-rippled pavement, snow flurries like deranged white blossoms blown about her ducked head and shoulders. We waited for her to call a cab, but she didn't. We watched her walk away in an agony of love. We didn't follow. We knew we must not follow! By this time giddy from the strain of the past hour or more, laughing breathlessly, grabbing each other's hands so hard it hurt. 'Oh. Oh, God. She spoke to us. "Marilyn Monroe." I touched her hand. Was it real?'

It was real: we had *The Selected Poems of Marianne Moore* to prove it.

That snowy early-evening in March 1956 of Strand Used Books, Broadway and Twelfth, New York City. That magic evening of Marilyn Monroe, when I kissed you for the first time.

bidisha

....

a taste of the east

The Asian Studies MA course was full of white people.
Shona sat down at her desk and smiled at her fellow
pupils – two pasty girls and a bloke with sun-bleached
hair and stubble. He winked at her and stretched his
arms out sleepily. 'Man, what a summer,' he said in a
surfie-dude accent, 'I just got off a flight from Bali. I
really needed to get there and, you know, sort my head
out.' Other pupils filtered in and started chatting with
each other, but apart from the stoner guy nobody talked
to Shona. She looked around and realised she was the
only Indian person in the room. Up on the walls were
prints of ancient carvings and etchings from the sub-
continent, along with a selection of traditional, native
costume.

Then the tutor walked in, and it was lust at first sight.
He clocked eyes on Shona and almost dropped his bona
fide yak-skin carry-case – bought after some hard bar-
gaining in an actual Bedouin hut. She was perfect: long
brown hair, long brown limbs, long brown eyes. He took
up his position at the head of the class and fiddled nervously with the silver Om stud in his right ear. 'Well,
welcome, everyone, to Asian Studies. My name is Julian

Arnold-Culleford – call me Jules – and over the next three terms we shall be exploring the, the *incredible richness* of Eastern philosophy. We'll delve into the ancient customs, powerful rituals and strange practices of some of the oldest cultures in the world and, hopefully, we'll learn something *about ourselves* along the way. Any questions?' Shona put up her hand and asked, 'If I do this course in conjunction with Islamic Art, does that mean I've fulfilled my module quota for the year? I mean, I won't have to come back and repeat anything?' Jules was a little shocked. 'But I thought someone of your – someone like you – would be, you know, really into a course like this.'

Asian style had hit the shops big-time, and little white girls with pale midriffs decided the skirts-over-trousers look was the way to go. Clothes rails were a synthetic riot of paprika red and orange, and magazines said that it was cool to be 'ethnic'. One autumn night in the student bar Shona got drunk with Jules and decided that transgressive, tutor–student sex was better than no sex at all. He took her to his apartment in New Cross, and when he opened the front door and led her inside she almost laughed in his face: terracotta walls, woodcarvings, war-masks, little ivory elephants everywhere. There was a set of tablas by the fireplace, and a Moroccan rug on the floor. Jules put on a tape of Arabic chanting and said 'I always listen to this when I want to chill out.'

He lay back on the sofa and started rolling a joint. She came and sat on his lap, he wrapped his arms around her and stroked her hair. They took their tops off and rolled around for a while, until Jules pulled back and said, 'You know, I've often thought that I was Indian in a past life.' They smoked the joint and Jules started telling Shona all about his travels in what he called 'the East'. He told her about all the amazing folk-tales and superstitions he'd learnt about there, and the ingenious things the natives did to keep themselves happy in such tough times. He said he was certain that he was an old Hindu mystic in some ancient civilisation. He told her his plans to take the summer off and go and live on an ashram. He kissed her all over the face, then put his mouth to her ear: 'Talk to me,' he whispered, ' . . . in Punjabi.'

About a month after this, Shona was lazing about in her flat thinking about the last person she was in love with. They'd broken up five years before, and five years is a long time. Since then, she graduated, worked in a bunch of PR companies, got her own flat and gone back to college. But she hadn't loved anyone. Her best friend Runa would always say things like 'Okay, in the last five years are you telling me there hasn't been a single person who's lived up to your oh-so-high standards?' and Shona would think about every guy she met, every stranger in the street, every pal, every colleague, every friend-of-a-friend, and shake her head. She didn't want any of them. Runa would cry 'It's been *half a decade*, for God's sake!' But Shona only attracted idiots – some were nice, some were clever, most were beautiful. But they were all basically idiots.

The phone rang and it was Jules. In the time since their first shag events had taken a nasty turn. So urgent was his passion for the East that Jules had turned psycho, calling her up at all hours, rubbing up against her in class, making her collect marked essays direct from his office at college and then trying to get her to engage in a little cross-cultural dialogue when she got there. This time, he was babbling about this message he'd had from the skies: 'I went to bed last night, and as soon as my head hit the pillow I started dreaming about this amazing place with, like, amazing old buildings and a water fountain and trees with their branches sweeping the ground. I can't describe the feeling. It was like that's where I was always *meant to be* in my life. It had this incredible spiritual quality. It was definitely a sign.' He'd already drafted his resignation letter and didn't think twice about leaving the entire MA course hanging as he went off to fulfil his spiritual destiny on some ashram in the Himalayas that he learnt about off the Internet. 'It's got no running water! And no electricity!' he said, 'it's absolutely perfect!'

The next time Shona went in to college, there was a new tutor and word was out that Jules had upped and left in nothing but a sarong, with his passport in one hand and a pair of flip-flops in the other. Instead, the group had a series of lecturers borrowed from other courses. One day after class Shona was gathering up her stuff, looking at the posters on the wall of the seminar room: *Community Craft – Experience The Forgotten Delights of Sikh Artistry.* A voice next to her said, 'It's so fucking patronising, isn't it? As though it took the English to come along and unearth all the buried talent of Asia, and even then they present it as the kind of stuff made in little mud huts by illiterate peasants taking time off from working on the land.' Shona turned around and clocked one of the finest young men she'd ever seen in her life. He was tall and athletically built and you could prise oyster shells apart on his cheekbones. His manly face wore a red, disgruntled expression as he inspected the poster. 'It really pisses me off,' he fumed, 'it's so racist! Don't you think so?' Shona shrugged. The young man introduced himself as Gilbert and invited her for a coffee in the common room. He was a PhD student, writing about colonialism, who went to all the lectures the college gave for postgraduates. 'Every day I sit there,' he frowned, 'listening to these do-good, oh-so-liberal people yapping on about their precious East, standing there in their all-natural-fabric clothes and their big dangly amber earrings. Paying out to so-called third world charities every month by direct debit. Yap yap yap, patting themselves on the back the whole time.'

It also transpired that Gilbert was a very, very rich young man with a pad in Chelsea and a family house in the country, complete with staff and horses. When he took his jacket off he tried to hide the label with his hand, but he couldn't possibly cover up the stink of all that money. His bag was soft tan leather by Mulberry, his overcoat was lined in the classic Burberry check, even his winter gloves were cashmere. Now, all Shona had ever wanted was a big house in the country and a strong, friendly sort of horse to ride. She made a deal with herself: she'd sit and listen to all of Gilbert's colonial guilt and, in return, she'd make him give her a chance to see a bit of the life she'd always craved. It seemed like a fair exchange. So she sat in the common room and nodded and agreed and sympathised as Gilbert went on about orientalism and exoticism and all the rest of it, and she could see how he thought they were just right for each other, how he thought he could *really talk* to her, how he thought they 'shared' the same political views.

That Christmas break Gilbert invited Shona to the country house – 'my bloody parents absolutely *force* me to go up there every year' – and drove them up there, his face dark with distaste, complaining about the political implications of keeping staff, of having the house itself 'like a huge wedding cake in a field, with ridiculous small-time balls and summer fairs and hunts. Pathetic,' he sneered, 'all those pathetic, pompous signifiers of English privilege.' But he still wore his cashmere gloves, and he still took the allowance his parents gave him. Shona gasped as they rolled up to the house. It stood there as proud as an army general, laced in white with thick columns and five steps leading up to the front door. There was a fat Christmas tree twinkling behind one of the windows.

Gilbert's parents didn't talk to Shona, the servants gave her strange, disrespectful looks and conversation was stilted. There was a darkie in the White House. Christmas Eve and Christmas Day passed silently but Shona was happy. She looked at the antique candle-holders on the table, the Christmas decorations which had been preserved since Victorian times and were pains-takingly unwrapped and reused every year. She looked at the morose row of portraits hung along the staircase – father, grandfather, great-grandfather – and the faded photographs in their heavy frames on the dresser in their bedroom. 'I've always wanted to live like that and wear clothes like that,' she said, pointing at the faded photos, and Gilbert gave her a strange look.

They kept it together for the rest of the course but by the time she left college and the first year of his doctorate was over, it was apparent that they only shared a bed, not a world-view. On the last day of the third term they were walking out of the college. Shona couldn't believe it was all over: she'd get her MA and be rid of this dump for ever. She could get on with her life, have some money in her pocket and have a good time. Gilbert grabbed her hand suddenly and asked, 'Look, I've always wondered, but why did you choose to do this course in the first place?' Shona shrugged, 'I'm Asian. The course was Asian Studies. I thought it'd be easy.' 'But you couldn't care less about – about colonialism, or your culture, or your roots or anything,' spluttered Gilbert. Shona looked at him. 'You're just as bad as Jules was,' she sighed, 'bad in a different way, but just as bad.' She disentangled her hand and walked off, out of the college, leaving him staring after her.

In the car park she spotted a familiar-looking Beetle. 'You're back,' she said quizzically to Jules, who was slowly getting his bags and a box of files from the back seat. He wasn't looking so hot – his eyes were lined and wrinkled and his mouth had a sour expression. 'How was India?' Shona asked, and he went even whiter. 'Oh, don't ask,' he said, and his voice was like a sad old man, 'I couldn't hack it. I thought it'd just be, you know, meditation and drawing some nice water from the well and getting up and looking at the dawn, but I got there and nobody spoke English or anything. They just studied all the time, in total silence, and nobody made the effort to help me out. I mean, how am I supposed to suddenly get there and understand Sanskrit or whatever?' Shona gave a slight, crisp smile, and said, 'Well, there you go. That's what happens when you go to a country that doesn't want you.' 'What are you doing now?' asked Jules, swallowing the insult whole. 'Getting a life,' said Shona, 'but I think I should tell you, Gilbert's inside and he's really keen to hear to all about your adventures.' She patted him on the shoulder and strode away, through the gates and down the road.

It was New Year's Eve, 1999. A colleague of Shona's from the fashion PR company where she now worked was throwing a huge party at her Clerkenwell 'loft'. The company was called Orchid and consisted of a bunch of honeyed blonde nice-girls who carried little tote bags and wore Miu Miu boots. They were all friendly enough but Shona wasn't really one of them. Since she left college she'd felt real life open out perilously beneath her feet once more: the sense of having to fill up your days, to get out into the loop and show yourself to people. Otherwise your identity hung by a thread. People forgot you existed. The work at Orchid was good fun and Shona went to a lot of parties. After Jules and Gilbert there was a string of good-looking, smart, funny, interested men – none of whom she really wanted.

She walked into the apartment and started greeting her pals, kissing them on both cheeks, taking a glass of champagne. Loads of people had gone away to celebrate the new millennium in more spiritual places – Malaysia, Thailand, India – but the place was still crammed. People were exclaiming over her outfit. That evening she'd taken a long bath, put on some music and slowly braided her long hair into cornrows tight against the scalp. She put on tight indigo jeans and pulled the turn-ups high on to her knees, then laced up her DMs. She slipped a T-shirt she'd got from a tourist stall over her head – slim-fitting, with a garish Union Jack on it. A stylist from a glossy magazine came over, staring at her like a dog on the hunt, and said, 'God, I just love it. I totally love it. Bovver-girl style. We should run a story on it.' The room was full of fashiony types in sari-fabric dresses, sarongs and complicated structures printed with photographic images of Shiva. A couple of people had henna tattoos. Shona grinned and said, 'Well, you know, I'd heard a little bit of multiracial cross-pollination was in, so here I am. You take my culture and I take yours.' She glanced down at the ugly boots and the severe, tight trousers. 'Aren't you proud?'

nicholas royle

....

empty boxes

The gallery was one of those places where you had to ring a bell to gain admittance. Simon instinctively disliked such places, but he was attracted to this one by the framed movie posters on the walls. He knew that the girl sitting behind the desk at the far end of the room, although very attractive, would instinctively dislike him, but it was cold and raining heavily, so he paused to have a look.

Posters for *Vertigo*, *Performance* and *Some Like It Hot* could be seen from the street through the plate-glass window. The prices, of course, were printed far too small for him to read without going in, and there were several more posters further inside that the angle did not permit him to identify.

He pressed the buzzer.

The girl looked up and reached under the desk to operate a switch. He pushed open the door and slipped inside as a gasp of warm air escaped past him into the street. He avoided the girl's gaze by turning straight to the nearest exhibit, a set of lobby cards for *Point Blank*. As he moved forward to read the price he glanced left towards where the girl was sitting. Her head was bent over the desk, her face concealed by a dark, twisting curtain of velvety hair. He could see her ankles and feet under the desk. As he watched, one foot was raised slightly and crossed behind the other. Was the sound he heard the indistinct rasp of her nylon or the grazing of his own sleeve against his jacket as he lifted his hand to massage his temples?

There were three other men in the gallery. They all held the same position in relation to the walls of the room. Each was standing straight, head back, chin up as he examined the poster in front of him. Their hands were either clasped behind their backs or kept close by their sides. The general attitude was one of silent reverence. It was as if action had been called on the set of *Last Year at Marienbad*.

The girl uncrossed her ankles and the effect of the nylon *swish* was like someone physically pinching his arm. He turned to glance at her and to his horror saw that she was looking directly at him, her hair already sliding down over her forehead. He looked away, heart thumping, and concentrated on the poster for *Vertigo*, which was in French. The little card on the wall revealed that it was linen-backed and priced at £2000. It made Simon dizzy just to imagine handing over that amount of money. It made him dizzy to imagine ever owning that amount of money.

As he moved deeper into the gallery, stopping to admire a poster for the film he had thought of only a moment earlier – Alain Resnais' *Last Year at Marienbad*, card-backed at £800 – Simon suddenly caught a vague whiff of something in his nostrils. He tipped his head back to sniff the air and suddenly became aware of a presence behind him. He turned around to see the girl standing very close to him. She then leaned even closer to speak and when she opened her mouth, he saw that she had a slight overbite and that her bottom lip was a little heavier. With better lighting it would jut. The tip of her tongue was bubblegum-pink.

'We have some special items in the back.'

Simon swallowed. 'Special items?'

'Follow me.'

She turned on her heel and stilettoed across the blonde-wood floor, the staccato reports ricocheting off the white walls, towards a short staircase twenty yards away. How could Simon not watch her legs and the way her skirt moved over her bottom as she crossed that short distance? He followed her up the half-dozen steps, mesmerised by the sway of her hips.

With an ironic flourish, she showed him a glass case filled with ticket stubs, velvet swatches, thimblefuls of carpet dust and cigarette ash.

Simon pointed to a frayed square of white canvas. 'Presumably from a screen?'

'The Coliseum, Harrow Road. Closed 1956, demolished and site redeveloped.'

'Very nice,' murmured Simon, looking more closely at the brass upholstery studs, obsolete lenses and strips of 35mm advertising trailers.

The girl turned to look towards the front of the gallery. He sensed that she was bored. She'd misjudged him, had thought he might be a collector with cash to flash, the scruffy attire the signature of the true eccentric.

'Everything is for sale?' he asked.

'This kind of stuff is currently fetching very good prices,' she pointed out. 'If you'll excuse me, I must be getting on.'

The mild flirtatiousness had been replaced by a hint of businesslike ruthlessness. Simon realised his viewing of the special collection was over. He turned to meet her gaze.

'If you wouldn't mind,' she said, gesturing towards the main part of the gallery.

He negotiated the steps and stopped by two more posters – *Get Carter* and *The Lavender Hill Mob*, each conservation-paper-backed and priced at around three months' wages – before opening the door and swapping warm air for cold once more.

Back at Gloucester Terrace, Simon sat watching that evening's continuous programme out of his window. One train after another pulled out of Paddington, their amber windows single frames, the gaps between the wheels sprocket holes, in strips of film. As they blundered through the forest of points, Simon recognised the familiar snag of the celluloid in the gate of the projector. Actor-passengers rocked in silhouetted rows, cut-outs against the tawny light pouring past them.

There were Great Western 125s bound for Bristol, Cardiff or Penzance, diesel multiple units terminating at Reading but stopping at every station in between, six-car Hammersmith & City line tubes that would henceforth remain above ground all the way to Hammersmith. Each was a movie, with a hundred different lead actors and a thousand narrative strands. From his magnificent vantage point, sat by the window in his director's chair, Simon felt in control. He believed that a single word from him would bring them all to a grinding halt. But he chose not to exercise that power.

Sometimes he rode on the trains. He went down to Paddington or Royal Oak and boarded a train. He'd been to Bristol, he'd visited Swindon. He'd travelled to the airport and back on the Heathrow Express. And many times, late in the evening, he'd taken the Hammer-smith & City line round to its western terminus. As he trundled past the rows and rows of Edwardian terraces and Victorian conversions, he was both in a film and watching one – or many. Wherever the curtains had not been drawn or blinds lowered, he was offered a window on to another world. A man standing next to a bed in an orange room. A young woman lying on another bed in blue light fully clothed. Two people sitting across a kitchen table eating. Banal but vital images of everyday existence, glimpses of bearable lives.

Sometimes the rooms he passed were empty. The curtains were open, the light was on – and so the film was running – but there was no one on screen. He would project himself into that empty box and improvise.

Returning home to Gloucester Terrace late at night he'd always manage to find a vacant carriage where he'd sit and wait to see who would get on at the next station. One night a young woman not unlike the girl from the gallery boarded his empty carriage at Ladbroke Grove and sat down on the opposite side one row of seats down. He framed her with his joined hands and closed one eye to compose the shot. He zoomed in silently, not too close, just enough, but she switched to the next carriage at Westbourne Park.

Maybe the girl from the gallery made such an impression because she reminded him of the woman on the train, or maybe it was the cynical way she had reeled him in, then cast him adrift. Whatever the reason, he found that he couldn't stop thinking about her. As he sat watching the nightly movie show outside his rear window, he saw her head in every frame.

He turned away from the window and trailed his fingers along the lines of video boxes on his shelves.

Meticulously labelled and sorted, the spines of the sleeve-inlays announced their contents, but not a single one promised distraction from the enduring image of the girl. The way she leaned forward to tempt him, then withdrew almost as abruptly. He picked out a video box from the top row and opened it very carefully, just wide enough to sniff inside, then snapped it shut and replaced it, his index finger lingering on the lettering under the plastic sleeve on the spine.

The flat was in darkness, as usual when he was not working. Mostly in the daytime he was out, researching, adding to his maps, walking the streets. Nighttimes he sat and watched the trains or he looked through his collection or he worked on the maps. There was enough of the city's light coming in at the window to cast shadows behind the few things he had in the flat and so make them stand out. A dust-furred cooking ring, filthy sink and minibar-style fridge. The bed. A large pile of empty video boxes ready to be filled when the need arose. His ancient 16mm projector perched on top of its stand, a small pile of film cans underneath. A table bearing the equally ancient Remington typewriter on which he wrote the endless letters that he hand-delivered to the BFI, the Film Theatre Association, English Heritage and other toothless bodies. Also on the table, his maps of London and press cuttings that had accumulated. Finally, threatening the safety of the wall perpendicular to the window, the shelves holding his large and ever expanding collection.

The window was kept shut, even in summer, and a substantial draught excluder lay along the bottom of the door that led to the stairwell and the bathroom he shared with two other tenants from neighbouring bedsits.

He woke in the morning curled up on the mattress

clutching two video boxes. Both, he was relieved to see, were tightly closed. It was early. The light from the window, which faced north, was weak and lustreless. He could hear the constant rattle of the daytime commuter trains, which were of little interest to him. This was how he knew he wasn't going mad: he was capable of discernment. Night trains – interesting. Day trains – boring. It was all to do with the light.

Huddled over the table with a lukewarm cup of coffee, Simon pored over the west London maps. He had yet to plot the abandoned cinemas on the Harrow Road that he had been on his way to find when distracted by the vintage poster gallery. That his research and a possible harvest had been slightly delayed was not a major problem. He could even spare the time to go back to the gallery, if what he was about to check on the map turned out to be significant. He plotted the locations, as best he could for the time being, of the demolished Coliseum, the Prince of Wales (now a bingo hall) and the former Regal, all of them on Harrow Road, and extended lines from them across to the sadly unplugged Electric on Portobello Road, the Gate and the Coronet on Notting Hill Gate, and the former Twentieth Century Theatre on Westbourne Grove, now restored and Grade 2-listed, but bereft of chairs and screen, an empty box.

As he had suspected, the lines intersected on Talbot Road, more or less at the spot where he judged the vintage poster gallery to be situated. He picked up his coffee and took it to the window, where he stood watching the traffic on the Westway for a good five minutes.

The gallery was less busy, Simon the only customer. The girl had looked up and buzzed the door to let him in, but whether or not she had recognised him he couldn't be sure. She bent over her work, her sleek hair falling slowly down over her face like a ruched drape.

In Simon's voluminous coat pocket was an empty box.

Every corner of the gallery was within sight of the desk where the girl sat. Clearly, that was the point. But by standing in front of a large poster for the Italian release of Hitchcock's *Frenzy*, which was located close to the door to the street, Simon was able to slip the box out of his pocket away from the girl and open it one-handed. He waited a moment or two, then moved the box up and down a couple of times before snapping it shut, masking the sound with a little cough. Replacing it in his pocket, he secured the two little catches, then withdrew his hand.

He strolled across to where the girl was sitting. 'Hi,' he said.

She raised her head very slowly, her hair twisting and somersaulting like eels in a dark river.

'Do you have a poster for *Eureka*?'

She thought about it. 'I don't think we do.'

'Or *Don't Look Now*.'

'No. Roeg fan, are you? Have you seen *Performance*?'

'Do you mean the film or the poster?'

'I mean the poster. I assume you've seen the film. Everybody's seen the film.'

'Both. But I hadn't seen the poster before I saw it here. Can I ask you something? Why are they so expensive?'

'Film posters are only just being recognised as works of art in their own right. At the end of a run, they used to get binned, or worse, burned.'

'I suppose you have to have *Performance*, given the location of your shop.'

'Why do you say that?'

'Because Roeg's local. Because the film was shot just around the corner.'

'Only the exteriors were done in Powis Square.'

'Of course, but still.'

They were silent, but he sensed that he'd got her interest.

'Do you think it's the case,' he went on, 'that where a film is seen is more important than where it is shot?'

'I'm not sure I follow.'

'Some people are obsessed with knowing where films are shot. The precise location of a shoot. I think the place where it is exhibited is far more significant, far more important.'

He saw something light up in her eyes. Her mouth opened slowly. He *had* misjudged her. The professional appearance was a disguise. She was a slightly looser cannon than she gave the impression of being. He began to feel excited.

'Round here,' he said, 'west London – what's your favourite cinema?'

She shrugged. 'The Coronet?'

'Too smoky.'

'The Gate?'

'Too stuffy. And the front row's too close to the screen. Where do you sit when you go, the front row?'

'Of course.'

'Me too. But at the Gate it's just too close, so you have to sit behind people. The illusion is shattered. Don't you find?'

'I used to like the Electric,' she said, looking off to the side.

'It's very sad that it's dark.'

'There's talk of it reopening.'

'It could happen. But I doubt it. It's one of an endangered species.'

'Rep cinemas.'

He nodded. 'Remember the Scala? Soon to reopen as a club. A nightclub. The Roxie? Became a novelty shop, then a sandwich shop; now it's empty.'

'The Lumière.'

'Not a rep cinema, but a beautiful space. Closed down. Single-screen cinemas will soon be just a memory. The Parkway and the Plaza in Camden – both gone. The Pavilion, the Palladium and the Galaxy around Shepherd's Bush Green – what are they now? A bingo hall, an Australian bar and a shop selling empty boxes – cheap suitcases.'

The subject of their dialogue was depressing, but the manner of its exchange was increasingly animated. Arclights shone in the girl's eyes. Simon bubbled with confidence.

'It's not all gone, you know,' he said. 'Not quite.'

The girl's mouth opened slowly. The pink tip of her tongue severed a gossamer-thin string of saliva. Her overbite hovered. The Béatrice Dalle lower lip trembled.

'I've got a special collection of my own,' he said.

Her eyes widened.

'I live near by. If you wanted . . .'

She turned to the wall, thinking, gazing blankly at an extremely rare poster for Michael Powell's *Peeping Tom*.

At Gloucester Terrace, she followed him up the narrow stairwell.

'Almost there,' he called over his shoulder into the darkness. The light had never worked as long as he had lived there. It wasn't the kind of light that mattered. The stairwell was a transitional place, insignificant.

'It's not much, I'm afraid,' he said, pushing open the door to his bedsit and pressing himself back against the wall to allow the girl to go first. As she squeezed past him, her hair brushed his face and he caught the slightest trace of the essence he had detected on his first visit to the gallery. He fingered the video box in his coat pocket. As soon as she was inside the tiny flat, he closed the door carefully behind them.

She went straight to the window and looked out.

'All those thousands of lives,' she said, watching two trains pull out simultaneously.

Simon's breathing was fast and shallow.

'I don't even know your name. Mine is Simon.'

'Claire.'

'Was your hair always this dark?'

Standing behind her as she watched the trains, he had taken a handful of her hair and held it against his face. She turned around.

'You brought me here to show me something.'

'My collection,' he said, turning towards the shelves.

She looked at the whole collection for a moment, taking it in, then started reading the spines on the sleeve-inlays.

'*Diva, Les yeux sans visage, The Shout, A Matter of Life and Death, The Texas Chainsaw Massacre* – good films, you've got good taste. Am I missing something?'

Simon took down one of the video cases – Christopher Petit's *Chinese Boxes* – and handed it to Claire.

'It's empty,' she said, weighing it in her hand, and a new light sparked in her eye.

'Don't be afraid,' he said softly, placing a reassuring hand on her arm. He took the box from her, held it in his two hands and slowly prised it open, just a crack. 'Please,' he whispered, holding it up to her nose.

She turned her dark eyes anxiously up at him and breathed in through her nose.

Simon gently lowered the box and closed it. He turned it over in his hands and showed her the spine.

'*Chinese Boxes*,' she read. 'Roxie, 9.12.86.' She frowned.

'The Roxie closed in March 1987,' he said. 'It's empty now, dark; you can't get in there. But this is part of it.'

Claire turned to look at the rows of video boxes on the shelves.

'All of these boxes are empty?' she said.

'You can tear down the screen and bulldoze the walls, but you can never destroy the space itself. This is a small part of that space.'

'Space?'

'The space between the walls and the floor and the screen and the people watching the films night after night. You think that space can remain unaffected by all of that emotion, all of that drama? It's not invulnerable that space, that air. It mutates. It's organic. Each new screening adds another layer, another infusion, each fresh outpouring of emotion saturates it further.'

Simon had taken hold of Claire's hair again and was stroking it as he explained. She didn't resist.

'And *Chinese Boxes*?'

'*Chinese Boxes* just happens to be the film that was playing the night I carved out my piece of history, the night I sampled the Roxie. Hence naming it on the box. If I open this box, I get *Chinese Boxes*, sure, but I also get the Roxie.'

'Don't you have any real videos?'

'What would I want with real videos? These mean more to me.' He gestured to indicate the entirety of his collection. 'This is a more faithful record of my experience of *Chinese Boxes* than a copy of *Chinese Boxes* itself.'

'But every time you open the box . . .?'

'I am very careful not to open it too far or keep it open for too long. I can sip from these wines for the rest of my life. There are no draughts in here. Air does not circulate unless it has a reason to.'

She smiled.

'Why are you smiling?'

'You're mad,' she said, still smiling. 'But in the nicest possible way. I like that. This is all fascinating, completely fascinating, but it's making me thirsty.'

He cupped his hand against the side of her face and she rested the weight of her head against him.

'Just a second,' he said and walked across the room to where the minibar forlornly sat. He withdrew from it a bottle of Scotch and took two mugs from the draining board. He poured two generous amounts. Claire was running her fingers along the spines of his video boxes.

'Will you stay?' he asked her.

'Do you think I should?' she asked with a sidelong glance.

'I think you should,' he said, refilling their mugs.

She stayed. The trains that ran outside ran through his head. Although for once he didn't watch them, he found he didn't need to. The hum of the projector, the crackle of the carbon arcs – the films were screened on his retinas. He directed their love scene like a *maître*, intercutting it with Roegesque snatches of dialogue. They talked about the lost cinema of Talbot Road, how rumours of its location surfaced from time to time but no one knew exactly where it had been. Built in the 1900s, demolished by 1914, and no record anywhere of its precise address. 'I think *I* know where it was,' he told

her. 'I think we *both* know where it was, don't we?' He
confessed to having taken an empty box to the gallery
that afternoon. They talked about his dream, his belief
that all of the old cinema spaces had been saved, either
by an agent of the state or by a secret society or by a
committed individual, and were stored somewhere, like
enormous Rachel Whiteread sculptures in gaseous form.
'I'm close to finding that place,' he said. 'I'm almost
there. You can help me. Just imagine it. Every film that
has ever been shown on every London screen that has
since been torn down plays there constantly and continuously and simultaneously. Each scene is played out at
the same time as the next. And each film is reacted to
by every audience it has ever had within this city. Every
tear that has been shed, every laugh that has echoed
around the walls of any London cinema that has ever
existed – they are shed over and over and they resound
endlessly within the walls of a single building. I just have
to find that building and you can help me find it.'

Sleep brought dreams that so closely resembled the
madness of his waking life he had no idea when he
slipped from one state to the other. He slept deeply and
woke to the clatter of the morning trains, the boring
morning trains – and an empty space in the bed beside
him. He called her name, knowing the only response
would be the echo of his cry. He looked at the empty
shelves where his collection had been and didn't know
whether he was relieved that his first assessment of the
girl now seemed to have been correct, or dismayed that
his reassessment had proved over-optimistic. In any case,
he was pleased that he had taken the precaution of
switching the sleeve-inlays from one set of video boxes
to the other before inviting the girl back.

The unmarked boxes piled up by the bed were the

boxes that had previously been labelled according to film, venue and date. Reidentifiying the blank boxes was a simple, if time-consuming, task for Simon. He had often tested himself by taking down a box at random and opening a corner for a sniff. He had yet to be wrong. Claire, of course, had taken – and was no doubt already installing in her gallery – two hundred and thirty empty boxes.

christopher kenworthy

....

the death of blonde

If it wasn't for the plait of hair they'd found in Janelle's apartment, I would never have stayed in Prague for December. The previous month had forced me to redefine the word *cold*. Even when it's windless and free of snow the air in Prague gets through your clothes and robs your body of heat. It's the sort of cold that makes it difficult to breathe and numbs your jaw, so you can't be certain whether it's the beer you've drunk or the weather that's slurring your speech. Not that I had anybody to talk to. Since Janelle had left me I'd struggled to find anybody else who could speak English. I'd resorted to sitting in cafés and staring at people, hoping a conversation would be struck up. At my age. The whole time I'd been with Janelle, I kept fantasising about how easy it would be to meet new people if we split up. But as soon as she'd left I felt remarkably ugly. I knew when I looked at women they were thinking *creep*. Or the Czech equivalent. It was a difficult time, so given the sad state of my social life I'd planned to go back to England for Christmas. But now that the plait of hair had been found among her discarded belongings, I had to stay.

Apparently the hair had been cut off with a knife

somewhere above shoulder level, and it was held together at the base only by an elastic band. My chances of getting hold of it were slim, because three competing parties were struggling for ownership. The police were the current holders, trying to determine whether there had been any foul play. Her disappearance looked innocent enough, *post-amour*, but they wanted to be sure. Secondly, a wigmaker from one of the opera companies said he'd paid a good fee to the apartment owner for the hair. His vehemence probably came from the fact they were about to stage the Ring Cycle, and his work was in demand. More determined, however, was the Curator of the Hair Museum, who invoked some ancient treasure-trove law, which states that all precious materials unearthed without a named owner belong to the state. Janelle's hair was far from gold, but in value it was higher.

There are museums for everything in Prague. Dolls, music, matches, cardboard. Whatever your interest, or lack of, there will be a tiny museum that pays homage. They're cheap, informative, and thankfully lacking in the interactive bullshit that's ruined most Western museums. But they suffer from the same belief in progress. Go to any museum and you can see that the Darwinian zeitgeist has infiltrated the psyche so deeply, we even think of matches and books as evolving.

I'm not a creationist, and I balk at calling myself a scientist, but I know the holes in evolution are still so huge that it's an embarrassment to science. I just wish the creationists would shut up, because it's now become a matter of scientific honour to defend evolution as The Only Truth. I don't doubt that something like evolution is going on, but we don't know how it works. Darwin himself said that if we couldn't find evidence of interspecies states his theory was probably wrong. But we ignore that and make excuses for the fossil record. I try not to sound too fanatical, but evolution is a *theory* and it's never been tested. All we see are fruit flies and moths turning into slightly different fruit flies and moths. You never see one turning into a fish. The truth is, I don't know what's going on. Which is something you never hear most scientists say, and that's all I ask.

But in every museum, you see evolution charted out like a map of facts. Remember those diagrams of horses, going from a sort of pygmy-baby horse to a big modern stallion? They're made up. The evidence indicates that several of those horses came from disparate ancestors, and the leaps between species are far from smooth. But the progress chart is a great diagram, and makes evolution seem natural. Hence the drawings of apes turning into upright hominids, and eventually into something resembling a naked businessman. Forget the missing links; the gradual unfolding of modern man looks so convincing when drawn, you'd have to be a religious maniac to doubt it.

Even the Prague Hair Museum was a victim of this belief system. I'd been there as part of our research into the nature of recording, shortly after I arrived in Prague. I was still officially working in London, but managed to spend long weekends with Janelle by focusing my research on the Czech Republic. It was before the death of blonde began, so the Hair Museum's display was quite predictable. There was only one room, a long corridor with high windows; everything was muted, except for the shine of hair, and the place smelt musty like a scalp. The curator was busy behind a desk, working on something I couldn't see, and didn't even acknowledge my entrance, even though nobody else was looking around.

Hair out of context seems impersonal and dead. There was a tray of braid weaves and silver barrettes clasped around hair that had kinked with age. Ringlets were displayed according to their spiral ratio, split into subsections of colour. Spit curls had been pressed against faceless mannequin cheeks, while finger waves and tresses hung from tiny hooks. Curl paper and ribboned lovelocks were set around a display of ebony combs and scissors. The history of the pigtail, from its Manchurian slavery origins to a modern Asian fashion, was almost convincing. I was less impressed by a chart showing the development of the bikini line in terms of fractal geometry. The advances in hair styling were shown through diagrams, and there was a section of peculiarities, such as hair that had turned white overnight. The rack of baby curls amused me, because they reminded me of the pale twists of hair I'd seen in countless Scottish museums, professing to be shorn from the head of Bonnie Prince Charlie. He must have been half bald by the time he was thirty at the rate they used to take hair from him. Famous cases of conviction by hair were displayed, where DNA testing from the plucked root had revealed the profile of a killer. This was compared to the common home-usage of a hair, stuck across a cupboard door or left on a diary, to detect unwanted openings. It was also pointed out that many an affair had been discovered by a stray hair.

The only surprise was that there were no wigs. When I asked the curator, he said, 'A wig is a fake memory of hair.' I expected him to elaborate, but only when I pressed him did he dismiss me by saying, 'There's a wig museum on Templová, if that's your interest.'

I swore that it wasn't, trying to reduce the offence I'd caused, but he continued working, methodically cleaning a strand of hair. He was wiping it down with an alcohol cloth, and it reminded me of the way film-restorers wash ancient strips of celluloid. His English was so good, I thought it was safe to ask him what he was doing.

'Emotional spectography,' he said. 'The recording of feelings in people's hair.'

I must have looked blank, so he said, 'Have you ever been in a room where people have been arguing? You can feel the anger hanging in the air. It's the same with hair. Emotion lingers. Like tree rings.'

Despite his vagueness I knew what he meant. When we'd been in the Natural History Museum in London, we'd found a display called History in Nature. Tree rings blackened by the Fire of London, rock slices that showed the aftermath of floods, core samples that revealed catastrophes as a smudge of discolouration. Fossils were displayed as memories of species locked in rock. It was the museum's attempt to show that even nature records, as though to justify its endless cataloguing. The politics offended me, but I knew there was some truth in it. Important events leave their mark on the world. According to the curator, it's the same with people; moments that move us are left in the structure of our hair.

Once treated, he would shine light through the strand, then look at the colours to glimpse the feelings. It was, he admitted, an inexact science. For a change, that didn't bother me.

Shortly after Janelle and I met we went to the Natural History Museum. We'd met at a hotel in London's Docklands, where they were holding the *Aping The Victorians* Conference. We had such similar ideas on our subject that I knew we'd either get along very well or become quite cold with each other. I hate to admit it now because it makes me sound shallow, but I was attracted to her by three things; her accent, her long blonde plait and her makeup. I'd become so used to women wearing little or no makeup, especially at academic conferences, that it was strange to see somebody wearing so much. The weird thing is, she was far from plain, and could have got away without makeup, so I couldn't work out what she was thinking of. I always used to be one of those men that hassled women about it, until I realised they meant it when they said they were wearing it for themselves. Even so, I preferred women who wore almost none, and was confused to find myself attracted to Janelle. Mostly she wore dark makeup, to offset her blonde hair, and her lips were red. It was incredibly bold. I told my friend Michael, and he deconstructed the attraction, saying I found her appealing because she was a cross between a porn-queen and a teacher. I didn't speak to him for the rest of the weekend.

When I next spoke to Janelle alone, I left the subject of our shared interest, and asked about her face, as politely as possible.

'For us,' she pointed East, presumably meaning Eastern Europe, 'this is quite new. We didn't have many luxuries for a long time. Giving things up is easy when you've had the fun, but we never got much chance to be glamorous. Until I was twenty-five, I could barely afford good makeup. So now I wear it all the time.'

'But you'd look fine without it.'

'Probably better,' she said, 'but I enjoy it. This way I save the real me for just one person.'

We managed to invite each other out. The Natural History Museum was an obvious choice for our first date, so we went early on the Sunday morning.

Annoying for its assumptions and fact-peddling, the
museum was startling in its racism. In the 'Development
of Man' section we found that the peak of evolution was
represented by a full-size model of a naked white man.
With blue eyes and immaculate blonde hair he looked
healthy, well-fed and underworked. Further back, by the
apes, there was a jet-black woman, breast feeding, with
hoops through her nose.

I remembered my Biology teacher showing remarkable
honesty when he'd said, 'Progress is so appealing because
it leads to us.' Us being white men, of course. Women
and other races were, by definition, primitive

Janelle had a story to match that, and as we walked
on we began talking eagerly.

'Museums are an insult to the imagination,' she said,
expressing disgust at the stuffed animals. She would have
preferred a description, a paw print, and an opportunity
to imagine, rather than a waxed carcass. 'They think
recording is meaning.' I didn't realise at the time that in
one statement she'd summed up her obsessions.
Recording as meaning, she would say, *is the myth of our
time*. Which is pretty ironic, because that lunchtime we
received a perfect demonstration of the myth in action.
Before we knew it we'd talked the rest of the morning
away in the coffee shop, and she started looking
uncomfortable. I asked if she had to go.

'No, but I am meeting somebody. I don't want you to
go, but maybe you don't want to meet this person.'

'Who is it?'

'My uncle.'

We established that I would stay. She didn't mind me
being there while she saw her uncle. She didn't really
like him, and he wasn't her proper uncle. He was a
Londoner who'd spent time with her family in Prague

when she was a child. So I thought that would be all right.

Her uncle turned up wearing a thick suit that stank of dust and dried rain. He offered to buy lunch for both of us, and I knew I'd be torn between feeling sorry for him and being bored. While we ate he talked to me as though we'd met before, asked Janelle a few questions about the family, and then got his video camera out. His wife, he said, wouldn't believe he'd seen Janelle. He then started filming, and asked her to speak. Nervously, her accent stronger than ever, she said hello, pointed to the museum around her, said why she was in England, and then stalled, shrugging. He turned the camera on to me, and effectively requested the same sort of response. I said something about only just having met Janelle, and he kept filming for a few seconds after I stopped talking. By then he'd managed to get a few people in the museum watching us, so it was perfect timing when he pulled out the view screen, and rewound the video for a public performance. The sound was turned up loud enough for everybody to hear, and we had to watch, smiling, hoping people wouldn't stare too much. I'd never realised just how bad my posture could be when I was feeling awkward. Worst of all, there was a big marble statue of Darwin behind me, as though we were sitting together.

Janelle's uncle was delighted though. He had his proof. The experience was real, because it was on tape, and that was more important than actually remembering it.

When he'd gone Janelle said that nothing could have bothered her more. 'This is exactly what I write about,' she said. 'If catalogued, something is real. Like this museum. If we put all these animals on display, evolution is a fact.'

She probably had no idea how much I liked her for saying that.

I became acutely aware of incidents of recording, where people refused to experience, but preferred to monitor their existence. At Waterloo station I saw a couple of girls go into a photo booth, leaving the curtain open wide enough for me to watch them. They pulled different faces, and made out that they were having a good time for the camera. Then they stood outside the machine silently with long faces, waiting for the photos to come out. It was as though recording a few moments of feigned joy was more important than having a genuinely good day out.

It was later that day that I saw the trainspotter at Milton Keynes. Trainspotters are a curious breed of person who stand on railway platforms and note down the numbers on the sides of train carriages. They spend years pursuing the impossible goal of collecting every single number. That day I saw a trainspotter with a video camera. I felt sick at the thought of him going home and watching that tape, proving that he'd witnessed those numbers.

The obsession with recording is insidious. Throughout London, tourists held video cameras so tightly to their eyes, it must have been like watching television for the whole weekend. People don't trust their own experience, or their memories, so they make their lives real by logging them. I wanted to smash their cameras and tell them to be there in the moment.

Half the problem is that people believe in images. If something is filmed, it is real. My parents, when watching made-for-television specials, would rant about the injustice of a particular drama, occasionally saying,

'I know it's only a film,' but you could tell they were having trouble seeing it as anything other than reality. We're so used to CCTV and video evidence that film has come to stand for truth.

Janelle and I were happy enough to experience each other; we ignored the language barrier, put aside the fact that we were living in different parts of Europe, and began a relationship.

We were at the age where going through the process of getting to know somebody is becoming a bit dull, so we didn't even bother relating our histories. Two weeks had gone by, and I'd told her nothing about my childhood. A world record. We preferred instead, to concentrate on the present, to learn about each other from our responses. So we talked about what we thought, and told stories, but we didn't get into *so what do you think about...* That way, when facts about each other emerged, they were usually more startling. Waiting for a cab one night, I was looking at the stars, and Janelle told me she couldn't see them.

'Well, not directly,' she said. 'I have eclipse burns.'

A few years previously, despite knowing the risk, she'd gained a couple of deep burns by staring at the sun during an annular eclipse. The burns were right in the centre of her retinas, obliterating the fovea. The parts that perceive detail were effectively removed, meaning she could only see things in her peripheral vision. If she looked at stars, they winked out. Even reading, she'd scan over the letters, letting the meaning occur to her in complete sentences.

'This is why I'm not interested in facts. There are very few specifics for me. If I look at something, it disappears.'

'Can you see me?'

'Yes, but not by staring. If I stare at your eyes, they

aren't there. I can only see them by taking your whole face in.'

She explained that she could see the stars, faces, details of all kinds, but only if she avoided looking at them directly. 'It's like passive effort,' she said. 'If I strive for something, it gets away from me.'

This minor disability didn't affect her much, but made me feel peculiar when we were looking in each other's eyes. I kept wondering what I must look like, blanked out. But it wasn't much of a problem, and we grew closer.

Rather than planning for the future, or cataloguing our past, we thrived on each other. It was serious from the outset, but never dour until the day she left for Prague. She had to go home, and from what we could tell we wouldn't see each other for months. So before we got too miserable I made the commitment to go to Prague every few weeks. Our parting at Heathrow didn't feel too bad, but when I got back to the flat I found that Janelle had cut off a piece of her hair for me to remember her by. She'd left a note saying it was a custom to give presents upon parting, to aid memory. Rather than take it from a layer that was out of sight, she'd cut it from the hair that was closest to her face. That way, she said, she'd have something to remember me by as well. It was then that I realised how much I missed her.

For the first few days the hair smelt of her, but soon it smelt of nothing but my hands. It was the softest hair I've ever known, but I could barely touch it, for fear of separating the strands and losing it forever.

We'd been together for over eight months when hair colour went viral. Euphemistically at least. We're fairly sure now that DNA had nothing to do with it, but that patterns for form were being passed in water, and DNA was re-coding accordingly. Whatever the truth, hair colour was spreading, and darker shades were favoured. Even synthetic dyes were being encoded and passed on as pigment. Within a few months there were hardly any blondes left, and of those that remained, their roots were beginning to darken. Janelle was one of the few people to have unblemished long blonde hair, and by November, she was one of the last remaining blondes.

You'd have thought that would make her appealing to people, a rarity, but the few blondes who remained felt like freaks. They were the ones awaiting the change, and nobody wanted to be around them. It reminded me of those personal ads that state *no baggage*. Nobody wanted to be near the blondes because trauma was obviously pending. But although Janelle was no more attractive to strangers, she became a curiosity. People would stare, some jealous, others just relishing one of their last views of a natural blonde. She was hassled occasionally to sell her hair before it grew darker, but she never showed any interest.

We were happy through that period, until an afternoon in mid-November. The weather in Prague had turned unreasonably cold. There was no snow, but you got the feeling that deep ice ran through the concrete. Passing the river, a frozen breeze lifted from its surface, making my lungs hurt. And we were completely miserable without knowing why. We weren't argumentative or disagreeable, but there was a malaise about us that made everything an effort. We walked up behind the castle, heading for the park. We were planning to go to the science museum – we'd been meaning to for weeks – but were so cold that we stopped in the park café. We didn't talk, but drank slowly, warming up. By the time we made it through to the museum – a building that looked like a car park – I felt close to tears. It was a hilarious museum, with five floors detailing the evolution of ships, cars, military equipment, animals and cameras. Normally we'd have had a great time, but we found ourselves bickering.

It took all day for us to confront the issue, but on the walk back down the hill, we began to talk. It was still early afternoon, but darkening, a grey mist over the whole of Prague. The arc of the river, crossed by so many bridges, looked motionless. Talking was difficult, because of the numbness in our lips, but we were both trying. I said there was nothing wrong with me, except for worrying about her mood. She said the same about me.

'Maybe I caught your mood,' she said. There were rumours of stray feelings and thoughts being spread, like the patterns that had spread hair colour. Mostly, though, they were occasional images and fragments of thought, rather than perpetual emotions.

'And anyway, maybe I caught yours,' I concluded.

In an attempt to salvage the day we went to the Radagast pub, an underground corridor with cheap beer and cheese. We'd been there the night before and had a great time, so we hoped it would serve the same purpose. We had to share a table from the outset, which made talking difficult. By the time the couple had gone, we'd both drunk a bit too much. We tried to talk about other things, but started arguing again. On the walk home she said she'd only let me into the flat if I left in the morning. I wasn't having that, so said I'd leave immediately. She seemed willing to let me do that, so I feigned illness, and slept in the bath. In the morning I picked up my bag and left, checking into a hostel before she even opened her curtains. They were still closed when I walked past at lunchtime. That night there was still no sign of her being in. Her phone wouldn't answer, the lights remained out, and nobody came when I knocked. Eventually I kicked down the door, which was easier than I'd always been led to believe. She'd left quite a lot of stuff behind, mostly in boxes. But there was no note, which surprised me more than anything.

I wanted to trace the point of loss. Who did she see that afternoon? What thoughts had ruined her mood? What had happened to change her so suddenly? I went through every theory, wondering if her impending change from blonde to dark had affected her somehow. But I couldn't image her being that bothered.

I let the police do the legwork, searching through her belongings. They kept me informed, and called me straightaway when they found out where she'd moved to. She was alive, they confirmed, and getting on with her life. I'd got to know them quite well, so they let me know roughly what area she was living in. She was still in Prague, and after Christmas she'd be carrying on with her research, so tracking her down should be easy. They also told me about the plait, putting odds on the museum curator being granted ownership. I'd been planning to go home for Christmas, but the presence of Janelle's hair gave me a chance to understand why she'd left.

The museum was more popular now, hair being graded throughout by colours; great swathes of blonde plaits, ponytails and bobs were arranged on pedestals as the prize exhibits. All of them were in vacuum cases. It was difficult to get the curator on his own, and even more difficult to get him to admit to owning Janelle's plait.

'I only want one hair.'

'For what?'

'Last time, you mentioned emotional spectography. I want to know what was going on in her mind. I need to know what she was feeling.'

'Wait until we're closed,' he said.

When the museum was empty, he turned down the lights and went to the safe. Janelle's plait was in a sealed plastic bag, awaiting display preparation. It took him about five minutes to pull one hair free, he was so gentle with it. We talked while he cleaned it, his movements as smooth as if he was stroking a cat.

'Do you know how close this was to her scalp?' he asked.

'I think she cut it off at shoulder length.'

'Then we're wasting our time. Her recent memories will be in the hair that's still on her head. Can you bring me one of those?'

'No, not for a while anyway. I won't be seeing her until the New Year.'

'Well, we can look at this, but the memories will be months old.'

'It's a start.'

'Do you know why she did it?'

'Left me?'

He shook his head, and made a scissoring motion with his fingers. I shrugged.

'You know the cutting of hair is generally a signal of starting over. New beginnings.'

'Yes. But even so.'

He secured the hair in a glass straw, then illuminated it. Holding a marble-lens close to his eye he moved in, squinting to get a better view. He moved gradually up the hair as he took in the years of her emotions. His face lit up as he reached the top.

'Can I see?'

He passed me the lens. Looking through was exactly as I imagined it to be. Magnified and polarised, the light from the hair looked like sand and spectrum lines. After a moment, though, I could see deeper colours, and with them came sensations. It was like struggling to remember something; when I moved on, I caught the glimpse of the memories I'd passed. I rushed the process, moving straight up to the place where she'd cut. Just before the top, there was a glint of gold. I heard myself gasp, and the curator said, 'See, she was in love.' As I pulled the lens away there was a vague afterimage of my own face.

Janelle agreed to meet me before Christmas, which was a sign of progress. It wasn't completely hopeless if she was willing to do that. Her supervisor had passed my message on, and she'd contacted me at the hostel. I went to the café half an hour earlier than we'd arranged, but she was already there. I'd pictured her turning dark overnight, but her hair was still mostly blonde, only the roots showing signs of shadow. The biggest difference was in her face. At first I thought she was cold, but then realised she wasn't wearing makeup.

'Are you all right?'

'I'm fine,' she said. 'I didn't really want to see you though.'

Meeting an ex-lover after a break-up up fascinates me. The person still feels so familiar, and you know you could make them laugh, but you can't even think about touching them. They are more estranged than when you first met, because there's less willingness to be open.

We didn't bother with the pleasantries of what we'd been up to, but got straight to the point.

'It wasn't me,' she said. 'It was you.'

I didn't respond, so she said, 'Think. Think about what you did.'

'I didn't do anything.'

'I was watching you more than you thought. It might seem like nothing to you, but it hurts. You understand. It hurts me.'

I could tell I wasn't going to get a complete hair from her, or an explanation, so I said, 'Meaning what? What am I meant to have done? I was perfectly happy until you started being so miserable.'

'You were in my peripheral vision,' she said. 'Even when you thought I couldn't see you, I was taking you in. Everything you did was sinking in to me.'

'So?'

'So work it out for yourself.'

'Please,' I said. 'Come to the Hair Museum. Help me to understand.'

I explained what had happened, what I'd seen, and she looked so upset that she put one hand over her eyes, and held a palm up at me to keep me away.

'All right,' she said.

The curator looked at Janelle with sympathy, which must have been annoying for her. He talked about her hair, said it would have looked beautiful on her. I expected her to be short-tempered, but she was kind to him.

'Have you come to try again?' he asked.

'No,' she said. 'This isn't about my hair. He can look at his own.'

She put her hand on my scalp, secured a hair, and pulled it free.

'That's not what I want.'

'Until you can do this, there's no point in looking at mine,' she said.

While we debated, the curator took the hair, cleaned it, and threaded it into the glass tube.

'Start at the root,' he said, illuminating it and passing me the lens.

I couldn't make out anything at first, because the feelings were so recent. It was only as I passed down the hair that I could sense the time passing back. It was easy to find the afternoon in the park, and although I sped through it to get past the emotions quickly, I slowed as the memories reeled back towards morning.

There was a glint, and then a smoky blue. My hand was trembling, but I stilled it, and she was walking by me, and I was watching to the side. A young girl, probably about seventeen. I didn't look at her for long, but I held on to the image of her face, wishing I could kiss her. If Janelle and I split up, it would be so easy for me to meet new people like her. Then I saw Janelle, her face slightly soured; she was getting older.

I pulled back from the lens, letting the image fade.

'Were you jealous? Is that all it was?'

'Not jealous, no. I felt abandoned. It wasn't that you looked, but that you hoped. You were hoping for a future with them because you were miserable with me. Look at the rest,' she said, pointing back at the hair.

I drew the lens down, letting images flicker past, hundreds of faces coming back to me, each memory tinged with a desire that said I'd done more than glance at them.

'The whole time you were with me you kept fantasising about how easy it would be to meet new people if we split up. That day was the last time I'd put up with it. I still cared, but I couldn't stay with you while you were wishing yourself away from me.'

The curator switched off the lamp.

I can't remember whether he left us alone, or stayed in the building while we talked, but I remember sitting there, realising how she'd been able to see the desire in me, and how she must have felt. And I remember leaning over, feeling Janelle's breath in my hair as she held me. I was saying sorry and trying to cry, but nothing came out. All I could feel was a sting in my scalp, and the stroke of her hand down my back.

tony white

....

the jet-set girls

Chipperfield Road
Bovingdon
Herts
21st Jan 1998
Dear Tony,

Thank you very much for your letter which arrived
shortly before Christmas. Tom tells me that your writing
is interesting; 'good stuff, good bloke' were his words.

I'm really very flattered by your obvious knowledge of
my 'work' (as you put it). You mentioned the NEL edition
of 'The Jet-Set Girls' – I had forgotten all about my brief
incarnation as 'Penny Douglas', most of 'her' titles were
in fact written by Jim Moffat (as you probably know) but
that one was definitely mine.

Now, to your question. How I got started in the business – the attached should answer this. Probably the same
way lots of people do – I was in the right place at the
right time. My advice to any young writer trying to be
published (not to yourself, of course) would be this: try
and find a way in through the back door.

If any of the enclosed is useful to you then you are
welcome to it. Chop and change as you wish.

As for your second request – If you think that the

Literary Quarterly would be interested in an interview, I'd be happy to do that with you, just give me a ring and we'll arrange a time.

Best wishes,

Hughie

Editor's note: – The following episode is presented largely in the form in which Hugh Johnston submitted it to me shortly before his death in March of last year. I have made only one or two very minor corrections in the interests of clarity. In his day, Hugh was well known for his ability to write a novel 'in one go'; he was reputed never to correct or re-draft one of his manuscripts. So it is in that spirit that I introduce what we had come to hope might form a chapter of his autobiography – sadly this will never now be completed. I am grateful to Tom Aitchison, and the Literary Estate of Hugh Johnston for allowing us to go ahead and print this story. We all felt that to publish this episode now would be a fitting memorial to one of the most successful, if least recognised, British writers of popular fiction.

The following story is dedicated to the memory of its author:
'Hughie' Johnston, 1940–1999

I suppose I was shooting my mouth off. It was another night in the West End's lesser establishments. Off the radar as usual. I imagine things have changed a bit now, but back then if you wanted to be out of reach of the police, the gangsters, the whole *demi-monde*, you had to drink with them. Anyone else was considered fair game.

Well, maybe I was wrong, on reflection, but that's how it seemed to me.

It must have been morning by the time I got to the Spotlight. It was a bit of a haunt in those days. Used to pop in and have a whisky with the touts; it was on their route from the gambling clubs to a half-hour kip over bacon and eggs in that little Greek café opposite Foyles. With Linda, I think her name was. She was there for years; certainly until Raymond put the rent up and she moved out. Sweet girl. She was then. Pretty little thing. Hard as nails. That was usually enough for me; back home to sleep it off until the next night. To be frank, I didn't have the where-with-all to carry on. More a lack of 'the old LSD' (pounds, shillings and pence) than a lack of stamina. But those chaps never seemed to sleep. I don't know how they did it. By half-past nine they'd be back out on their pitches. It was as if they drew some sort of energy from their trade, in lieu of ever actually resting themselves. Part of the transaction, so to speak.

Anyway, the Spotlight. Weird place. You wouldn't know it was there unless you knew it was there. If you know what I mean. Just a door down some steps in that alley next to Denmark Street. No bar or anything. Couple of tables and chairs and some bottles of pale ale in the corner. Something stronger if you wanted. Little Cypriot called Tony used to run it. Poof, obviously. No one paid cash. Well I did, but all the bigger boys just 'ran up tabs', not so much a slate as a retainer. So much a month just to keep him open.

I'd always fancied myself as a writer. Hadn't actually done it though. Had anything published, I mean. I suppose I just enjoyed that certain 'low life' thrill of doing what I imagined it was that writers did. Penguin in the jacket pocket, you know. Reading cheap translations of the French stuff over halves in the French. Even wore a polo neck: I shudder to think of it. I normally kept my ambitions to myself though, in that kind of company. So I must have been half-cut. Still I wasn't the only one. There were one or two other people there who fancied themselves as something they weren't.

They were all at the Spotlight that night. Tony was mincing around with a grubby tea towel over his shoulder as usual. Una Pearson was there – that was part of the attraction of the place. Bit of a fading beauty by then, of course. Still called herself an 'actress' though. She could drink me under the table any night of the week. A couple of the Bazalgette brothers were lording it at the corner table. On one side was Mo. 'Shakey Mo' people called him – something to do with his temper. No one said it to his face of course. Next to him was Charles, the eldest. Big chap but very softly spoken. The Bishop. That was his nickname, because if he was thinking about something he'd always get out this rosary; mull things over while he ran the beads through his fingers, counting them – and your options – off. Very slowly. Never saw him drink. His one vice – if you could call it that – was an incredibly sweet tooth. Spanish Phil, the king of the touts, once told me that Charlie was diabetic, but I never had any inclination to try and verify this.

I was bragging to Una about what I used to call 'the great British novel' – moaning about Greene and Amis and Waugh, telling her what was wrong with them, and why my first novel was going to be better, even, than the likes of Orwell. Of course it was no such thing. And Una, bless her, was too far gone to care.

Even though I drank there several times a week, I'd never spoken to any of the Bazalgette family. So, when Mo sent a boy over to ask if I would like to join him and Charles for a drink, I suppose I was too flattered to do anything other than accept. I excused myself from the conversation with Una and followed him over. I shook The Bishop's hand, nodded a silent greeting, then sat down on the chair which Mo had pushed out from under the table with his foot.

'Charles wanted a quiet word, Hugh. Between ourselves.'

The Bishop didn't say anything for a while. He was thinking. Pushing his beads around, occasionally looking up at me, or at what was going on in the club behind me. Then he put the beads down and took a Mars Bar out of his pocket. Tearing the wrapper, he took a bite, then looked at Mo and nodded.

'You can write, Hugh, can't you, eh?' asked Mo.

I looked from one to the other. Charles had his mouth full of Mars, but was staring straight at me.

'Charlie and me . . . We heard you was a bit of a writer,' Mo persisted.

I said that, yes, I was writing a novel.

'Lovely. Thought so, didn't we.'

The Bishop looked at me for a while without saying anything, then nodded, before taking another bite.

'Thing is,' Mo continued, 'We're looking for a writer at the moment. Tell him Charlie.'

He swallowed his last bit of Mars, then spoke for the first time.

'We're looking at a new game, Hugh. Maurice thought you might be interested. Excuse me.'

Perhaps the nervousness showed on my face; I didn't want to know about any of their games – old or new. People had a tendency to wind up dead in the kind of games that the Bazalgette brothers played. Ignorance is bliss, as the saying goes. He threw the empty wrapper on the floor, then pocketed his rosary and stood up, whispering something in Mo's ear before leaving the table. Mo turned and caught the eye of one of the younger lads, this real 'hardnut', as we used to say then, called Davey, who immediately nudged his mate. They put down their bottles and opened the door for The Bishop – Davey went out first, then came back in and nodded. The other two followed him out.

'Publishing,' said Mo, as the door shut behind them. 'We've been looking into it. And we figure there's a fucking mint to be made. Cost fuck-all to print, if you do enough of 'em. Couple of bob a piece at the fucking most. Sell a few thousand copies at twelve and six each. You can work it out for yourself, Hugh.'

I didn't hide my surprise. This was the last thing I'd expected to hear. I said that I supposed there was quite a lot of money in it, but that depended whether the book was well received, how the critics responded. A great work of literature, I ventured, could probably earn its publisher and its writer a good deal of money.

Mo laughed at this.

'What do your mob get paid then?'

His question took me by surprise. 'Nothing,' would have been the most truthful answer I could have given, and frankly, until I heard the question phrased in Mo's inimitable style, this wasn't something I'd even considered. Until that moment I had been firmly of the conviction that one wrote for the love of literature. I decided to take a stab in the dark. It varied, I said. Depending on the fame of the author. But at a rough guess, I would say that advances on royalties could probably be anything from twenty quid to a thousand guineas.

'How does a hundred and fifty nicker sound?' he asked. 'Up front of course.'

I could only agree. Yes, I should imagine that any writer worth his salt would be pleased with a sum of that kind. After all, I added, let's not forget that a novel can take anything up to several years to write.

Mo nearly choked on his pale ale.

'Years?' he exploded. 'Several fucking years? You taking the piss, Hughie, old son? We was thinking of a week!'

A week? I was astounded and told him so. I had been working away on my own manuscript for nigh-on a couple of years, and I was nowhere near to finishing it.

'So you ain't interested? Shame. Find some other cunt then, I suppose.'

'Well no, I didn't say I wasn't interested, Mo . . .' I backpedalled, suddenly realising that he hadn't been talking generally, but actually making me an offer. 'But it takes a while to set up as a publishing house, you need editors for one thing, a reputation, before people will take you . . .'

'We've got a fucking reputation, Hugh. What you trying to say?'

'No, I mean a reputation in the literary world, Mo.'

'Who the fuck said anything about literature? Forget that shit. That ain't gonna bring in the LSD, mate. Here.'

He picked a briefcase up from the floor, opened it, and took out a number of luridly covered paperbacked volumes. Put them on the table in front of me.

They had titles like *Schoolgirls Who Do, The Desire to Dominate, Lesbian Love*; all were published by imprints I'd never heard of – Luxor, Hanbury, Ship, Tallis.

'Go on then, have a fucking flick through.'

I did as he suggested. The quality of the writing was fairly perfunctory – decidedly unerotic even, some had photographic inserts to pad them out.

'And this is the quality end of the market,' he said, pushing a copy of de Sade's *120 Days of Sodom*, and an Olympia edition of something called *The Story of O* across the table. 'Now, *this* stuff fucking shifts. If you can copy it, not too fucking obviously of course, we might be getting somewhere.'

I looked up at him quizzically, pointing at first one, then the other title. Mo pointed at *The Story of O*.

'Listen,' he said, 'Charlie's done a bit of asking around on the blower, and it looks like this mob are only gonna be doing *O*. What do you say?'

I couldn't believe my ears A hundred and fifty was a couple of month's wages. I was sobering up fast. Mo looked over my shoulder.

'Oi, Tone. Come on, son.'

Tony appeared with two glasses and a bottle of Maltese brandy.

'Leave em, Tone, eh.'

'Let me get this straight. If I write one of these— *books*—you and your brother will give me a hundred and fifty quid?'

'That's right, Hughie old son. If you want to. More than one, though. We're gonna need a few.' He nodded at the assembled drinkers. 'The lads say you're trustworthy. Just bring it here same time next week and I'll pay you for the next one. Think you can manage that?'

He began to pour two glasses of brandy.

He was offering me more money than I'd ever earned before, to write a book. Suddenly the failings of the modern British novel began to seem less and less important. I felt myself nodding enthusiastically, heard myself speaking: 'Thanks, Mo. Course I can.'

He grinned and we shook hands.

'Keep the books, Hughie, use them for research. Money's in the bag.'

'But how are you going to get them into the book-shops, Mo?'

'Leave that to us, son,' he said, pushing the glass towards me. 'We *own* the fucking bookshops. Hang on though,' he pulled some pin-up magazines out of the briefcase, flicked through to the Classifieds. 'You might want to see this. Look.'

His grubby finger was pointing at an advertisement.

The Story of A, it said, beneath a half-tone dolly bird. 'By Anonymous. 12/6 ea. + 6d post & packing. Kali Books' with a private box address in Wardour Street.

'Kali?' I asked. Surprised at the brothers' knowledge of the Hindu pantheon. 'After the goddess of . . .'

'No, it's personal, Hugh. Family thing.'

'Wait a minute, Mo. You've got one title already then? Do you want me to start with "B" or what?'

Mo laughed as he drained his glass.

'Don't be daft.' He jabbed the ad with his finger. 'That's your first book, son. Orders are good and all. So don't go letting your readers down, will you, eh?'

I drained my brandy. Mo poured another for both of us.

There was a commotion at the doorway. I turned around and saw Davey coming back into the club; he had blood streaming down his face. Tony yelped, then rushed over, sat him down, and dabbed at the wound with his tea towel, chattering away in Greek or whatever it was. Charles Bazalgette walked over and rejoined us at the table. He raised his eyebrows in my direction. Mo nodded.

The Bishop smiled briefly and put his hand out, I shook it. Then he looked at his brother. Mo picked up the briefcase and stuffed the books and magazines back inside before pushing it across the table towards me.

'Come on then, son, best be off, eh? You've got work to do.'

I was woken the next afternoon by a knock on the door of my room. I staggered out of bed, tripping over Mo's briefcase as I did so, and quickly put on a dressing gown to make myself half-decent. When I opened the door I was surprised to see Una Pearson standing in the hallway outside. She was carrying a shopping basket, in which I could clearly see a bottle of wine.

'Morning, darling,' she said. 'Thought you might like some breakfast before you start work.'

'Una, how did you . . . Excuse me, I was just getting up. Come in.'

Before I start work.

'Mo told you, did he?'

'It was me that suggested you, sweetie. Looked as if you needed the money.' Una placed her hand briefly against my cheek as she squeezed past me. I was suddenly aware of how stuffy my room was, and immediately went across to my desk. Reaching over the typewriter, I opened the curtains and struggled with the sash, lifting it a couple of inches – enough to allow a thin blast of cool air in.

While I was doing this, Una had put down her handbag and her shopping basket, and was busily rinsing a couple of glasses which she set down beside the sink. She began looking through the cutlery drawer.

'It's on the table,' I said, clearing my clothes from the chairs.

She pulled the cork and poured, then handed me a glass whilst looking around at the room.

'At least it's cheap,' I offered.

'I should hope so too, darling.'

She took a new pack of Embassy from her handbag, opened it and offered me one.

A couple of glasses later I was beginning to feel a little more human.

'It was very sweet of you to come and wake me.'

Una said nothing, just smiled, then got up from her chair, walked the few steps to where I was sitting and took the cigarette from between my lips. Stubbing it out in the ashtray, she leaned over to my ear.

'I had my reasons, darling.'

I could feel her breath on my cheek. Smell her perfume. I turned and kissed her, I might have been a bit green but I wasn't stupid – I knew what this was about.

Straightening, Una began to unbutton her twin-set. She placed the cardigan on the back of her chair. Reaching behind her waist served to push her ample bosom toward me, and I could see the outline of her dark nipples through her slip. To be honest, I felt like a kid at Christmas! How many men had rehearsed this moment in their minds? She unzipped her skirt, pushed it down, stepped out of it. Then she slowly lifted the slip above her head. She was wearing a pink, one-piece girdle, which emphasised her voluptuous, hour-glass figure, and – I was surprised to see – nothing else, save her stockings. Her pubic hair was dark and thick.

'You like what you see, darling?'

'Very much,' I rather superfluously replied, for Una was already tugging at my dressing gown cord to reveal the confirmation of my words. She kissed me once again, and I slipped my hands into her brassiere, pushed the straps off her shoulders. Standing suddenly, Una walked over to where her handbag was left, beside her chair. She reached in and took out a lipstick. Without taking her eyes from mine, she applied it to her lips, smacking them in the way that all women do. Then to my surprise she delicately outlined her nipples with similarly deft strokes. My desire was now more aroused than ever, and Una knelt quickly between my legs and set to polishing my glans with her tongue (the image of her licking and biting at my swollen, ripening fruit has sustained me for years). She frenched me then, and I gasped as she took my entire length in her mouth. When she was satisfied with my resolve, Una gave my prick one last lingering kiss before clambering swiftly up on to my lap. Grasping her *derrière* in both hands I helped her to guide herself on to my proud manhood, which slipped easily and suddenly into the tight warmth of her silken sanctuary. While she caressed and teased me, with all the guile and art of the courtesan, I busied myself with the joys that I found before my face – taking first one, then the other tit into my mouth, lapping and sucking at her paps and completely mindless of the lipstick which must surely have been smearing my face.

There can be little more beautiful in this world than the delicate exclamations of joy which a woman in the throes of passion can emit. Soft as the petal-like skin of their inner thighs, these wordless imprecations can lead a man to the very brink of destruction. But nothing could have prepared me for the stream of expletives which Una, grinding ever harder on to my lap, began to scream. 'Fuck me harder, you bastard!' she screamed. She was pulling my hair and biting at my shoulders. 'Fuck me like a whore! I want to feel you come in my cunt!'

For a second or two I was taken aback, but then quickly redoubled my efforts, driving myself deeper and deeper until I seemed to be entering the very heart of her being. Our outlines dissolved then. Somewhere, far away, I could hear a cry of ecstasy, but I was aware only of a beautiful unfolding, as of a rose-bud, and I felt myself to be somewhere deep in the heart of that sudden flowering – a part of it, almost. I could hold my resolve no longer, and with a final thrust I emptied myself within her.

We spent several days and nights lost in the joys that each other's bodies offered. In her day, Una must surely have been one of the most beautiful women of her generation, and even now, all these years later, I still love watching *Passport to Pimlico*, and the other Ealing Studio comedies, just to catch a glimpse of her in her prime. The age difference between us seemed to me to be of little importance when we could pleasure each other with such urgency. Each time we made love I felt that she was teaching me not only about sex – though she certainly was – but about life itself. We steered clear of the Spotlight Club, venturing out only as far as the public houses and clubs in my neighbourhood off Westbourne Grove, and occasionally cabbing it down to a restaurant in Mayfair for a quiet supper. The money was burning a hole in my pocket I suppose, and we lived a high old life for a few days.

I was surprised then, as we sat over our early evening

drinks in the Grapes, to hear a familiar voice call my name.

I looked up and saw that Mo was carrying a tray of drinks over to our table. He was followed by a man of striking appearance. Dressed in the kind of restrainedly flamboyant Saville Row finery that only the richest among us could afford in those austerity days, Mo's companion had an arrestingly pale complexion, topped by a shock of white hair, which was cut in the Italian style – fashionably long across the ear. He was a young man, so his tow-headed appearance was all the more striking.

'Hugh,' said Mo, 'I want you to meet Mr Cornelius, an associate of Kali Books.'

I half-stood and shook the cold, slender hand that was offered.

They both sat down, and I followed suit.

'Mr Cornelius was wondering how your book was coming along, weren't you, Jerry?'

Cornelius nodded.

'Nearly finished now,' I lied. 'Only a couple of chapters left to write. I'll see you on Friday as we arranged.'

'He's been working very hard,' Una added. 'I thought he needed a break, bless him.'

Mo moved quickly, reaching over and making to slap her across the face with the back of his hand, but Una saw it coming and grabbed his wrist in mid-swing, held it there, then spat, 'Don't even think about it, you stupid little fucker.'

'Yeah, steady on, Mo.' I put my arm around her, but she shrugged it off, then snorted derisively and threw Mo's hand down.

'The thing is,' Cornelius spoke now, diffusing the tension with his quiet, even voice. 'We've just been to your place, Hugh, and there wasn't much sign of activity there. You've only got a couple of days to finish it, and from what we saw you haven't even started yet.'

'I . . .'

Mo put his brandy down, and sighed. I noticed that his hand was trembling very slightly.

'What you're gonna do now, Hugh, if you don't mind my saying,' he interjected, 'is go home and write this fucking book. I know you've been spending money like water, old son, so there's no chance of you paying us back, is there? Well, is there?'

I shook my head.

'So Jerry here is gonna take you home, and you ain't gonna fucking leave your place until it's fucking finished, son. Understand?'

I nodded. There was clearly no point in protesting.

'And you,' he turned to Una, 'are gonna leave the boy alone until he's finished. Fucking disgraceful it is, you'd drop him if he couldn't afford to keep you in gin. You're old enough to be his bleeding mother!'

If Una's glass had been full, I had the feeling that she'd have flung it at Mo. As it was, she stood up. 'You can fuck off, the lot of you!' she spat, then stormed out. I made to follow her but Cornelius grabbed my arm in a vice grip that was surprisingly powerful for a fellow of his build. I had no choice but to stay put, but not for long; a few minutes later I found myself being hustled unceremoniously out of the pub.

'G'night Mrs H,' Mo offered the landlady as we left.

'Ta ta, Mo,' she said, as if things like this happened every day, then, more deferentially, '*Mr* Cornelius.'

'How much have you got left?' Cornelius asked when we were back in my room.

I shrugged and pointed at my jacket which was flung

over the chair where Una and I had first made love a few days before. He reached into my breast pocket and took out my wallet. Opening it, he removed the two fivers that remained, along with a couple of ten bob notes.

'Don't worry about her,' he said. 'She'll have forgotten all about that in the morning. She'll be back, I know she will – she likes you. Mo thinks she was leading you astray. He has high hopes for you.'

He folded the notes and put them in his waistcoat.

'Keys?'

I took the fob from my trouser pocket and tossed it to him, then busied myself with feeding a sheet of foolscap into the Remington.

'Just going out for a couple of things,' he said, 'Since we're going to be here for a day or so.' Then, almost as an afterthought, he turned and added, 'This could be good for you, if you don't fuck it up. You know that, don't you.'

I heard him lock the door from the outside, took a deep breath, and began typing.

susan corrigan

mr pharmacist

There is a certain amount of reassurance in a cheese-burger. No, not *eating* it. Making it. Okay? Basically, you've got to form a mental assembly line: thawed quarter-pounder patty frying on the grill (pre-formed, not my fault) wreathed in chopped, golden onions. Flip, lay the cheese on the seared top, *a là* starlet's negligée. Pause while starlet removes undergarments on way to Hollywood casting couch. *Voilà*, the cheese softens; in – whoops, just checking! – let's see, the amount of time it takes your average mogul to give it a squirt of mayo. Spatula, burger, bun, plate, service! Gherkin optional.

I'm terrible. I really shouldn't be thinking like this after school, at work, age fourteen. Nor should I have smuggled the copy of *Hollywood Wives*, worn fan-like from household over-perusal, out of my mother's night stand drawer, because I can't stop thinking about the bit where the guy gets stuck *inside* this bimbo. Worse, I'm not even supposed to know this book exists yet my own mother has a secret copy she's pretending she never saw, much less bought. What am I supposed to do: 'Mom, have you ever heard of anyone getting caught in a vagina?'

Come on, people have to eat here.

Usual scenario: five old guys who move in slow motion, even after five cups of black coffee each, all happy to be of Swedish descent in the Scandinavian theme parks of suburban Minnesota. Ohhh, yah. You bet! All happy to work the hunter-gatherer look whether sitting in a drugstore's soda fountain or pulling Winnebagos attached to big Cadillacs out of this suburb and up to The Lake, which is where The Boat always is. All happy to 'talk shop' and pretend to flirt with Fritz' coffee-serving granddaughter. Fritz makes sure they tip at least a dollar each. Coffee is 60 cents with unlimited refills. Thankfully, they eat doughnuts – and lots of them – while they sit there talking about who owns what (and who) and how much it costs. Christ, the amount of Stan Petersons and Vern Johnsons in phone books throughout Minnesota. Thousands of the old guys, and they're all issued with Christmas lutefisk and those baseball caps made by Polaris or John Deere. My grandfather once claimed it all came from the central offices of a Lutheran relief charity and for a split second I didn't realize he was joking. How do they tell each other apart?

'Vern, why'n'cha get the little lady to bring you another Bismarck?'

'I got a better chance of calling Reagan on the Red Phone, Stan.'

You'd be surprised what happens in drugstores, especially this one. For a start, there's the fountain. There just aren't real soda fountains in drugstores any more now that every new shopping mall has a chrome-plated pseudo-1950s diner inside. This is probably the only one left in Minneapolis still located within a pharmacy, a place I've gone to buy chocolate my whole life, from the moment I could walk to the corner myself with 50 cents trapped in my fist, after school or after Sunday breakfast at my grandfather's house. My mother worked here once, flipping burgers in her starched white uniform when she was sixteen. 1960. You expect The Fonz to put in a cameo, really, somewhere between the prescriptions counter and the Revlon stand. Mom lasted six months before the pharmacist fired her; she doesn't elaborate on the reasons for dismissal but hasn't set foot inside the place since, preferring to send me or my sister as emissaries bearing the following note:

Dear Al,
Please sell my daughter a carton of Marlboro Lights. These cigarettes are for my use only.

Then her name, signed with a flourish I find difficult to duplicate on forged school excuse notes.

My grandfather cronied me into this job by leaning on Al, the pharmacist, a nervous little man who wrung his hands together whenever he wasn't washing them. Germ freak, with a pushy wife who actually owns the place and acts like it's the Grand Duchy of Cornwall. Al is cheap, probably because it's all wifey's money and she'd probably chop his nads off if any of us was paid *above* minimum wage, since that would seriously deprive her of essentials like enough Giorgio to bathe her dog in. I wonder if she knows the surveillance cameras are fake. My sister certainly realizes, and I'm dreading what happens when she does a klepto raid on my shift. Makeup, magazines, laxatives, fake nails, Doritos, baseball cards and Hershey bars exit the store each time safe in the bat-wing sleeves of her winter coat. She knows about serious amounts of Valium and Dilaudid locked in Al's safe, there to tempt drug robbers and agitated housewives who get along with their doctors better than their husbands, a basement full of stock and walk-in freezers, no-frills toilets with massive 'Employees Must Wash Hands' notices at eye level. Neatly folded and permanently creased white pinafores and aprons in a cupboard full of various uniforms. At work there is only me, Al, a cashier called Tracey and the stock boy, Bobby. He's sixteen and 'a bit slow', as Glenda says. If Glenda could speak in anything other than half-truths and whole clichés, she'd simply state that she and 'Alvin' gave Bobby a job because they wanted social rewards 'for giving him the chance'.

Sometimes I worry, because Al once accused me of shoplifting a piece of *sports gum* – as if! – and made me feel like scum while he asked me to turn out my pockets. When I came home with the story of what happened, my mom told me I should have made him call a policeman to search me – that's the law. Anything else was like an old man asking a kid to take their clothes off.

I think that was a hint.

Obviously, I didn't find employer-hating (and baiting) a completely alien concept. Shared family values and all that. 'Take This Job And Shove It' had recently sat atop the pop charts. Serving as cook, soda jerk and waitress simultaneously was borderline child slavery, legal so long as I clocked out by seven. The sartorial demands of Junior High and my extreme distaste for babysitting the neighbors' hyperactive brats forced my hand, so I have this job. Unlike absolutely everyone at school, I have a mother who doesn't believe in pocket money, mostly because she can't afford to. So with a job I can hold my head up high, walking past the mall girls. They're into lip gloss and nothing comes between them and their Calvins – if anything did, their parents would kill them.

The sartorial demands of Junior High. I'm into red lipstick and plagiarize the wardrobes of movies starring women called Hepburn, and rather than worship at the church of cheerleaders or the temple of teenage, I find having my own pursuits makes the natives restless. They don't like me wearing my granny's old but fancy cashmere cable-knit cardigans back-to-front, for example. I can't show up each morning without some feather-haired moron in Gloria Vanderbilts shouting abuse. If I just 'ignored' them, I'd turn into one of those pasty girls in thick glasses worn down by I-stink-and-everyone-hates-me paranoia. Instead I exhale grandly and fire off an insult prepared earlier by Oscar Wilde. When I do this at home, or she catches me pulling faces in the bathroom mirror, my mother calls me 'Norma Desmond'.

So despite my obvious interests it wasn't intentional Schwab's Drugs, discover-me-like-Lana Turner stuff getting a job flipping burgers and building ice cream sundaes, even though I'm good at that part of it. My milkshakes rule the five-state area. I'm probably too good at eavesdropping and not good enough at looking busy to really last, like the women on the lunch shift who've been adding hearts and flowers to their name tags for thirty years, who sit there fueling my grandpa's small-business pals while their talk veers from golf to real estate 'deals' to how the walleyes are biting on Moose Lake. Nobody wants to be discovered here, least of all me. I refuse to wear a name tag because I dread the scenario where I meet some faceless customer whose name I don't know, calling mine from behind shrubs. When I walk home in the dark, darting from street beacon to street beacon for three blocks of pure torture, I forget that nobody on our street locks their front doors.

The clock's nudging 6.45; further Bismarcks would

spoil the dinners of Stan and Vern. My grandfather's tired of surveying his kingdom in his limited-edition (possibly Pierre Cardin, more like Liberace) Lincoln so offers to wait for the end of my shift to spin me home. This happens more often since my grandmother died, but he's more bored than in mourning. His friends down cups and clear off, tipping heavily. Luckily, Al's training Bobby to do the cleaning tonight because the fountain gets too busy for me to manage complete Alvin-standard sterilization before seven p.m. Sling dirty mugs into dishwasher, make the international 'five minutes' sign, collect my tips and fly downstairs to the toilets to change into the yellow shirtwaist dress that reminds me of the one Katharine Hepburn douses in *Summertime*, embarrassing herself by falling into a filthy Venetian canal under the gaze of Rossano Brazzi. These are the kind of problems I want to have someday.

As I change, I plot the return of *Hollywood Wives* to its hiding-place in Mom's nightstand drawer, making a mental note to cross-reference the medical book for the name given to permanent, stuck erections caused by heart attacks.

Frankly, this stuff isn't ever in the pamphlets sent discreetly from school to our parents. School is like the Hays Office, America's cinematic bureau of prohibition; most parents resemble Mr Hays, the Postmaster-General appointed to see that loving couples in movies kept both feet on the floor in bedroom scenes, or that matinee gangsters' crimes landed them in Pokey. Public censorship overseen by the people paid to deliver love letters and bills, covering Mae West's tits and ruining the film of *Breakfast At Tiffany's*. Typical! So these sexy books fly around the back of classrooms with the good bits marked out in highlighter pen and everyone feels guilty or embarrassed just thinking of getting caught in the middle of a yellowed-up passage. I bet the nuns at the Catholic school across the highway tell their students God is watching, and this is how it feels when He does. Sometimes it's so much easier to run with the crowd here. Was it any wonder people turned off the lights to focus on sexy arrangements of light, or sounds, or words in compartments? Exile real or ugly things, relegate them – or, like me, put them back where they belong without detection from anyone save the like-minded. Up to you, even if you're still a virgin. Yet the more you pretend a thing doesn't exist, the harder it whacks you over the head when you realize it actually does.

Outside, in the storeroom, there is a crash, the muffled sound of thin, clear plastic on cement. Then a whisper, nervous. This can only be Al. And of course he isn't alone. I hear the noise of a smile almost transforming to a belch of a laugh.

Somehow I knew I was safe, whether or not Grandpa was waiting on a stool upstairs, knowing Al to be chaperoned by the unknown in the basement. Al probably wasn't thinking like me. Dressed, I turned off the light in the bathroom and allowed my eyes to adjust long enough to make out the edges in the door-jamb, the outlines of appliances, the hygiene order on the wall. Just this once, I refrained from washing my hands, turning the door-handle gently, tiptoeing in the hopes that I wouldn't find myself falling into some river of shit while wearing this dress.

In almost imperceptible silhouette, Al trembled. Instead of anger at violating one of his stupid rules, there was this strange aura of fear surrounding him. Also floating in this browny darkness was Bobby – the one who'd made the babyish gurgle. On the floor, lipsticks still in their rack-cartons arranged themselves in satellite around gentle lumps of fabric which I took to be Bobby's jeans, unbelted and dropped.

Like I said, I'd seen enough movies to construct most of the missing visuals. Since Bobby could barely initiate the act of tying his own shoelaces, this had to be Al's bright idea. I wondered if Al had taken one of the lipsticks and smashed it into his lizard-lips before wrapping same around his employee's confused, exposed boyhood. And to paraphrase Mom's favorite lady writer, did the member weep, or spurt exultantly?

Exhale. Nothing needed saying, so after mouthing the word *bastard*, I summoned a composure I often mistake for an application of the Stanislavsky method to real life, walking with absolutely no emotion cluttering my footfall. At the stairwell, still moving, I snatched a carton of Marlboro Lights from a cardboard delivery box, took the steps up two at a time, stuffed the carton into my book bag and collected my grandfather.

Once home, once my grandfather had been despatched with a wave of thanks, I hurtled through the unlocked door so solid it whooshes whenever it's pushed. My sister sat passive in the glow of some wretched programme like *Alice* or *Happy Days*, blue-collar laff-riots that reminded me of Excelsior Drugs; the dog bounded across my path in zig-zags as I searched for signs of intelligent life elsewhere in the house.

My mother and my aunt, who lives four houses away but across backyards, sit in our kitchen surrounded by shopping bags from Southdale, the nation's first mall, where my aunt once had a job waitressing at the 'sidewalk café' when she was a Sophomore. This hinterland Grace Kelly, married to a policeman who's head of the Vice Squad, is basically a life-support system for several credit

cards, aware of this fact and up to the job. It's probably
hard to be her little sister. In front of them, two more
cups of steaming Swedish gasoline. Ever since I started
thinking about stuff like this, my aunt's sex life *seems* a
bit Hitchcock, as it were, because she went spastic at me
and my sister for teaching our five-year-old cousin the
words to 'Physical' by Olivia Newton-John. I got a back-
seat slap for sneering 'Forewarned is fore-armed' after
she shouted at us, which had enough English on it to
shock my brain into realizing her attitudes probably
didn't come from the police reports my uncle left on his
desk in the den.

Usually she's a good aunt who presides over dinner
parties in Halston halter-neck jump-suits, with a library
waiting for my cousin's cognizance and ten years' worth
of *National Geographic* in glass cupboards. If she hadn't
been born on this side of the creek – her saving grace –
I'd swear the woman could have been an emissary from
the other side, where the lady who wrote 'Ordinary
People' has a big Tudor house, snotty preppies lounge
all day in tennis whites and they still have problems with
selling 'their' empty houses to Jews. I've noticed she
and Mom haven't bitched at each other much since the
divorce from my dad came through. Nobody's smug
about any of it.

'Hi, how was work?'

'Fine,' replied my mother, aware somehow that this
question did not apply to her sibling. My grandfather
photographed them once in bad light, for a photo where
Mom, holding my infant sister, gazes balefully into the
lens while her oblivious sibling applies three different
types of nail polish immediately behind her. 'School?'

'Boring. Next question?' I hate how my mind can be
free to spin out at work but when confronted by family

members in my own home, shuts down. I believe this is also why groups of older Minnesotan men take fishing trips together.

'Work?'

'Grandpa drove me home, his friends came in. Good tips.' I explained, taking off my coat, prevented from dumping it into a vacant chair by the automatic pointing mother-finger which really says 'Put it *in* the closet.' I glanced at my aunt. 'How are you doing?'

'Fine. I should go back,' she paused to gather her shopping bags. Only one of them, from Target, belonged to my mom. I flinched; at school we called this K-mart clone 'Targée Boutique' and tried to pilot our shopping mothers to nicer places on the annual run for school clothes. 'It's getting late for Kelly to still be with the neighbours.'

After Continental kisses on both cheeks for me and instructions to call her later for my mom, she was off. Instead of a slam, the door hissed shut. Instantly I wheeled around and found the schoolbag, rummaged inside, and held out the Marlboro Lights like an offering.

'These are for you,' I insisted.

'But I didn't send you a note for Al. Did you – '

'No,' I cut her off. 'If you're wondering whether I'm smoking, I'm not. No way.' My anti-tobacco diatribes went nowhere with her and I knew it was useless to start since, in her defence, she's tried to quit at least four times. Divorce and nicotine usually go so well together, don't they? Somewhere in St Paul, my dad was on his second pack of the day, the fat slob. If I wanted to be really pathetic, I could blame my need for gainful employment on his absence.

Whatever. For my mother, smoking is a form of yoga where people sometimes get lung cancer by accident.

That's the last thing anyone thinks about, except me, as the hot cherry burns down to the filter and the smoker's annoying life takes five while the ashes gather, flicked with precision and impatience into their tray. She peeled open the carton, drew out a packet, tapped and unwrapped it, bit a jutting Marlboro filter and lit her cigarette in all of three seconds. She exhaled smoke, blew a ring, and sent another shaft of smoke through the ring. Very naughty. Then she looked straight at me. 'The last shift I ever worked at Excelsior, I stole a whole carton of cigarettes too.'

Pause. Mentally prepare leading question. This is not the time to be nosy. 'That's why Al fired you?'

'That's not why I left,' she smiled, colored slightly by embarrassment. 'But every time I sent one of you girls in for my smokes, it reminded him why I did.' As punctuation, she took another drag, exhaled, caught my eye and winked.

Nodding a form of 'good night', I picked up the book bag, conscious of *Hollywood Wives* hidden at the bottom, ambled into the hallway, grabbed the careworn medical book from its place on a bench and shut the bedroom door behind me. Do mothers know *everything*?

matthew de abaitua

....

the stock exchange

At twenty-one, Richard Else was the youngest of all eight passengers on the flight, a short hop from the island of St Kitts to the island of Nevis. He sat behind the pilot, behind his sunglasses, and closed his eyes, removing himself from the excited clamour of the golf widows behind him and placing his concentration squarely upon the sensation of take off. The acceleration of the small plane was matched by an equal velocity within him, a sympathy between the speeding tarmac and the blood in his veins. His spine searched for solid earth. When his coccyx sensed the emptiness rising below, his nerves reared up from the seat, unwilling to settle their entire weight upon such precariousness. There was no mistaking the feeling of being airborne.

Richard was fresh from university and chasing a job offer faxed to his father from an old business acquaintance called Tom Carter, a single page of which he carried in his briefcase. The fax promised work experience, accommodation and expenses, but the position itself was unspecified. Even though the exact nature of that position had yet to be revealed to him, he knew he would excel at it regardless. It was in his nature to excel.

He removed his sunglasses to appreciate the ascent – so sudden, Richard felt that he must have left something behind. Instinctively, he checked that the briefcase was still there, knocking against his calf, and finding it, he realised he was missing some less tangible property. Some watermark of his self, torn from him quite unexpectedly, persisted in the heat haze of the runway.

This sense of loss lasted only as long as it took for the plane to bank and bring Nevis into view – a cloud-wreathed volcano, thickly clad in rainforest, dominated the small island. The ocean below sped from deep to transparent blue before being replaced by a beach, fringed with palm trees. It was immediately apparent he was heading for some sort of paradise.

According to the fax, he was to meet his prospective employers at the Hamilton Plantation Inn, but when he arrived, it appeared deserted. Reception was closed. Tentatively he went up to the windows of the dining-hall. Places were set, with the silverware arranged in the traditional formation; the room was even decorated with Bach, whose early Brandenburg Concertos wobbled out of an antique gramophone. But no one was there. He moved on to the gardens. They were astonishing. He wandered in between the palm trees and riotous blossoms, laying down his briefcase to run the ridged spine of an enormous leaf between his fingers. The plants had the presence of beings: when he came across a Traveller's Palm, an eight-foot-tall apparition whose brief trunk had been expertly splayed into a fan of tense stalks, he started, as if encountering an upright manta ray. Beside it, there was an avocado tree. He picked one of the heavy fruits and the recoil of the branch disturbed a parrot –

which ca-cawed, screeched, and set upon a defiant sweep of the gardens.

While watching its ill-tempered flight, Richard saw a rusting contraption, raised on a moss-covered brick base. Once he had hitched himself on to it, he could see that it was the remains of a steam-powered engine, connected to a sequence of large iron rollers which – judging from a set of new, polished pipes – someone was restoring. It was placed over a well, which he presumed ran under the tall stone chimney in the centre of the gardens. The machine and chimney appeared to be the sole relics from the time when the plantation was used to refine sugar, as the main house and attendant villas of the Inn had a whiff of '80s design, despite the best efforts of the architect to make them appear colonial. As he set about clambering down from the contraption, he noticed a woman sitting at a pagoda on the edge of the garden. She was waving at him. He took up his briefcase, and went to join her.

The woman was wearing a light white dress, which contrasted with her deep tan. She took a slim brown cigarette from a silver case, placed the gold band of the filter between her lips, and motioned for him to sit.

'Lou-Lou told me you had arrived,' she said, removing the cigarette to speak, then replacing it.

'My name is Richard Else,' he said offering a handshake.

'I know who you are, Richard,' she said, her cheeks hollowing as she sucked the cigarette to life. The match was shaken twice, and extinguished, before she returned his handshake.

'I'm sorry, I didn't catch your name.'

'You were expecting Tom Carter, weren't you? He's busy with the infernal Mr Bougas and a gang of

Cossacks, so I'm afraid you'll have to settle for me for the time being. I'm Anna. I own the inn. I believe you'll be staying with us for some weeks.'

She pushed the cigarette case toward him. He declined silently.

'Oh yes, I forgot. The young don't smoke, do they? It's only the old diehards like me who stick with it.' The weathering of the skin about her collarbone and the looseness of her triceps were the only indications of age that she had permitted, for her face and body had been so scrupulously maintained he couldn't place her any more precisely than mid-thirties to late forties. But then he wasn't experienced in placing anyone much older than twenty-one.

From the pagoda, Richard could see that the plantation was set upon one of the four knuckles that encircled the great volcano. A thick cloud was feeling its way down through the forests of the great peak.

'You have a very beautiful place,' he said, 'I was admiring your gardens. Are you restoring the sugar refinery?'

'Not personally. I have a man who is looking into it. I find the idea of authenticity appealing. I had the inn built on the footprints of the original plantation, which didn't survive the emancipation, of course.'

Her manner was metropolitan, her flesh ruthlessly pared back: but such latent ferocity had been baked in the sun for a decade until it had softened into a sophisticated languor.

'I have to warn you, there aren't any other guests at the moment. Today is the first day of the hurricane season, no one visits for pleasure until the winter. The next five months are very slow and very humid, what little one can face doing in such heat is usually spent preparing for the storms. The Nevisians have a little poem, it's very important to remember it.' Anna propped her cigarette in the ashtray, and recited. ' "June too soon, July standby, August you must, September remember, October all over".' She took up her cigarette. 'It's the first thing everyone learns when they move here. You should make a note of it.'

A black maid brought them a jug of Pimms, and a plate of cinnamon toast. Anna took a nimble bite, then broke off a small piece, and held it before her. Nervously, Richard reached out to accept it.

'What are you doing?' Anna laughed abruptly. The parrot glided down and gripped her wrist with its claws, wrestling the toast from her fingers. She petted it. 'It's for Lou-Lou, isn't it, Lou-Lou?' She cooed to the bird 'Say "hello mummy", go on, say "hello mummy".' After swallowing, the bird obediently imitated her with blinking incomprehension – hellomummyhellomum-myhellomummy. Richard took refuge from his error by sipping at the tall glass of Pimms. The ice audibly winced under the heat. The bird regarded him balefully while Anna stoked its breast feathers with the curve of her index finger.

'You're very young to be mixed up with Tom Carter. How did you meet him?'

'I haven't. He made me an offer, sight unseen. He's an old partner of my father's.' The misunderstanding with the toast made him feel quite angry. He didn't like to be mocked, and suspected Anna was inclined to patronise him, which would make him furious.

'An old partner? I've known Tom for at least a decade, and the only partner he's had in that time is Mr Bougas. Do you know William Bougas? No? Oh you're in for a treat. He's very much the dark star of our little set. He's a very unique individual.'

He nodded, still fuming.

'Help yourself to the toast,' Anna passed the plate to him. Her parrot was chewing at the shoulder strap of her dress, which she had to correct. When Richard took a slice, the bird transferred its attention to him, calling for a share. He ignored it.

'How long have you lived here?'

'God, since the mid '80s. Tom and William moved out here a few years later, just ahead of the recession in London. We were what you'd call yuppies, I suppose, but we're a proper community now. Very tight. Nevis is such a small island that everyone knows everyone else's business, which is the second thing visitors should learn. Anything you do or say will circulate, we can be quite the gossips. Especially during hurricane season, when we get very few outsiders.'

'What kind of people come here?'

'Not many young people like yourself. Unless they're honeymooners, and of course we see little of them. It's mainly businessmen from all around the world, doing their little deals. Inevitably everyone is rich. Do you like rich people, Richard?'

'I don't mind them. I haven't known many. But I don't have a problem with people having lots of money. I hope to myself one day.'

'For me, it's not just about being rich. It used to be. Now I like to think it's more about a person's soul. I can feel a good soul. I like to attract a particular type of person to my inn. They have to fit in with the island. Nevis is a very special place, and if you're open to it, and you have the soul to appreciate it, then it can be the greatest place on earth.' She gestured to the volcano.

The thick weather rolling about its caldera was spilling over into the rainforest, a signal that the afternoon was cooling, and that dusk was on its way.

Anna left him at the bar with the news that Tom Carter was still detained by his meeting, and would be along as soon as it was finished, but in the meantime he was to relax. 'Have a drink, whatever you want, it's on the house.' He confined himself to the local beer, which had the same sweet cane aroma as the island itself. He drank two bottles, swiftly and self-consciously. He made a stab at bonhomie with the barman, who was polishing champagne glasses, but his efforts were rewarded with only a dark nod, and further polishing – each glass turned in the light, then deliberately placed in rank on a silver tray.

He wasn't very good at waiting, he took it as an implicit insult. He wasn't very good at relaxing either. His elder brother was more suited to the static life than he was. Richard turned the empty beer bottle around in his hand and thought briefly of his family, continents away. If he was successful in Nevis, it would be a while before he saw them again, which didn't really worry him. His father was retired, though that was a euphemism, for really he had been defeated by redundancy, and his brother was still piddling around with sculpture, the dole a regular insult from a society that – rightly in Richard's opinion – put little value on his efforts. If his mother, while she was still alive, would scold him for being severe in his judgements of other people, it was only because he was being too public with them, as she herself – when he was alone with her – would make similarly cutting remarks, especially after the divorce. He missed her, but like her, he disliked sentimentality, and honoured her by avoiding it. These thoughts were interrupted by the approach of two young men and their loud conversation, which made Richard bristle with a desire to be included.

'You put in two million, ten million, whatever you've got lying around, and you get a forty-five per cent return and the beauty is that you don't even have to do anything. The money takes care of itself.'

They were Canadian – Josh and James. While James summoned the barman, Josh removed his tan cotton jacket, hung it deliberately around the back of his stool, and took care of the introductions.

'Are you here for business or pleasure?' With one hand, Josh rummaged through the pockets of his jacket before producing a softpack of Marlboro Lights.

'Business,' replied Richard, with some pleasure.

'What area are you in?'

He puffed out his cheeks to express the difficulty of answering such a question simply. The last thing he wanted to admit was that he had no idea what business he was in, and indeed was sitting around in a bar, on his own, waiting to find out. Fortunately, Josh didn't press the matter, and instead offered him a cigarette.

'You don't smoke? You must be new to the island. Everyone here smokes, except for the Nevisians, of course.'

'You can't get lung cancer in Nevis,' James passed Richard a beer, 'the air's so sweet it cleans your lungs right out.' The two of them were in their mid-twenties, and had affected the same post-preppy look of *haute* leisurewear, though where James had a sub-military severity, close-cropped and gym-fierce, Josh had an elaborate fringe and an extravagantly coloured silk lining to his jacket. With disdain, Josh dismissed the fruit from his cocktail, flinging the pieces into the ashtray. 'Who're you working with, then? Can you tell us that much?'

Richard said he was working with Tom Carter, Josh whistled as if impressed. 'The big man himself. Wow. No wonder you can't tell us what you're up to – Tom would eat you alive if he knew you were letting the likes of us in on his business. I've drunk with him a few times, I throw the whole bar at him and he just gobbles it up and doesn't let us in on a single thing.'

'He's kind of outside the main business of the island,' said James, taking a seat, so that Richard was between the two of them. 'We see him around but our worlds don't really meet.'

'What are you in?' asked Richard, hoping he was handling himself convincingly.

'Off-shore registration, not banking – that's all St Kitts. The usual off-shore stuff. Capital flows around the world like tides, it needs somewhere to rest on its journey and someone to look after it.' This riff amused them both. 'We're just sailing on the tides of money,' added James. 'There are oceans of dollars and we steer it into the lagoons, yeah, the deep still lagoons of capital just off the main drag of capitalism.'

'And what would you two know about capitalism?' This remark came from a new voice, a sarcastic drawl, English but indeterminately so. Its owner insinuated himself between the Canadians and offered a handshake to Richard. 'William Bougas. Anna said I'd find you here, and so I have. Welcome to Nevis, Richard.' Bougas was a stocky, energetic man, with a satyr's gut and an unruly, extravagant head of black curls which marked him out from the more disciplined figures of Josh and James. Also, he had astonishingly bad teeth, with the front two forced into retreat by a pair of thick incisors.

Despite his unruly appearance, the Canadians clearly deferred to him, proffering meek goodbyes to Richard when Bougas swiftly led him away. 'How are you feeling after your flight? Not too tired? Good, you've arrived just in time for Anna's weekly gathering; you'll get to see all the regulars.'

The volume of the bar had increased with Bougas' arrival. A cork popped, and out poured the evening. Waiters appeared and began serving the host of new arrivals. Richard had never seen so many nationalities sharing the same space – a trio of Nigerians pushed past them ('Oil money, don't even consider dealing with them' remarked Bougas, as he ushered Richard through the room), a withered, sweating man with a hearing aid vainly tried to drag Bougas aside ('Californian, made his money in hydroponics, forever seeking investment to set up an operation here. Never listens when I tell him that no one invests in greenhouses on an island that suffers from hurricanes. But then he is deaf'). Bougas indicated a huddle of black men ('Nevisian politicians. Not like British politicians at all. All trained in law, but strangely passionate. In Nevis, politics is as much the national sport as cricket'). There were Argentinians ('Beef, obviously. Useful to know if you need to buy a racehorse'), more Americans ('New York Jews, a hotline to Wall Street. Can't take their liquor'), and there was even a famous English journalist, who Richard recognised from broadcasts from war zones ('Old-fashioned Reithian liberal, doesn't like to be seen to be here. Don't stare'). To his frustration, Richard was out of the door without being introduced to any of these fantastic figures. 'Where are we going?' he said, half his body inclined back towards the hall. 'We have to leave,' said Bougas, unlocking the door of his Suzuki jeep. 'Tom's expecting you. He wants to see you first, before those jackals get at you.' Richard climbed reluctantly into the passenger seat. 'Don't worry, we'll be back in time for brandy and cigars. Believe me, that crowd are only entertaining when they're drunk. No one does any business when they're sober. We won't miss a thing.' With a flourish, Bougas reversed the jeep, let fly an arc of gravel, and raced down into the island.

Bougas drove rhetorically, as if composing an argument out of gear changes and revs. Richard admired the performance in silence. Their progress across the island was swift until they ran aground at a street festival. An entire kitchen had been set up by the side of the road, with hotplates of sizzling meat and cauldrons of stew. Bougas sucked his teeth with frustration, and slowed the jeep to a crawl. He had to stop altogether when an old rasta swayed oblivious before them, a bottle of spiced rum held deftly between his long fingers. His dreds had aged into a single, thick rope which shook as he blew somewhat fruitlessly into a child's tin trumpet.

The moment they stopped, their path filled up with a crowd eager to get at the food. Other cars had already given up on the idea of progress, and had hitched up on an embankment. Bougas had no choice but to pull over.

It was a church festival; all of the congregation were wearing yellow pullovers, with the name of the church – Eastridge Marvian – emblazoned on the front, and their names stencilled on to the back. Richard watched one woman – her jumper said she was called 'Ardel' – carry a battered tureen up the embankment, and decided to follow her. She struggled up on to a lawn, dominated by a church, and what looked like a maypole. Red, white and blue ribbons flowed about the pole, their ends pinned to earth by rocks and bricks, which a pair of boys would adjust every time a breeze disturbed the ribbons. The sky was overcast, the dusk distinctly chilly, making the scene seem very English to Richard, both in its dourness, and in the way the Nevisians were suffering the weather in shirtsleeves. It seemed very uncharacteristic of the Caribbean, sedate and homely, with the sole rasta the only drunk and scoundrel. He turned back to share his amusement with Bougas, who just looked unimpressed, slouched with his hands still on the wheel.

Andrel pressed a Styrofoam cup into his hands. He took the opportunity to use her name and ask what she was serving him. 'Goatwater,' she replied, 'it's mutton and goat stew,' she added, after he took a tentative sip. It tasted of oxtail soup: a chop bone broke the meniscus and presented a side of fat to his tongue. He tried not to wince, offered exaggerated thanks, and peered at her when she turned to serve the other members of the congregation who were now gathering upon the hill. She was a hefty woman, so hefty that if she was white he would have thought no more of her. It was strange, but he decided that black skin disguised the worst of fat, which revolted him on men and women alike: it was the pallid slabs he couldn't stand. He fancied chancing his arm with her, after the long flight and the fallow months after university, he was in need of a casual fuck, what he referred to – when drunk and holding forth – as an empty.

The calypso gospel rattling the tinny church sound-system was abruptly stopped, and a tall, broadchested pastor, with the vigorous bearing of a God-fearing patriarch, took up a microphone. With disdain he sidestepped the rasta, straightened his back and proclaimed, 'Turn your eyes to the hills and you will see dancing at its very best!' Then, after a long scratchy run-in groove, Abba's 'Dancing Queen' trickled out over the green. Twelve dancers, six of each sex, pranced out from the church and up to the pole. They took up the ribbons, and began to dance. He almost laughed – this fragment of England played out beneath the volcano struck him as incredibly old-fashioned, and impressively naive. Ardel explained the moves to him; the dancers began with the single ribbon platt, then the single loop, then the double loop. 'Now this is very difficult,' said Ardel, 'the spider's web.' After one false start, the dancers shuffled back into position to reveal an expertly intertwined configuration. He couldn't help but join in the applause.

'It reminds me of home,' he said, detaining Ardel with a hand on her forearm. She asked him where he was from, and when he replied 'England', she looked annoyed. 'No, whereabouts in England?' she insisted. While he explained about Hampshire, she listened with distraction, confining herself to a remark that she had relatives in Birmingham, who she visited often. The conversation had reached a natural conclusion, so he tried to kickstart it. 'It's the last thing I would have expected to see here, I mean, Morris dancing in the Caribbean. Especially at a church festival, because in England we consider Morris dancing to be pagan. But here it's like you've remixed parts of our past to create your own traditions, which is very interesting.' This thesis had come to him suddenly, and although he'd only had a brief second to consider it, he still considered it sound. Ardel was unimpressed. 'It's a ribbon dance,' she said, 'not Morris dancing. There's nothing pagan about it at all.'

She was far less indulgent than he had anticipated, especially for a fat one. He was about to ask for a tour of the dishes steaming in the street kitchen when a commotion broke out on the embankment: the rasta had climbed on to the back of the jeep, and was simultaneously ranting at Bougas while fending off the efforts of the congregation to remove him. Ardel strode down to sort it out. Richard tagged behind, taking the opportunity to dump the goatwater, and consider the possibilities of her hips.

'Get down from there, Stamford Bourne,' shouted Ardel, bearing a ladle.

'Don tell me whad to do, woman.' The rasta towered over Bougas, who was easing the jeep through the crowds, beeping his horn to get them to disperse. 'Look at me, Mister Bougas, show me your eyes and tell me you don't owe me.' Then, when Bougas continued to ignore him, he leant forward and made a play for his curls. Bougas batted the hand away, beckoned Ardel to him. 'Get . . . him . . . off.' Swiftly Ardel marshalled the men into wrestling the rasta from the jeep; he didn't struggle, and they just dropped him on the embankment. As they drove away, Richard attempted a parting wave to Ardel, but she was busy delivering her recriminations. Shame. Bougas was laughing. 'Stamford Bourne! He told me he was called Rasafrica. Poor little Stamford. Typical rasta – just a petty crook with delusions of grandeur.'

They drove through the rest of the village, past dusk-idle Nevisians chatting out on the porches and pavements. 'In future, Richard, stay in the jeep.' As he spoke, Bougas scrubbed idly at his nicotine-stained fangs, as if to clean them. 'Our business doesn't require any contact with the locals. In fact, they're mutually exclusive. Unfortunately, I am a victim of certain laws of supply and demand, so I have dealings with the likes of Stamford, but there are numerous historical sensitivities between us and them that I don't want you treading all over. If you work with me, you stay with me. Understood?' Richard nodded, and resumed his silence. His seat was sticky with spilt rum.

Night settled. They drove up into the dark flanks of the volcano. Richard felt the nervousness of altitude, just as he had on the flight in. The higher they climbed, the darker it became, the more uncertain he was of the earth beneath. Soon, they were driving off-road. Richard steadied himself against the bounds and dips of the trail by placing his fingertips against the dashboard. The headlights revealed an enclosed tunnel, the forest cored into a vegetative artery. By now, they were deep into the cloud. There were no stars, the moon a mute disc drilled through the sky. Richard had long since lost any sense of position in relation to the rest of the island. Anxiety pulled at his collar, at his throat.

Around them, the trees and bush were alive with ticks and creaks. The call of the treefrogs were a playground of rusty swings and roundabouts. Maniac calls whooped above him. He realised he was now clinging to the dashboard. Bougas drove on with silent determination. With all this in their backyard, it was no wonder the Nevisians still clung to God. Richard was tempted to pray himself.

Eventually, they came upon a pair of low buildings shielded by palm trees. Bougas went inside. Hectic with nerves, Richard fiddled at the ignition. He turned the headlights back on, their beams forming one patch of illuminated certainty ahead.

He didn't have to wait long. When Bougas re-emerged, he was bearing up the large fleshy frame of a man. He struggled to heave the big man across the path and on to the back seat of the jeep, the suspension wilting under the dead weight of him. The remains of the man's hair were matted together by sweat, which also glossed the deep grooves of his face, weathered by years of booze-fuelled expansion and stress-driven contraction. It was a face that had boomed and busted a dozen times.

'Is this the Else boy?' bellowed Tom Carter, sprawled across the back seat like the catch of the day, still clutching a tumbler of martini.

'Richard Else,' said Richard, turning to offer a hand-shake which Carter limply reciprocated.

'Yes, yes, pleased to meet you.' Just as Richard was composing his first remarks to his prospective employer, he saw Carter undergo a violent spasm of pain that made him grip at his chest.

'Those fucking Cossacks with their fucking vodka have fucked my fucking heart. Swee-ee-t cunting Jesus, that hurt. William, get me home before my heart climbs out of my fucking mouth.' They drove back into the forest. Richard stared at Carter in the rear-view mirror, he seemed as much a force of nature as the wildlife about them. He noticed Richard was watching him. Grimacing, he unbuttoned his shirt to reveal a deep scar running down his chest.

'See this' – a blast of stale cigar and fresh bile – 'rite of passage. Your first bypass should come no more than two years after your first million – otherwise, you're nobody.' His laugh was a grinding of gears, until it was arrested by another spasm, which made him hiss. 'Until you've got this scar, in my eyes you're still an apprentice. Only a cock the size of a clarinet carries as much cachet as this scar. Fortunately, I've got both. That makes me the boss around here. While you're on the island, you keep your mouth shut, you watch me, you listen to

Bougas, that's all the education you'll need.' Carter reached for a packet of cigarettes, and thrust them at Richard.

'Fag?'

'He doesn't smoke,' said Bougas.

'Start now.' Carter knocked his finger against the base of the softpack, propelling a single Marlboro Red onto Richard's lap. He put it against his lips, accepted a light from Bougas, and puffed hesitantly. Carter grinned. 'I can see we're going to have to put this kid on to a course of the Cs if we're to make anything of him, do you know what a course of the C's is, Richard?' Carter reared up, his shirt still open. 'Cubans, champagne, cocaine and cunt. In that order. Always in that fucking order. Cubans, champagne, cocaine and cunt.' Richard realised he was grinning. 'How's your old man? Still fucking up his life?'

'He's taken up watercolours,' said Richard.

Carter exploded with laughter. 'It must be killing him knowing you're out here with us. I don't allow my own kids on the same continent when I'm in the middle of a deal. They're too young to see such horrors. If your father didn't still owe me, he'd never have let you go. To be honest, I really wanted the firstborn son, but I hear he's a bit of fuck up.'

'He's a sculptor. He makes things out of found objects. He's sold three of them.'

'Exactly. I won't have anyone with artistic pretensions working with me. Culture has its place, but it's not one of the big C's. You need focus, I don't want some moon-eyed kid with one foot in my office and one foot in some fucking dream about a screenplay. It just makes you susceptible to doubt. Do you have any doubts, Richard? Any pretensions?' Richard was adamant he did not. 'Well, I'm giving you three weeks to prove it, and I tell you, if you stick with us, if it works out, I'll make you a fucking rich man. Do you like the sound of that? Do you?'

He did. They drove back to Anna's.

Somehow, Tom Carter survived the evening. Between Richard and Bougas, they managed to get him to his villa, where Anna made sure that three of the four C's were brought to him. No one counselled caution or restraint. As the night wore on, Carter would receive guests from the main gathering. He sat up in his bed, exposing his bull chest and scar, sharing the odd line with whoever came by – a mirror, three ashtrays and four empty bottles of champagne lay on the duvet, their contents scattering and dribbling away each time Carter had a spasm. The two Canadians Josh and James had been shipwrecked by all the drugs and booze, and Richard had to step over them when bringing his boss another pack of cigarettes. 'This is true rebellion,' Carter said to him, fierce and deranged. It was four in the morning, and Richard was numb from the neck up. 'Fuck hippies. Fuck punks. Fuck your ravers and your anarchists and your artists. We changed the world – me, Bougas, your dad – Britain was shit, *shit* after the '70s. You couldn't fart unless the unions said so. The nation was stagnant. But it was us who saw the new age, we changed the way the world did business, for christssake – we destroyed socialism, communism, nationalism, monarchism, liberalism, class – the whole fucking works. We were the new breed. We were the most successful counter-culture there ever was. The only people who ever doubted us were the *grandes dames* of the bourgeoisie with their endless fucking dinner party whinges. All they ever brought to the table was guilt. We fucked them harder than art ever did. We did to them what Darwin did to religion. They're redundant, powerless, and we came out of it legends, legends, *legends*.'

Despite these binges, Carter survived the next few weeks too. The days were spent up on the flanks of the volcano, huddled in negotiation with the Cossacks, and the evenings were spent releasing all the frustrations and anger of these dealings, either in overwhelming indulgence, or in ferocious outbursts. Richard was not allowed to sit in on the negotiations. Instead he was given related research tasks. After breakfast, he would sit down at his computer and trawl the Internet. The deal that Bougas and Carter were putting together involved Internet gambling, a subject which they seemed to know little about. Sometimes the information Richard came up with would be received well, sometimes it would infuriate Carter so much he would shred the printouts in his face. 'The Cossacks have got PhDs in this shit. They've got top-drawer Communist educations. You're making me look like a fucking idiot.'

It didn't take long for Richard to become dependent on the approval of the two men. Sitting on the balcony, waiting nervously for them to return, the sound of the jeep approaching would make him start and bound around like the family dog. He would jump up from whatever he was doing, pace about, keen to see them immediately, but reluctant to be seen to be so dependent. When he felt that it had been long enough, he would gather up the research and stroll down to meet them at the bar, where he would wait for the conversation to lapse so that he could show them what he had prepared. One day, they ignored it. Just slung it aside straightaway. He sulked in his room all night, in his trunks and a T-shirt, methodically working his way through a bottle of spiced rum and a pack of cigarettes. By midnight, the sense of rejection had blossomed into defiance – he conceived of a hundred insults, and staggered down to the main hall to deliver them.

Anna intercepted him at the staircase. She put her hand on his chest. 'What do you think you're doing? You can't go in there dressed like that.' In her black evening dress, Anna was a silhouette against the sound of laughter and chatter blaring out from the hall. After an evening locked up in the darkness of his own obsessions, it was quite blinding. He stopped dead. She shut the door, muting the life beyond, and put her hand back on to his chest. It was the contact he had been craving all evening. 'They don't need me any more. I don't know why I'm still here,' he said, helplessly honest.

She took him by the arm and led him into the gardens. 'You mustn't take it personally,' she said, 'it's always like this when they are close to a big deal. They shut out everyone until it's just the two of them. I gave up caring about it long ago.' It was a clear and startling night, the air was warm and cane-sweet. Her sympathies made him want to sob, the weeks of drinking and stress had left him emotionally raw. Carter praised him, Carter damned him. Carter told him he was going to be rich, Carter told him he was born to be broke. Everyday, it was all boom and bust. The cracks were breaking out all over.

'You feel very cold,' he said, taking her wrist. He was keen to touch her. 'It's because I've been here so long. My blood has gone. Cut me, I bleed ice water.' She smiled and slipped her wrist free of him. She walked on until they came to a low set of ruins. The treefrogs were performing their nightly chorus.

'Listen. Close your eyes. Can you hear them?' Richard indulged her, even though the sawing calls were so loud he could hear them from his bedroom. 'They're very romantic, don't you think? Calling to one another in the dark, you really need the soul to appreciate their lust.' He opened his eyes. A concrete mixer and a set of tools lay nearby. The ruins had been marked into a grid by white tape. 'This is my next project. Once I have the refinery working again, I want to restore this building to its original state.' She stepped over the tape, ducking into the ruins. Richard followed. The ceiling was still partially collapsed, the starlight illuminated her. 'Before the original plantation fell into disrepair, this was the birthing hospital. This is where they bred the slaves. So many of the slaves were dying that the owners decided to increase their stock by holding a few studs here. They impregnated as many women as they could manage. Can you imagine what that must have been like? The sound of it, the smell of it – the plantation owner driving them together. Would he be able to contain himself when the slaves were fucking, or would the sight of them stir him up into a frenzy? Was it rape, or did the women join in willingly?'

The ruins were cramped, he began by touching her neck, across the clavicle, the voice in her throat vibrating beneath his fingertips. 'I'm aware of its insensitivity. The wounds of the plantocracy are still healing in the island's psyche. The prime minister wouldn't be happy at all.' She let Richard lick at her breast, she looked down at him, his eyes were closed, lost in the pleasure of it. 'But I'll restore it anyway. It might have been built just for breeding, but maybe love blossomed here. It's erotic really.' He looked up at her, puzzled that she seemed so unmoved by his efforts. 'Am I doing something wrong?'

he asked. 'No, not all, it just takes me a while to get going,' she stroked his hair and his cheek. 'You're very good at it. Keep going.'

She wouldn't let him take off her dress. It was too cold for that: she hitched it up to her waist, yanked down his trunks, and goaded him on there and then, with her legs propped on the rotted molars of stone.

Afterwards, she took him to her bedroom – he lay naked on her grand four-poster, watching her through the mesh of the mosquito net while she poured a pair of hefty brandies.

'I know you've thought of leaving, but if I were you, I'd wait to see how it all turns out.' Anna unclipped her earrings and replaced them with a new pair; she corrected her hair and stirred the ice in his brandy with her forefinger before handing it to him through the net. 'I don't think the deal is going very well. Not this time. Carter has totally fucked up.'

Richard was surprised. 'Bougas told me last week it was a done deal.'

Anna winced, and drew her cigarette case from a minute black bag. 'Oh it is. But I don't think it's the deal he thought they were making. What do you know about it?'

'I've been looking into what equipment they'll need. How many programmers they'll need to write the code, how many designers they'll need. There are lots of gambling sites, I've had a few ideas on how this one can really stand out. They'll need a few servers, of course, and it'll cost money to buy up decent domain names, but it seems a sound proposition. You're running a casino but without the huge overheads. Even better, if the local laws change, you can pack it up into a truck and move it to another island.'

Anna looked over the length of his body, he hiked his palms behind his head, tensing his abs to show himself off to his best advantage. But when he searched for her appreciation, he saw something else. 'You really sound like you know what you're doing. Tom doesn't have a clue about the Internet. William tries to teach him, but he's a beast of a previous age. He won't learn.' She drained her glass, refilled it, and slipped through the net. She ran her hand up his thigh, back down again. 'I've had affairs with both of them. A year with each. You'd expect them to be jealous of one another, but they're not.' He lifted his leg to encourage her hand down his thigh. Briefly she played along, tweaked his cock and smiled at how easy it was to turn him on. How little he understood about what was going on about him, paddling away in the shallows of his innocence. She withdrew her touch, 'It makes me very tense. Not knowing what they're up to. It's a small island, one mistake could cause us so much trouble.'

'I'm going to ask them, face to face,' the sex and the brandy had replenished Richard's store of bravado. 'Right now, I'm going to sort this out,' he jumped out of bed and pulled on his trunks. Anna remained, flopping wearily into his imprint on the bed. 'Please, Richard, wait.' He stopped, half-hoping she was going to beg him not to confront them. 'Do change into your evening suit first. Nothing would be more absurd than the sight of you losing your temper in a pair of trunks.'

When Richard stepped into the dining-room, he was surprised to find the room strangely hushed, with the dozen guests seated in a circle beside the bar. Bougas saluted him. 'You're just in time, Richard. Come and join us.' A waiter fetched a chair for him, and he shuffled his way into the circle, between Josh and James. 'This is going to be so cool,' whispered James. 'The coolest,' agreed Josh. They were chewing, their eyes bright and expectant. Richard asked them what was going on, but they shushed him: 'Just watch.' All the gang was there, in that small circle, the Nigerians, the Argentinians, the New Yorkers, the Nevisians – but there was one new addition, a blade-faced Cossack, who was adjusting his jewellery, book-ended by two mammoth guards. There was no doubting the malignant confidence of the Cossacks, no questioning of their presence. While everyone in the room radiated wealth, and a few degrees of power, the Cossack had assumed a position of superiority over all of them – it was he who gestured to Tom Carter to begin. The gathering was his to command.

Carter stood on his chair. He was sober, his shirt tightly buttoned, his bow-tie straight. In place of his normally raging complexion, there was something paler, and subdued. 'First of all, it's my pleasure to introduce you to Alexander Antipov, who is very prominent in the Ukrainian business community. I've had the pleasure of his company for the last few days while I've been negotiating with him to secure considerable investment in a venture that – I am pleased to announce – is going to bring a great deal of money into the island.' Minor applause. On to the second sheet of his speech. 'When I first arrived in Nevis, I had come fresh from a city that was about to collapse into recession. I was fortunate to escape that: indeed, by escaping the recession, it meant our appetite for business was unscathed, and that we could bring to the island the same vigour and drive that had propelled us to the top in London. It didn't take long to attract many talented people here. You were all quick to grasp the new opportunities both in tourism and in off-shore investment. We've all done very well out of it. But now is the time to expand our horizons. Economies are cyclical. They boom and they bust. It's a fact of nature. What emerges is never quite the same as what went before. I made my money in property and in the City; indeed, I look about me and see that all of us here have made a success of the traditional areas of capital. Now though is a period of renewal, new forces have arrived. A whole new economy has emerged, that of the Internet, and that is the area which we – in partnership with Mr Antipov – intend to explore.' Major applause. Carter sat down, he corrected the crease of his trousers. Richard caught his eye, but he looked right through him. As he slid his speech into his inside pocket, Richard saw a pronounced tremor in his hand, the fingers stiff and unwieldy.

Antipov moved outside of the circle. He walked over to the antique gramophone, and took a record from a slim leather satchel. 'We have a tradition in my country of playing the national anthem on occasions like this.' Delicately, with the record between his fingers, he slid it on to the stem of the player, and made a show of blowing dust from the grooves. 'It's been a while since the last deal,' he said. Everyone made a show of laughing, except for Carter. He was holding a Cuban cigar, staring at how the tremor of his fingers was magnified along its length. Bougas leant over to him, inquired if he was all right. Carter nodded. He placed the cigar on his lap, took out a box of matches, and lay them apart on his thighs. They sat before him like a revolver and a single bullet.

Antipov dropped the needle on to the record. The sudden crack and spit of the warped vinyl. 'It's customary also amongst my people to show goodwill at the sealing of such a deal. The coming together of two business operations is very like a marriage. I think of myself as the bride, I am losing my innocence in getting into bed with such experienced businessmen.' He waved down the laughter. 'Of course, this means it is also customary for my family to pay a dowry, I believe.' From behind the gramophone, he pulled out a large parcel just in time for the opening fanfare of the anthem. 'In here there is one hundred thousand American dollars. I trust you all know the rules to pass the parcel. Let's have some fun.' He chucked it first to the Nevisians, who were clearly taken aback by the amount of money Antipov had promised.

Collectively, the calculation of its potential reward against the potential risk to their image moved between them, their legal minds searching for precedents, and finding none of any use, they passed the parcel swiftly along. It landed on James' lap. He held it before him, shook it: 'Feels like a hundred thousand dollars to me.' He handed it to Richard. Everything he had ever wanted was right there in his hands. Gift-wrapped. His plan to demand an explanation as to exactly what was going on evaporated immediately. How could one even think of questioning a world that contained such prizes?

The music stopped, the circle craned forward as Richard tore aside the first layer of paper. 'To make it fair,' said Antipov, 'I shall turn my back from now on.' He faced the wall, and returned the needle to the record.

Josh received the parcel with glee, 'I never know whether to pass it quickly or slowly. The tactics of pass the parcel completely elude me.' Whereas the younger men saw only the thrill of the game, when the parcel moved to the hands of the older businessmen, they regarded it warily. The distinguished journalist was unfortunate enough to have to unwrap the second layer:

he did so while staring furiously at Carter for involving him in such a dubious matter. Clearly, the establishment were uncomfortable with the game, but no one was getting up to leave. It was not only the promise of the parcel that kept them pinned to their seats: who would walk out on a man who could toss a hundred thousand dollars aside like that? Who would risk offending him?

Again, it landed on Richard's lap. By now, the parcel was thinner by four layers. There was no way of guessing how many layers there were to unwrap before getting the money. Josh was right. When you had it in your hands, you just couldn't decide whether to pass it on swiftly in the hope it would return to you in time for the next hiatus in the music, or hang on to it. Maybe Antipov had been lazy when wrapping it, and he was just a millimetre away from a fortune.

When he passed it to Josh, the Canadian whispered to him: 'Exactly what Internet operation are they setting up?' 'Gambling,' said Richard. He handed him the parcel, and Josh passed it briskly on to the trio of Argentinians. 'Oh wow. That's nasty. Listen to this, James,' he pulled his friend close to him. 'Calculate this equation: Russkies plus off-shore island multiplied by a couple of Internet gambling servers equals . . .?'

James sneered, 'Put it on fast spin baby, we've got a lot of dollars to wash.' 'Carter's out of his depth.' 'Tides have caught up with him.' 'Did you know about this?' Richard was ricocheting from one to the next. 'Know about what? You can gamble here. It's legal. What do you mean?' 'Russkies plus collapsed domestic economy equals get my hard currency out, you motherfuckers.' The music stopped. James was holding the parcel. He winked at Richard. 'It's a good job I don't give a shit.'

He tore the wrapping free and winced when he saw there were more layers to go. 'Fuck.'

As each layer of the wrapping came off, the tension of the circle increased. They suffered longer and longer bursts of the anthem. Antipov was chatting to Anna, and gave the impression that he had forgotten about the game altogether. After a huddled conversation, the Nevisian politicians decided they would leave. 'Tonight, you have crossed the line,' said one. Anna tried to placate them as they strode from the hall, but they were adamant. 'This is a humiliation!' The English journalist also stood up, and stepped back from the circle. 'I will not be bought,' he announced, with the hauteur of the BBC statesman.

Antipov appeared unmoved by these two displays. He lifted the needle from the record so that the journalist had to make his exit in silence, each footstep pronounced clearly on the varnished wooden floor. Richard realised that these sudden exits had left him holding the parcel. 'Go on,' said Josh. He tore off the brown paper to reveal thick, shiny wrapping. 'Double fuck.'

Antipov was smoking one of Anna's cigarettes, Richard recognised the gold filter between his thin lips. 'There is only one layer left. Anyone who has any moral objections to playing pass the parcel should leave now. I wouldn't want anyone to feel compromised. It's only a game.' He replaced the needle. Now, it was as if there had been a sudden build-up of gravity within the parcel, so slowly and laboriously did it drag itself from hand to hand. Fingertips adhered to the wrapping, the whorls of their sweat persisted upon the paper's mirrored surface. It came to Richard. It was another instant of take off – sensation rushed within him to fill the moment. He looked squarely at the parcel and willed the music to end. It didn't. The anthem continued, and when he finally passed it on, the nerves and excitement of the earth rushing beneath him came to an abrupt stop. He almost vomited.

Carter appeared equally nauseous. He had removed his bow tie, his neck was slick with sweat. Deliberately, he took up the cigar. Bougas passed him the parcel. The music stopped. Antipov started a round of applause, that slowly spread across the circle, until they were all on their feet applauding Carter furiously. While he fumbled to unwrap the silver paper, Bougas held a light beneath the twitching end of the cigar. Once the wrapping was removed, Richard saw that Carter had, in his hands, a string-bound stack of what was undeniably a hundred thousand dollars. 'You've won, you've won,' Richard jumped up to congratulate his employer. Carter closed his eyes, took a hefty drag on his Cuban cigar, dropped the money, and collapsed.

It was the first day of hurricane season. The air was thick and had curdled into a heat haze above the runway. Richard Else sat behind the pilot, behind his sunglasses, and closed his eyes. He had been working hard all week: his staff were an unruly gang of ex-hackers, which made them impossible to trust. He had picked them up from a failed counter-cultural webzine in Vancouver, so while their expertise was impeccable, their attitudes were unpredictable. Most of the time, their suspicions as to the exact nature of the operation could be allayed simply by throwing money at them. Or by a good course of the C's. But it was only a matter of time before one of them cracked. They would discover that the virtual casino had thousands of virtual customers and only one real one, who lived somewhere in the Ukraine. Carter had missed this technicality until the very end – by which time, he was in no state to adapt to it. Bad break. 'Cut down,' as the minister said, 'in his prime.'

With the hackers, you could never predict when the scales of profit against principle would tip, or when risk would suddenly supercede reward. Their idealism was either submerged, which was bad, or it had flipped into nilhism, which was better but still pretty bad. So Richard had a policy of changing his staff every three months, a sudden clear-out would be followed by this flight to St Kitts to meet a new batch, arriving pasty and breathless, at the international airport. An injection of new blood never did any harm. Indeed, it was necessary for survival.

Bougas tapped him on the shoulder and offered him a cigarette. He refused, and took out a cigar.

He was airborne.

emily perkins

....

let's go

Let's go to Roxy, we say. Let's go to FX.

I try to learn some of the language, but don't get beyond 'diky', which means thanks. Informal. Casual. Friendly. The formal way is 'dekuji vam', but it's easier not to bother with the distinction. I find myself lost, wandering up and down a block looking for the Globe Café (I am two crucial streets away from it, but I don't know this). I stop people and ask, Do you speak English? and they shake their heads and smile. Diky, I call after them, diky, diky. Diky for nothing!

We go to Roxy, we go to FX.

Grunge, announces Hal, hit Prague like a soggy mattress.

He's right. It looks like it's here to stay, in every bar and café we visit. Americans, Americans. Thousands of dollars but they dress as if they're slumming it.

We stand outside the theatres and study the black and white photographs. Scenes from Beckett, Anouilh, Ionesco. Seriousness. Raised fists. Absurdity. We laugh.

We come across a candles-and-flowers shrine commemorating the Velvet Revolution. There are poems which we cannot read. Some tourists wander up and stand behind us, at a deferential distance. We don't speak until they are gone. We want them to believe what we briefly believe, that this is our memorial, our pain, our revolution. They back away with the hush of the guilty. We look at each other and we laugh. Hal reads a poem out loud in nonsensical Czech phonetics and we laugh again.

We're hungover at Segafredo and I'm cross because they don't have hangover food. I order a hot chocolate without cream.

The waitress doesn't understand me.

Without cream, I say. No cream.

She looks at Hal for help. He finds me embarrassing.

No cream, I say louder. I don't want any cream with the hot chocolate.

She frowns.

Cream? I don't want any?

I mime pouring cream out of a jug. Thick, I mutter.

Her face is blank. She tells me, It does not come with cream.

I make a mental note of this, for next time.

We go to Roxy, we go to Globe, we go to FX.

Look! says Hal. Poetry readings!

We get a cab to FX for the Saturday night poetry reading. The cab driver has a more explicit collection of pornographic pictures than most. I think about what might be in his car boot. He has a high colour and when someone cuts him out at the lights I think I see specks of foam in the corner of his mouth. His moustache makes it hard to be certain. I worry about apoplexy, and how hard it would be to gain control of the car if he were to clutch at his chest and then collapse suddenly around the steering wheel, inert.

We sit in the big armchairs at the back of FX. Some

very beautiful women are there. They are all Czech,
which is unusual. A – that they're beautiful (no tan
stockings encasing ham-like thighs, no tasselled suede
pirate boots, no lurid artificial blush applied over unde-
mure cheeks). B – that they are here in FX, which like
every other place we go to is usually inhabited by young
people from everywhere in the world except Eastern
Europe.

Their eyebrows are plucked excruciatingly thin and
without exception they have those fashionably swollen
big lips. Hal says there must be a special machine in the
girls' loos – press a button and a boxing glove pops out
and hits you to create that perfect punched-in-the-mouth
look. He mimes being hit by it, his head jerking back in
a whiplash movement. Again! I say, clapping my hands
together, Again!

The beautiful women drift in and out, past our chairs,
talking intently to each other in low voices. Sheets of
paper – their poems! – dangle casually from their
fingertips.

Czech chicks, murmurs Hal longingly.

Learn the language, I suggest. That'd be a start.

Diky, he says, morose.

Actually I think the language barrier is no bad thing.
It provides a lot of scope for meaningful looks. But it
does mean that what we understand by a 'poetry reading'
is not what the Czechs understand by one – after much
quiet and tender-sounding talk between themselves and
passing around of the pieces of paper, they stand up
and flowingly, waifishly, leave.

We go to Roxy, we go to Roxy.

Hal dances. I don't, won't, can't. The vodka is cheap.
It works out, per plastic cup, at 90p. Or a buck and a
quarter. Or two dollars fifty. In any currency, it's a cheap

shot. Ha ha. Later, we hear that there is some poisoned Polish vodka floating around the city. It was transported from Kracow in rusty vats. More than seven shots a night, the papers say, could kill a grown man. Even so, we do not die.

The receptionist at the hotel says, There is a message for you. We're excited – a message? Who could it be from? Perhaps it is from our friend Louis who is running a bagel factory somewhere outside the city. Perhaps it is news from home, except that nobody knows where we are. Maybe, I think, it could be from the German boy I gave my number to in Chapeau Rouge last night.

But – unhappy travellers! – the message is from the hotel management. We have chipped a corner off the wooden tag attached to our room key.

You have broken this, the message says, and it was new last week. You must replace it.

We are bewildered. I hand over some kroner.

Now? I ask, unsure what to do.

As you wish, the receptionist says, taking my money and giving me a receipt which she first stamps three times.

Sorry about that, we say, and we laugh.

Prague is not a good place to be vegetarian. We go to dinner and order three or four different kinds of meat, which all arrive on the same plate but cooked in different ways. It is a flesh-fest. Hal pretends to adore it but even he is unable to finish the last piece of liver. Vegetables, we say. We want vegetables. When they come they are recently thawed diced things from out of a packet: carrot, sweetcorn, peas. Vodka, we say. We want vodka. Ha ha ha.

Apparently, there are a number of things I do which infuriate Hal. I embarrass him in cafés (the hot chocolate incident); I embarrass him in bars (the German boy incident). I talk too loudly in the street and I can be 'pretentious'. Pretentious, *moi*? Hal's objections surprise me. We are like an old married couple. He says 'huh' too often (he claims to be unaware of this) and his jaw clicks when he eats. Or is that my father? I can't be sure.

It's too hot in our hotel! The radiators are up full blast. Gusts of warm air chase us down the halls. Our room is a little heat pit. I wake up with gunky eyes and burning sinuses.

The hotel is large. We suspect that there are no other guests. Every now and then – sometimes very early in the morning – we hear the distant whine of a vacuum cleaner on another floor. Who are they vacuuming for? They never vacuum for us. We lie on our beds, stifling in the thick air, rubbing at our sticky eyes. The windows do not open. I decide it is sinister that the windows do not open. After the broken key tag situation it is hard for me to trust the hotel staff. Perhaps the room is bugged. They have our passports, after all. Every night I expect to come back to some fresh damage and another bill for repair. A hole punched in the wall, possibly a broken chair. The suffocating heat does not diminish my unease.

Dear Alicia, I write on a postcard to my sister, We are having a wonderful time in Prague and looking after our hotel room very well. The Czech hospitality is marvellous.

I hand it to the receptionist to post. I smile at her. Diky, post, please, I say. You post?, nodding – Stamp? Diky.

Don't shout, hisses Hal from behind me. You'll ruin everything. You post, I say, please, diky, read it, you silly Slav cow, diky.

We make a new friend at the Globe. His name is Dick and he's American. A New Yorker, he tells us, but will later under the influence of vodka admit he is from 'Joisey'. Dick and Hal play backgammon while I write letters I will never send, and drink tumblerfuls of red wine, and listen. Dick's just been in Vietnam.

Oh yeah, he says, it was beautiful. Like going back in time, man. This incredible French architecture, women in long silk pants. Unbelievably cheap, you know, everything. He snickers. And I mean everything.

Hal snickers too. I look at the rain on the Globe's windows and try to imagine Saigon.

We take Dick back to our hotel, where I get changed, and on to the Whale Bar. Vodka, vodka, we cry. Dick pays for everything in American money. In Vietnam, he tells us, he decided to become a dong millionaire. He exchanged however many hundred US dollars into Vietnamese dong, until he had a suitcase filled with great bricks of money. He kept the million dong locked in this suitcase in his hotel room for a week, not touching it. Then he got crazy on Long Island Iced Tea one night after this little Spanish senorita he'd been going with left town. He gambled every last bit of the money away, ha ha ha, playing poker and twenty-one.

I challenge him to a game of twenty-one, feeling lucky because it's my age and besides I'm rather good at it, but Hal cuts in and says I'm not allowed. Dick and Hal both smile at me, like older brothers, like members of the same team. What can I do?

Czech chicks! Czech chicks! Hal is getting desperate. It is difficult for him, travelling with me in tow. He accuses me of sabotaging all his flirtatious encounters. I can't help it. Mostly I try not to, but sometimes when he goes to the bathroom I look at the girl he's been eyeing up and I give her the evils. I'm only protecting him from himself, after all. Things got nasty once, in Warsaw. Hal fell in with a bad crowd, turpentine, death metal, etcetera, and I had to bail him out. This short Polack girl glommed on to us and wouldn't leave our hotel. Crying, carrying on. Baby, she kept saying, baby. Either it was the only English she knew or it was a serious accusation. Some meat-faced guy who said he was her brother turned up on the scene, ranting and raving. Hal didn't like the idea of a big Polish wedding so we shoved some cigarettes at them and split town. I'm not ready to leave Prague yet, so Hal will just have to keep himself in hand. Ha ha ha.

Petrin Hill. What a climb! The heels on my boots stick into the earth and I skid on wet leaves. Hal has to drag me up most of the way while Dick strides on ahead. By the time we're at the top my arms are only just still in their sockets. Something awful happens. Hal doubles over outside the observatory. It could be his back problem. Or it could be liver failure. It makes a good photograph. Aaoow, he says, aaoow. I say cheese while Dick clicks the camera. Tears come out of Hal's eyes. I hold his hands. I feel that I should because some nights he sits on the edge of his bed while I sit on the edge of mine and he holds my hands. (Those are the nights I can't breathe or speak, the nights when the world is spinning way too fast and giving me the shakes. Vodka and cigarettes fail to stop these shakes any more but Hal holding my hands sometimes helps.) It doesn't seem the same rule applies to his back pain. Aaoow, aaoow. Poor baby. I make him lie flat on the damp ground and wipe the sweat off his face. I look around for Dick but he's not there. Help, I shout to the passers-by, *Au secours*! They keep on passing by. Hal pants and whimpers some more. It hurts to watch him. Then Dick reappears with a hip-flask of whisky. Hal drinks some and shuts his eyes and smiles. His whimpering subsides. He gets to his feet and laughs. What a relief! We love Dick! We jump around. We run all over the top of the hill taking photographs of each other. We are a music video.

Franz Kafka was one skinny guy. Kind of good-looking though. Huh, says Hal, you think so?

He thinks I'm shallow. To prove him wrong I buy a copy of *The Trial*. I will read it soon, right after I've finished *Laughable Loves*.

Dick has hours of fun reading the Police Service note on his street map. 'Dear friends,' he shouts to us in a cod Czech accent as we walk up to meet him outside the usual place, 'for the answer to your question, how the crime in Prague differs from the crime in other European cities, it is possible to say: in no way!'

Or, hysterically, in Whale he will tell the barman, 'In the number of committed criminal acts counted for 100,000 inhabitants the Czech Republic is in the order after the Netherlands, Germany, Austria and Switzerland. Therefore Prague is a quiet oasis basically.'

He has memorized it. Hal groans and wrinkles his nose but I could listen to it over and over again.

Dick also likes to remind us that, 'Prague has street prostitutes, too. You can see them in Prelova Street and in a part of Narodni Street. We do not recommend to contact them.'

Hal and Dick have left me alone! Meanies. They've gone 'out on the town' and didn't let me go with them. You better not leave the hotel, they said to me. It's not safe for a young girl alone in the big city.

Life is a cabaret, old chum, they sing as they swing down the stairs of the hotel, leaving me standing forlorn in the doorway, calling out, We do not recommend to contact them. We do NOT recommend it.

I go to Whale, I go to Roxy.

At Roxy I am drinking vodka and not dancing. I am wearing tight Lycra and am highly groomed in order to stand out from the babydoll T-shirts, grubby denim and ornamental hairclips around me. I look *fantastique*. A boy of I guess about seventeen makes eyes at me. I make eyes back. Then I ignore him, kind of cool. He walks past me. He has a nice body. He turns and smiles at me. I smile back. He walks back past me the other way. I laugh into my vodka. He beckons me to come and sit with him and his friends. I saunter over.

Hi, I say.

Hi, they say. One of them lights my cigarette.

Are you having becher? says the one about to go to the bar. They are Czech! This is perfect. It is cultural relations. Foreign affairs. They buy me drinks even though the money I nicked from Hal's secret supply at the hotel would probably pay their rent for a month. They are economics students.

After the revolution, the one who is still making eyes at me explains, we all wanted to be businessmen. Yuppies. They laugh at this, and I laugh too. Now they would all rather be poets. It is more romantic. But they've enrolled in their courses and they must finish them, or their parents would be disappointed. They ask me what I do and I tell them nothing. They are jealous. They are stoned.

This grass, my boyfriend says, is extra strong. Do you know why? It is because of the acid rain that rained down on all the plants after Chernobyl. The acid gets into the dope and makes it extra strong.

I stifle a yawn.

The friends go to dance and leave me alone with my boyfriend. He has a beautiful smile and a slow blink so I kiss him.

That'll show Hick and Dal.

The Hunger Wall. So-called because at the time it was built there was great poverty. Those men who worked on the wall were guaranteed food. Therefore they did not go hungry. Therefore it was a good thing to heave boulders up to the top of Petrin Hill for days on end. Without machinery or anything. Oh! it is too sad. Aaoow. We carve our initials into one of the rocks with my boyfriend's Swiss Army Knife. It is a gesture of solidarity.

Prague 3 contains student accommodation. I know this because I spend a night there, even though I am no student. I stay in the dorm, in an empty room vacated by a friend of my boyfriend's for the night. We stay there together and I wish I could remember more of it but the truth is I don't. I do remember that he says, You are the first older woman I am with (he is eighteen; I am twenty-one). He also says, I suppose you have read *Unbearable Lightness of Fucking Being*. And, When I have a girlfriend my studies go well and my room is tidier. He spent last summer in New York – actually in Queens, working in a Greek restaurant. It did not improve his English. He says, I know the black slang – fuck you, motherfucker. I laugh. He is nice. He is sweet. He blinks slowly and he waits for a taxicab with me in the morning. You should take the tram, he says, which is a million kroner cheaper than a taxi, but I have never taken a tram in this city before and I am not going to start now. It is enough of a struggle to get back to where the hotel is and find Hal and Dick without this tram business. He kisses me goodbye and I cry in the taxicab because I am lost and he was nice and sweet and I am not sure where I am going to find Dick and Hal and what sort of mood they will be in when finally I do.

Places where Hal and Dick are not. They are not at the hotel. They are not at Globe. They are not at FX. I think I see them on Charles Bridge but it is not them, just two Australians who look worried when I cry. I have to find them. Whale. Globe. FX. I even go to Chapeau Rouge but it's too early and there's nobody there but the bar staff and a girl smoking a pipe. (It is a good look, and one to consider adopting later.) Where could they be? I ring the hotel and when the receptionist hears me talking she hangs up. I am lost in a city where I don't speak the language and I can't find my only two friends in the whole world. This must be the price of casual sex – my eighteen-year-old, whose name I didn't ever quite hear properly. I need somebody to hold my hands.

In Vietnam, Dick told us, there are beggars who bang their heads on the ground, harder and harder until you pay them to stop.

In Chapeau Rouge again I find them. They have not been back to the hotel. They are still on their bender. Welcome to the lost weekend, they tell me. You naughty, naughty girl, what are you doing out of your room? Dick has two Swedish girls on his arm and Hal is sulking. He is out of Marlboros and is smoking the local brand which he complains is ripping his throat to shreds. Dick has been beating him at backgammon, drinking and girls. I tell them what I've been doing and they berate me for half an hour about the dangers of unknown boys, unknown drugs, unknown addresses and unprotected sex. I didn't mean to tell them about that bit but I'm so happy to have found them I don't care.

Don't care was made to care, Hal tells me.

Yes, says Dick. Don't care was hung.

We have to see Dick to the airport. I don't like city airports, always on the edge of town past flat rust-coloured buildings and low trees. I don't like seeing so much asphalt all in one place. Big airport hotels. Hangars, and shuttle buses. Rental car places. Corrugated iron manufacturers. I know it's not fashionable to think nature is beautiful and that these man-made monstrosities are a waste of space. You're so un-modern, Hal will say. This is the future, this is real. You are such a girl.

We all cry a little, saying goodbye. Well, we make the sounds of crying and that's enough. Dick is going to Kingston, Jamaica. My heart is down, he sings, My head is spinning around.

But that's the leaving Kingston song, I say, not the leaving Prague song.

There is no leaving Prague song, he says, because I am too bowed with grief for music.

Oh, I sigh, and feel a single tear running down my cheek.

Huh, says Hal.

Goodbye, says Dick.

Au revoir! Au revoir!

To comfort ourselves we take a walk by the river. It is grey, and glimmering (it never stops glimmering). We see a man fishing down a grating with a hat out to collect money. There is slightly too much of this sad-eyed clown culture in Prague, if you ask me. Paintings on velvet, puppets on string – that sort of thing.

Take my picture, I tell Hal.

I pose next to the fishing clown and look mournful. We have six rolls of black and white film. It is *très romantique*. Me on the Charles Bridge, me with the Vltava in the background, me in front of the cathedral. *Très* Juliette

Binoche. We don't take photographs of Hal. *Il est trop laid*. We did take some of Dick, Dick and me in pornographic contortions in our hotel room. We can sell them to the taxi drivers if we ever run out money. This won't happen. Not as long as we stay in Eastern Europe.

What are you feeling, Hal asks me, surprisingly, back at the hotel. What are you feeling? F.e.e.l.i.n.g.

I shrug, giggling.

Search me!

Hal can sniff out an exhibition opening at twenty paces, in any city. They are the same the world over, unlike poetry readings. The tricky part is timing it so's you're not conspicuous out-of-towners, but not getting there so late that all the free drink is gone. We throw back as much as we can, look at the art a bit, and leave. This show involves a lot of perspex and fluorescent light. It's conceptual. We don't understand the concept. There is a cultural divide.

Hal is losing patience with my spouting of inside knowledge of the Czech people, gleaned from the night I spent with my sex Slav. He accuses me of trying to make the best of a botched situation. Yes?, I say, not sure quite what is wrong with that. It comes out that he is still cross with me for doing it, that he thinks I took a stupid risk, that he believes 'it's different for girls', i.e. worse, and that as he's responsible for me I should respect his wishes. Then he actually says, 'act your age not your shoe size'. Excuse me? Hello? He can't tell me to grow up. I'm twenty-one. I am grown up! But I do shut up, mainly because I've repeated everything the sex Slav and his friends told me and everything I've read in *Laughable Loves* (which after all is fiction, and quite old) and I've run out of inside knowledge about the Czech culture. Damn.

I miss Dick. No amount of cajoling or wheedling would persuade him to delay his ticket. Have I been let down by him? Yes. Has he used me? It's dawning on me that, most probably, he has. It's not that I thought it was love or anything, I just felt like – we had a special bond. The time when we snuck away from Hal and ate sausages in Wenceslas Square, and Dick said that Prague was the most romantic city in the world and I held my breath, then had to let it out after a minute because nothing happened . . . The times when I'm sure I caught him looking at me in a certain kind of way . . . The enthusiasm he showed for our dirty photo session . . . I could have been wrong. I must have been too gullible. I have no instinct about Dick. Perhaps I'll get back to the hotel and find a one-way ticket to Jamaica waiting for me. It's possible, after all; anything is possible!

I can see myself marrying someone like Dick – I can imagine the wedding, the honeymoon, the drink and the infidelities. The reconciliations, the anti-depressants, the children and the diets. The trial separations, the therapy. Dick reminds me of Robert Wagner. The glamour.

Huh, says Hal, when I confess my marital fantasy over vodkas at HP (a mistake, both the venue and the confession). You've been reading too many novels. And now I am confused because the old argument used to be that I didn't read enough! Hal is hard to please. I tell him so – it seems to please him.

How long is it since I've seen the sea? I wake up, adrenalin racing through me. Hal, I say, Hal, how far away from the ocean are we? He snores and rolls over. We have a map. I dig it out of the suitcase and spread it over my bed. In the faint light I can make out where we are. Then Hungary, Romania, Black Sea. Austria, Italy,

Adriatic Sea. Germany, Netherlands, North Sea. Poland, Baltic Sea – the shortest route. We're surrounded on all sides. The room is extra hot. My hands are prickling. I don't want the river. I don't want some dead old spa town or a lake. I want the ocean, the Pacific Ocean. The new world. This never-ending stone oppresses me. The cobbled streets, the ruins, the ancient tombs – it's all so much dust. You can have it. It smells like decay and chalk. Boulders being carried up mountains. Wake up, Hal, wake up.

Hey, says Hal, I know. Let's change all our money and become zloty millionaires. Ha ha ha.

I'd rather be travelling with the fishing clown than be travelling with this. I mean it.

I thought I saw Dick today, in the little café on the steps above the castle. We'd been looking at the tomb of Vladimir the Torturer, or whatever his name is. Again. Crypt after crypt, monument after monument, one fascinating piece of history after another. The guy I thought was Dick was actually the tour guide. You never know.

An old American man who has been hitting on me follows us out of Chapeau Rouge. Gross. He's forty at least. He totters along the street after us while we giggle, ignoring him. He's muttering something. We stop so we can hear what it is. He catches up with us, looks confused as if he's trying to remember where he knows us from. I lean towards him, into the mutter.

Is Roxy open. Is Roxy open. Is Roxy open.

This is what he has to say.

We walk through Unpronounceable Square for breakfast at Cornucopia.

What do you want to do today? asks Hal.

Go to the beach, I say.

Ha ha ha.

We go shopping. I buy a beret and Hal buys a fridge magnet, though we do not own a fridge. We walk up to the Globe, we read English magazines and play backgammon. We drink coffee and all the time I'm thinking the sea, the sea. The white light of home, the smell of salt and coconut oil, hot rubber and woodsmoke. Summer music from a car stereo. Roller blades and pohutukawa flowers, green hills and the green horizon of the sea.

You are as drunk as a rainbow. That's another thing the sex Slav said to me, that I'd forgotten. I'm not quite sure what it means – only, I suppose (an educated guess) that you are very, very drunk.

I am sick in the toilet at Roxy. I splash my face with cold water the way men do and tell myself it's only motion sickness.

'Pickpockets,' Dick was fond of telling me, 'prefer to work in a tight squeeze. It arises especially in department stores.' Then he'd kiss my cheek. Just remember that, honey, he'd say, they like nothing more than a tight squeeze. Ha ha ha. Diky, Dick.

Do you understand, says Hal, holding my hands in the hot hotel room, that we can't go back yet?

My teeth are chattering.

Look at me, he says. Do. You. Understand.

He waits. I nod my head, yes.

Okay, he says. Okay. Tomorrow we'll take the train to Budapest. Smile!

We go to Budapest. We go.

amy prior

....

miss shima

All day she had been measuring out chemicals – iodides and sulphates and nitrates and some things she couldn't remember and some things she'd like to forget – things that had been irritating her all day long (she felt some crystal's residue, even then, at the back of her nose – a strange rotten fruit smell that would remain until she left the building). She had been mixing too – powders with liquids with vapours – and making things disappear and reappear as something else: a grey fluid became transparent; a brown liquid transformed into white and irridescent crystals.

This was when she was most attentive to her work; coaxing the beautiful things from their liqueur was such an art. The coldness had to be just right and the swirling at such a rate and angle that fostered evaporation at a steady speed. And then, the moment she enjoyed most was just when the surface of the liquid began to glisten and the prospect of change became a reality. Even if there was only a low yield it was always worth it. Just a few perfect specimens would make her happy. Sometimes she would take them close to the window and study the way the light refracted through them, the way it deviated in the most mysterious ways.

Back home, of course, light was slightly different – clearer and less diffused by cloud. When she was a child May-Lee spent a long time studying the way it played on the surface of the river that ran past her bedroom window, how it formed such stark geometrical patterns. Now when she looked out into the backyard of her bedsit in Swiss Cottage she noticed the blurred boundaries that governed the edges of the sun patches, the ones that managed to filter through past the dustbins.

As she set some test tubes on a drying rack, she remembered her hairdresser's appointment, and then saw her stylist's face in the space between the fume cupboard and the window. And she stayed seeing it until some noxious fumes of an unknown substance began permeating the whole area.

'Fume cupboard, May-Lee,' her team leader shouted from across the lab and May-Lee attended to the situation.

'It's not good, innit. I'm doing it, okay?' May-Lee said, walking slowly towards the source of the disturbance. She was often distracted like this. Her work, though occasionally absorbing, was in the main quite mundane and often she longed for more colour and dazzle. Beauty at the Real Beauty Company was hi-tech experimentation: The creation of colour was a complicated process, one she had never imagined could be so time-consuming. In fact, for six months their team had worked on developing a new type of lipstick, one that would stick firm all day, however many glasses of wine the wearer sipped. The project was so secret that even May-Lee didn't quite know what the direction was. She just mixed and measured to order and hoped that the work she did was of some use.

May-Lee Shima was one of the quietest laboratory assistants The Real Beauty Company had ever employed. Colleagues talked of her focused determination – a product, they presumed, of a primitive upbringing. It was true, May-Lee's grandparents had worked the fields all day, but things had been easier for their offspring. Moving to Beijing had helped and so had an uncle with a restaurant. Soon after May-Lee was born, her parents were waiting tables full time and she was palmed off on relatives. Usually she stayed at her cousin's because they had lots of games and when she was older she liked watching their satellite TV. Her interest in science can be traced to one cousin Chang who used to buy chemicals from the druggists and make explosions and small fireworks behind the family house when his father was away. May-Lee liked to watch him create these beautiful things and wondered if one day she could too.

By now, the gases from the fume cupboard had touched the back of her throat and she felt it graze. Oh, she was so stupid. What she needed now was something to get rid of the taste. She liked to take a snack break at this time anyway, because it was just past three and if she made it a clean fifteen minutes, then there was only one-and-three quarter hours left and one-and-three quarter hours was not too long. Usually she went to the confectionary dispenser and dispensed herself something sweet for the duration. Some days it was Kit-Kat, others it was Crunchie, and maybe, just maybe (if she was very lucky) on a good day it would be a Star Bar. The type of snack made a great deal of difference to her break and today she was especially pleased that her favourite was available.

On the roof people looked small, like the woodlice in her kitchenette, and she enjoyed following their tracks from one end of the street to the other. She reached for the cigarettes from the pocket of her white coat, clean this week but now stained and perfumed from the various spillages and emissions that had befallen her already. She lit a Marlboro with little effort, a move she had been perfecting for a while now, ever since watching all the actresses on video, in the films made when smoking was still fashionable and no one had even heard of lung cancer.

'You were lucky,' she heard a voice behind her, one she recognised. 'That stuff could have got out of hand.' It was Maureen, her team leader.

'I just got distracted by something else,' said May-Lee, looking down at her shoes – Hi-tech trainers, once white and now grey at the edges.

In her too-small bedsit in her too-small house currently full of Irish men with too-large histories and too-huge capacities for whiskey, May-Lee sat and studied her reflection, a pleasant one but one that would go unnoticed in a crowd, especially round there, an area where there were so many people from overseas. She saw them buying Feta cheese and halal meat and baklava at the local shops, and sometimes she bumped into them in the hallway. Thai students who paid their way by handing out flyers on Oxford Street; refugees from Bosnia, rehoused from temporary hotels with babies who got sick; gypsies from Kosovo on the run from the authorities; Moroccan women with diplomat husbands who lived in the large white houses and covered themselves carefully so as not to offend. She saw them all and yet she did not speak to one of them, because they were never introduced.

Her hair was straight and long and hung loosely, gathered by a coloured elastic band doubled over twice. She liked to wear simple things that required little ironing because she had no iron and besides even if she bought one, there would be little room to set up the board in the room where she slept, ate, dressed, undressed and watched TV. Today she wore a checked shirt over jeans, fraying at the bottom and slightly less blue than when she had first bought them.

All morning she had been watching films. She had a whole stack borrowed from Blockbuster. She liked the musicals and today she watched her favourite, one she had viewed too many times to count. The plot was complex, but the main strand involved a spoiled heiress who was torn between her new fiancé and an old ex-husband. Of course she found true love in the end, but only after a journey involving many clinches and crinolined dresses and songs that, afterwards, rang in May-Lee's head for hours.

As she cooked lunch she sang one of them, a bright tune they danced to in a large, panelled room. Oh, she just loved it and as she stirred the mushrooms on the gas ring (she noticed the meter was running low), she waltzed over to her fridge and then waltzed back, quick little steps which she took on her tiptoes, moving in time with the rhythm she had in her head. When she added the carrots she did so with a flourish, arching her hand at an elegant angle as she raised the fish slice from the pan. The onions were chopped to the beat of an up-tempo ballad duet sung by a sassy blonde in a twin set and her soon-to-be husband, around a table laden with polished silver and crystal glasses.

There were no tears, as usual.

And as she moved over to the bed to eat she drifted into a slow dance, cradling her plate as the heiress had cradled her long-lost husband in the pre-wedding party, as if this were really the last time before fate pulled them apart. She traced a path of circles, round the orange vinyl sofa, pirouetting the lamp that spotlit her for an instant, arcing the silvery tracks of the slugs who occasionally popped in from behind the sink, finishing around the laundry, which had been sorted into piles – whites with whites, coloureds with coloureds, wools with wools.

'I'm having a simply wonderful afternoon,' May-Lee said to her reflection, imagining a camera catching her most flattering angle, and again she repeated this phrase, elongating the vowels and raising the pitch, watching her lips move as she spoke.

Her hairdressers was in Chinatown, somewhere between an all-night grocery shop and a casino. May-Lee wanted her usual stylist, but it was Dana's day off. May-Lee liked Dana because she either did all the talking or did not talk at all. She heard about her fashion shoots for the magazines, how it was such hard work, the old days in her father's salon in Tokyo. She learnt she liked to live alone, even in Brixton which was so on the edge; how one day she would like to live in the country with lots of cows. May-Lee had found out all these things during the few times she had visited the salon, and on each occasion she would listen as attentively as a friend, nodding her head cautiously in comprehension at points when the scissors were not angled in a dangerous position. In fact, sometimes May-Lee thought she and Dana had some kind of special connection, that secretly Dana wished she might eventually become a friend, and often she waited for opportunities to arise in conversation that provided the possibility of social events outside the salon. Once Dana mentioned she liked jazz and May-Lee thought she could ask her to Ronnie Scott's; another time she said she liked rollerblading and May-Lee wondered if she would enjoy the ups and downs of Hampstead Heath. Despite May-Lee's ideas to the contrary, Dana remained just a hairdresser, though her trim became secondary to the sparkling conversation. Every time, May-Lee emerged with the same down-to-her-shoulders-almost-one-length-natural-colour style she'd had since she was fifteen years old and her mother stopped having time to plait her hair.

Instead of Dana, May-Lee got Muki who wanted to know everything about her and said little about herself.

'What can I do for you today?' she asked first of all, looking at May-Lee's reflection. May-Lee thought for a moment. Dana had never asked this question. Dana would say: 'Just a trim today, huh?' and then wheel her over to the basins before she had time to answer.

'I want something different,' May-Lee said. Her voice surprised her, like she was listening to someone else speak.

'You want some colour?' Muki ran her hands through to check the condition. 'This is good. You have good hair. Sometimes our clients, they have damage but you are okay. You could have anything. You want to go lighter? I can see it lighter.' She fetched some samples from the side, then held several up beside May-Lee's hair. 'This one is gooood. I could mix it with some red or brown. And we could do some highlights.'

May-Lee thought for a moment. She looked up at Muki's hair. It was long too, but cut in a layered style at the front that made her look seventies like Suzi Quatro. The flicks were accentuated by blonde highlights, but the contrast between the blonde and black was too strong.

'I want it all over,' she said, 'like this,' and she reached into her bag and picked out the video to show her what she meant.

'You want it like that?' Muki said, her voice suddenly high and disbelieving, though tempered with a professional respect of customer rights.

Muki began sectioning her hair, clipping then painting, clipping then painting. It was a long and difficult process and she needed distractions; every so often she'd disappear to the far corner of the salon to change the tape or rewind to a track she particularly liked. Muki was from Osaka and had lived in London three years. She wore skin-tight blue jeans and a black T-shirt and sometimes a leather jacket indoors. Her knowledge of contemporary Western music was limited to the late '70s. She liked the greats – Earth, Wind and Fire, Sister Sledge, Donna Summer. 'That's Grace Kelly, right? You like those films?' she said, moving her head slowly to the rhythm of the current song.

'Yeah. They help me improve English,' May-Lee said.

'Can't you go to college?' said Muki. 'My sister goes and she teaches me.' She twirled, briefly, knocking a metal comb against her side in time to the beat, then peering at May-Lee's reflection. May-Lee saw her stepping left then right. She took up a great deal of floor space.

'I haven't got time. My job is long hours and I get tired,' May-Lee said.

Under the heater her scalp was on fire. She could almost

imagine the top layer of skin being stripped away. Always in life she had relied on nature's way to keep her hair looking good. She remembered her mother, the way she brushed her hair when Aunt Mee visited from England – long, steady strokes; how then she smoothed it down, tied it into plaits. She saw her father in a business suit (sharply pressed), with his hair oiled back, gratefully accepting the gifts. Always, there would be lots for her: a floral print smock from Laura Ashley or stripy leg warmers or Bendick's Mints in their glossy gold and green box. She remembered a dress – one in particular, made from a thick blue-green shimmery material that looked like the ocean, decorated with beads that curved round the bodice. She thought of sitting perched in the corner on a high, stiff little chair in that dark room, modelling it for them all, making a show of adjusting her collar or straightening her hem, chewing, then twirling the ends of plaits tightly round her little finger, making curls that stayed. She remembered how Aunt Mee dabbed her pulse points with Chanel No. 5, how even days afterwards she could smell it on her wrists, long after the dress had disappeared into the depths of her mother's wardrobe (deemed unsuitable for day wear). How later, at odd moments, like when she was walking the dusty track to her sister's, she thought of the dress, saw herself wearing it, felt it almost – the cool silkiness of the material against her skin, imagined how the others would gaze, smiling and waving her way.

Another present, one she remembers well, was a book called *Glamour World*, a hardback with gold-embossed pages rich with details about good grooming for girls. For months she pored over the illustrations, practising step-by-step just the correct way to apply mascara, how to gloss with no fuss; when to glitter and when to matt.

The text was littered with tips from actresses who had tried-and-trusted ways of making up. From Veronica Lake she learnt about eye liner, from Doris Day about colour and coordination.

Her mother became concerned – May-Lee spent every day buried in her book. But it was the summer of the separation and she was preoccupied with other things. Uncles and cousins and friends would appear for concilatory visits. In the afternoons they would sit in the dark, curtained front room, eating Dim Sung and drinking tea. Sometimes May-Lee would walk past the closed door, listening to the clink of their china and their voices, serious and hushed.

Aunt Mee had the one stable marriage of the family. She and Jonathan had been together twelve years. He had found her twenty-six minutes into the tape, a nineteen-year-old girl from Beijing (hobbies include Chinese painting, flower arranging and cookery) whose small stature betrayed her large personality. Just from the way she spoke, he realised her competence in social situations, and as he watched he pictured her beside him at a client's dinner; how she would look at the high-rank executives with those unblinking eyes, hypnotizing them into deals that were only marginally profitable. He collected her soon afterwards en route to a business trip to Malaysia. He remembers arriving at her house; the meal with the sweet dumplings, damp sponges that emanated a sweet, sickly liquid when squeezed into the tiny crevice of his mouth; the way she pared meat from the chicken feet, scraping it off carefully the way a dog cleans a bone, a process that prompted his awareness of their wide cultural differences. She had been taking English lessons, and each time she spoke (she liked the idioms) her grandmother would nod proudly. A grand woman whose silence accompanied a ruthless streak, it was she who had encouraged Mee to get on to the books of the marriage agency. There was no future for her on the farm; they all knew that. Now Mee's husband's business, the Real Beauty Company, was multinational. Aunt Mee shopped at Harrods, Knightsbridge and had her groceries delivered by van.

When May-Lee emerged from the heater, washed hair hanging loose and combed through, her first feeling was one of disappointment. The darkness was only slightly tempered, a sandy hue in place of a golden blonde. But as Muki proceeded to snip and trim, tease and curl, the hair dried and the emerging colour grew lighter and lighter until there was little difference between May-Lee's shade and the one on the front of the video. Then she squirt, squirted the lacquer until the style stiffened like sugar cake frosting and waltzed over to the other side of the salon to get a mirror.

'How do you like it?' Muki looked expectantly at May-Lee's face, revolving the mirror through numerous angles to provide the most expansive view.

'I couldn't be happier,' she said, pouting her lips slightly and wishing she had re-applied colour earlier.

She found it at the back of the wardrobe, still wrapped in plastic from the journey here.

Unzipping the back, she thought she smelt fragrance, an expensive brand, engrained in the fibres and now floating her way. She stepped into the skirt, then fiddled with the zip. It was hard to get it all the way up, and she struggled at the top, holding her shoulders back to keep the blades less obstructive. Once it was done she saw it was still a perfect fit, contouring with just the right tightness, and she gazed at the blue-green shimmer of the material, glancing at herself from an unusual angle in the mirror, golden hair still frozen into delicate waves at the back, and whispered: 'It's right off the Paris plane. A steal at eleven hundred dollars,' elongating the vowels and raising the pitch, watching her lips move as she spoke.

Now, in front of the mirror, May-Lee tended to her makeup because, if she were to go to the movies, she must look the part. She cleansed first and looked, with disgust, at the residue of dirt that had built up. The bedsit was not the cleanest of places, but she couldn't imagine where it had all come from.

She smoothed on moisturiser and foundation (ever since she had arrived her skin had developed rashes – a product, she thought, of bad food and pollution), then defined her eyes – lids, lashes and brows. She checked her reflection and, noticing a stray hair had lodged itself at an awkward angle on her brow, plucked it with some tweezers. She applied her lipstick – plum shimmer – then pulled out a tissue from the box and blotted it once, then again. She took a final look and then said, to no one in particular: 'Oh, it's enchanting,' in the same voice as before.

Her usual seat at the Ritzy bar was occupied, so she chose another, higher than the others, and sat perched in the corner sipping her Tequila sunrise (usually she just had 7-UP but today she felt like something different), waiting for the seven o'clock showing – a silent classic, the name of which had long since escaped her. They were all there – the lady with the ice cream, smartly dressed in her peppermint-green uniform, a pink cap perched on her hat; the popcorn man, loading the cardboard boxes until they were way overflowing.

Ah, she thought, here are the others, looking at the

people taking their seats round the bar. The suited man, elegantly balancing a cigarette in the hand that was simultaneously holding a whisky. He turned and looked at her and, just for a moment, she thought she saw him smile, the kind of smile that hinted at recognition, and May-Lee looked at his face briefly and wondered if she had seen it before. It was so rarely in London you saw the same person twice. You could walk for days, weeks and meet only different people. As quickly as he looked, she turned away, and concentrated on rearranging the hem of her dress, feeling, briefly, the cool silkiness of the material against her skin, a sensation heightened by an alcoholic warmth. His girlfriend, so smart in her city suit and briefcase, joined at his side.

She went to buy some choc chip ice cream. The lady prepared a scoop and placed it into a tub and said: 'You enjoy that, dear. You look like you need cheering up.'

'Oh, but I'm already having a simply wonderful evening,' said May-Lee, elongating the vowels and raising the pitch, watching her lips move in the mirror opposite as she spoke. And the lady smiled at her and said nothing. She knew they would smile when she wore her dress.

She liked it, sitting here, eating her ice cream, surveying it all. She and the ice cream lady and the popcorn man and the suited man and his girlfriend were the stars. The others, they had walk-on parts when needed. And she could almost see the camera shots, they way the other actors would pose, the camera capturing her on that stool. She imagined the way the light would deviate, reflected from the shimmering fabric of her dress on to the mirrors and back again, so the screen was awash with a beautiful blue-green.

Just then she heard raised voices and turned, eager to

catch the drama that was developing between the couple next to her.

'What's she staring at?' the city girl said in a voice that carried. Then, after replenishing her glass, she added: 'Look at her. God, that dress. It's like something my grandma used to wear.'

She prepared herself a light snack before bed. Sometimes she had a Twix or a cheese toastie or a kebab from the shop over the road. But today she boiled some rice and green tea and combined them in one bowl and ate fast, the way she used to, using chopsticks to manœuvre the food to her mouth.

Then she sat at her dressing table, removing her makeup with a cotton pad soaked in lotion, smoothing it over her skin, thinking about the film, which was not as good as she remembered. She brushed her hair, long strokes that gradually loosened her newly curled style.

She unzipped the dress and carefully laid it on the bed. She sat there looking, in the dimness that had rapidly enveloped her tiny room this last hour, and saw that still even the moon managed to refract through her window on to its glassy beads, making patterns on the wall – stark geometrical shapes that intersected in such strange ways. She looked away quickly, picked up the plastic cover that was still lying on her duvet and carefully wrapped the dress, attaching a coathanger, then opening the wardrobe, hanging it back where it came from.

emily hammond

....

doko ni iki mas ka

In the middle of the San Joaquin Valley and flat as Kansas, Stockton, where I went to college, was foggy and cold in the winter, broiling hot in the summer. Callison College was actually just one program within the whole University of the Pacific, which couldn't have been more conservative. Which meant those of us in Callison felt a need to be especially flamboyant and eccentric, to counteract the fraternities and sororities just down the street.

Callison College had its own dorm, complete with coed floors and bathrooms, yet there weren't enough Callison students to fill the dorm, so we wound up with some interesting mixtures. My roommate, for example, was an acidhead anorectic poet from Seattle; next door to us were two black football players who played endless Isaac Hayes records and were visited constantly by girlfriends. Though every morning the football players and I brushed our teeth side by side and used adjacent stalls, often simultaneously (I used to study their huge white sneakers and wonder what they thought of my Indian buffalo thongs), we seldom spoke or communicated, except to pound on each other's doors and holler, 'Phone's for you!'

When I think of Callison now, I think of the classes. Chinese Brush Stroke Painting, for example: a twenty-yard roll of rice paper, ink stone, ink in the form of a clay stick, a brush. My semester was spent copying bamboo shoots out of a book, while the professor passed by, saying, 'Too much water, Susan.' Or, 'Susan, not enough ink.' I'd add more water or more ink, pestling it together to the right consistency.

It was never the right consistency.

Around me the other students elaborated on complex landscapes of temples and mountainsides, while I became distraught. The professor, attempting to motivate me, told me about the masters who would spend ten years perfecting a single bamboo shoot.

I dropped the course.

Another course I took: Japanese. At around the same time as Chinese Brush Stroke Painting, my major at that time being Asian Studies. The class was taught in two sections, small groups for grammar, pronunciation and practice in Hiragana and Katakana, for which there was a text; the other section of the course was reserved for Kanji, for which there was no text. For this we sat cross-legged in a long hallway with a blackboard at the front. The professor drew a succession of Kanji, labeled their meanings in English, and gave a little talk on each one – how over time and history, this or that stroke came to represent this or that element – most of which I missed, so frantically did I struggle to copy the row of Kanji – each one a complexity of angled strokes just so, one stroke off and you changed the meaning of the whole pictograph. Inevitably, just as I'd get halfway down the row, working furiously, the professor would erase all the Kanji and just as quickly – stroke-stroke here, stroke-stroke there – replace them with six or eight others.

I dropped this course as well. Surprisingly, many of my fellow students did quite well in both Japanese and Chinese Brush Stroke Painting (the same students who lined their dorm rooms with straw mats and sawed off the legs of their tables so they'd be low to the floor. Drank tea. Took their chopsticks to the cafeteria). They stayed up all night discussing the subtleties of the Kanji, all of us stunned by marijuana: 'This line represents a tree, can you see it? A flower here, there a bud.' Still I didn't get it. My pronunciation of Japanese was horrendous, too, only one phrase remaining after all these years. *Doko ni iki mas ka*: where are you going?

I survived the other courses. Japanese History. Varieties of Political Experience. Comparative Cultures of India, China, and the US Humanities (Callison-style, a lot of dance therapy and foreign movies). Slowly, though, I found myself taking other courses – Psychology, Photography, Geology, which I excelled in.

But when I think back on Callison, I don't remember the classes so much. I remember parties, lecherous professors. Fried brains, acid, Thai Sticks. Stoned. Watching *Last Year at Marienbad* over and over, and another movie, *Woman in the Dunes*, about an Japanese entomologist trapped in a sandpit. People dropping out, having nervous breakdowns, falling in love with self-professed warlocks, making love with everybody, anybody. Outbreaks of crabs, scabies . . . all under the guise of expanding our intellectual horizons.

Then one day outside my dorm I saw a girl who looked like my best friend from high school, Kiri – a bigger, blonder Kiri – walking toward me through the fog and drizzle, but this wasn't possible, she was in Eureka.

It was Kiri. She was huge. She was pregnant.

'Did I tell you Yoshi had a false pregnancy?' she said later in my dorm room. 'Grew teats and everything, a full swinging belly.' Yoshi was her dog she'd brought along with her, a white samoyed-collie mix we would be sneaking in and out of the dorm over the next several weeks. 'Susan, I didn't tell you? She was *lactating*, for God's sake.'

'You didn't mention that, no.' I couldn't help staring; Kiri had taken off her shirt and pants to show me what it was like, because I'd asked: pendulous breasts, a brown line running from her navel downward, her belly eggshell white and reaching out into the room like some other body part, a huge rubber nose or a knee, something bought at a joke store and attached. Kiri had started college a year ago and now would have to quit, for a while. She planned to give the baby up for adoption.

'The vet couldn't believe it. He really thought she was pregnant at first. Until I told him she was spayed.' She shook her long, thin blonde hair, causing Yoshi to look up startled and concerned from her nap by my bed.

'It's because I'm pregnant, that's what it was. Empathetic reaction.'

'What did the vet do?' I asked.

'Nothing. He said just let her be, so I did, and it went away.' She buttoned up her blue work shirt, which in the rainy green light looked almost velvety, and I wondered if she wished she could make her own pregnancy go away now that it was so evident. I was surprised that for all our old jokes about knitting needles (and throwing ourselves off horses, down flights of stairs), Kiri, when it came down to it, didn't believe in abortion. She didn't think it was wrong or anything; she just couldn't do it herself. As for giving up the baby for adoption, she didn't seem distressed by this in the least, or by the pregnancy in general. In fact her life seemed to go on as before – tonight, for instance, she had a date.

'Already?' I said. 'Who?'

Some guy she'd met on the Trailways bus. He was taking her out for a steak dinner. Kiri loved to eat and this guy said he would love to feed her.

As for the father of the baby, Kiri had broken up with him even before she'd discovered she was pregnant. She'd decided not to tell him – he would hover about, worry, talk marriage. No, let him go, let him live in San Francisco and be happy and ignorant.

Kiri didn't weep about her predicament; rather, she appeared almost jolly, as if this pregnancy were just another one of our adventures to add to the list.

'What shall *we* eat today?' she'd say as we stood in line at the cafeteria, meaning not just her and the fetus, but me too, as though the three of us were in this together.

My friends stared at the heft of her, but not too much. It was that sort of college, those sort of times – an alternative college in the early seventies, sort of the tail end of the sixties. Unwed mother? Cool. Whatever.

Men fell hard for Kiri and she didn't even try – no makeup or jewelry, in her Levi jeans and men's flannel shirts. Pregnant even, her belly like a balloon! It was that quality she had, the Madonna face, the sapphire eyes. A certain brand of innocence she exuded, even in the grungiest bar, five months' pregnant, carrying on in ways she shouldn't.

Every night was like this. Off to do an errand or go

out for a bite to eat, we'd get sidetracked to somebody's dorm room or a dark sticky bar, or a cubbyhole apartment off-campus with dirty dishes up to the ceiling, the same Doobies' record playing over and over again, some blonde lumberjack sort at Kiri's elbow.

Finally one night I got disgusted and left, went back to my dorm room to do homework for a change. Not that anyone noticed I had left, least of all Kiri.

We had it out when she came home, around three. I'd positioned a chair in front of the door, Yoshi at my feet, both of us watching the door like a couple of nursemaids awaiting Kiri's return.

'What do you think you're doing?' I said.

'Letting myself in the door.'

'What are you doing? You're pregnant!'

She cradled her belly. 'How observant of you.'

'Are you drunk?' I said.

'I only had a couple of beers, I swear to God.'

'A couple?'

'Look,' she said. 'I hardly drink. I gave up smoking. What do you want?'

'You're partying, screwing around. Everywhere you go there are men falling all over you. You're acting like this isn't even happening.'

'Jesus, Susan. You're not my mother.'

'*You're* the mother.' I sounded so like a parent, like Fred McMurray gone mad. I couldn't help myself. God! She was pregnant. I thought of the baby reeling around in all that chaos and liquor. I was revolted, scared.

'Our mothers drank all the time when they had us,' Kiri said. 'Smoked too. I mean, I didn't know my real mother, but one can assume. Look at us, we're fine.' She giggled. 'Just a little brain-damaged.'

'Shut up.'

'I'm just going out for a little fun,' she said petulantly. She flopped onto my bed, undid the safety pin on her jeans, belly protruding like a bowl. 'I've got to get maternity clothes.'

She started to cry. I held her while Yoshi blinked wetly, her black-rimmed eyes appearing mascaraed against her white fur. 'No,' Kiri said, 'I don't know what I'm doing. What am I doing? What am I doing?'

The following day we went into Stockton, to the Miracle Mile for shampoo and maternity clothes. I felt both proud and ashamed for Kiri. Her size was truly a miracle to behold – to think there was a baby, a living being in there! – her hard belly like a drawer that had been pulled out, which Kiri liked to rest her arms on ('Comfortable,' she said, 'and good shock value'). Two older women stopped to ask Kiri when was she due, did she think it was a boy or girl, could she sleep? When they didn't see a wedding band they scanned her face anxiously – was she married? attached at least? She wasn't going to do this alone, was she? They seemed to know not to ask about her 'husband'.

'Does it bother you?' I asked. 'People assuming you're on your way home now to paint stencils on the baby's crib?'

'Yes,' she said, sitting on a bench, legs apart, pointing and flexing her ballet slippers, the only shoes she could get on her feet by herself now. 'It bothers me,' she said, 'but not nearly as much as it bothers you.'

'That's unfair, Kiri, and it's not true!' I wasn't sure if it was true or not, but I knew it was mostly untrue. 'I don't give a shit what people think. You know that.'

'I wish I *was* going home to paint stencils on the baby's crib,' Kiri said.

'Seriously?' My heart leaped. That's just what I'd been

thinking – that I felt I knew this baby now, that when Kiri had to give him or her up, it would be like giving up a part of myself. I tried to sound casual. 'Have you ever thought of keeping the baby?'

'Every single day,' Kiri said. 'But no. I can't. I'm alone, I'm nineteen. I don't have any money. How would I do it?' Tears crept into her voice.

'I don't know,' I said, placing my hand on her belly. 'Sometimes I think about it too – think about how it *could* be done.' Through her dress I could feel the baby kicking.

After Kiri left for Eureka, I began seeing Nick. Seeing, not dating. Nobody dated.

I continued to think about Kiri keeping her baby. I would be moved out of the dorm by then, into an apartment. (I'd convinced my father I could study better there.) One bedroom, sure, but the living-room was large – Kiri and the baby could stay there, until Kiri got on her feet. Then she could move into another apartment, maybe in the same house; it was an old house split into four apartments.

It was fantasy, of course, and a lack of knowledge. What about a crib? A changing table? All we had in the living-room – we meaning Nick and me, we were already living together though my father didn't know – was a sagging couch. The place was drafty, cardboard over one of the panes of glass. No washer and dryer in the house, you had to lug your laundry four blocks to the nearest laundromat.

I didn't know anything about babies, mothering. My own mother was dead. I'd never even babysat; Kiri, at least, had.

'No, Susan,' she said on the phone when I told her my idea. 'It won't work. You have no idea . . .'

'Money isn't a problem,' I said, launching into part two of the plan. 'I have some income from my mother's estate. Not much and it's in some bank that only my father knows about, but I can get hold of it. It's my money.'

'Susan, no.'

'Why not?' I said.

'I can't keep this baby, you know I can't.'

'But I just explained to you how.'

'Susan, it's my baby. Let me decide what's best. Quit trying to save me.'

This stung for some reason, and I felt worn out. 'Okay, Kiri, but just think about it, okay? It's an option, that's all. Whatever you decide, I want to be there at the birth.'

'What?' She sounded tired, and a little put out.

'We've talked about that, remember? Please? I want to be there.'

'Right.'

'I want to be there,' I said again.

Despite Kiri's reluctance, I lapsed into long and drawn-out fantasies about the baby. Even though our living-room was a grayed flesh color, in my mind it was white. The couch was pink and rounded, smiling almost. The rug was gone; in its place, a beautiful hardwood floor. We would take turns caring for the baby, Kiri, Nick, and me. All our friends would pitch in; we'd go on picnics; the baby would be a loved and darling sort of mascot.

Amazingly, Nick said little to discourage me. Little to encourage me, either. 'Well, maybe,' he said in his vague and gentle way. 'We'll see, okay?' Mostly he was caught up in his piano, his composing, his jazz combo, their jam sessions. Often when I came home from my night class there would be fifteen or so people crammed into our apartment listening to the band, drinking, smoking hashish, cigarettes; overflowing ashtrays everywhere, and when the band quit, the stereo would go on, album cover jackets strewn about as Nick and friends would say to each other, 'Wait a minute, you gotta hear this.' On would go another record, another bottle of wine opened, another trip to the store for more liquor and cigarettes . . .

How I thought this would work with a baby, I can't explain. I just didn't think about it.

Spring arrived, and Stockton was a beauty. Within hours, it seemed, the fog dissipated, grass sprouted, trees blossomed. Every evening Nick and I walked to the Music Building; at ten minutes to six exactly, swallows swooped through the campus, round and round, picking up speed like airborne race cars. Then the six o'clock chimes would start, building to a crescendo with the birds. Then silence.

Nick and I were an established couple by then, a state mysteriously reached without words. We'd just come together at the city park one day, soon after he'd moved into my dorm room (my acidhead anorectic poet roommate had long ago dropped out to live in San Francisco), and it was understood somehow as we fed the ducks and watched them mate, that we would find an apartment together.

I was crazy about Nick. Crazy about sleeping with him. He was tall, pale, dark-haired, and warm-skinned. Shy and peaceful except when playing piano, or when aroused. Then he was noisy. I was noisy. It became embarrassing, a joke in the household. Our neighbors, our friends would listen, no, *hear* us – they couldn't help but hear us – and repeat back to us what we had moaned at each other. We blushed, grinned, hung our heads – had we really said that? So loudly? A vague memory of it . . . And the next time, later the same day even, we'd do it all over again.

They, our friends, didn't mind; we didn't mind – not enough to control ourselves. It was that sort of household. In our backyard lived T.J. Stone in a tent, complete with waterbed. Missing a front tooth (considered sexy by all the women), T.J. loved Boz Scaggs, steamed artichokes, and women. Slept with everybody. In the apartment below ours was Thompson, an aspiring filmmaker. He made movies of body parts. In one movie, legs. In another, women's breasts.

We all considered ourselves artists of some kind. Nick, a musician. Natalie next door, a potter. T.J., lover of women. Myself? I didn't always know how I fit in. Rock hound? I'd changed my major to Geology, in search of some stability perhaps. Rocks. But nothing about Geology was stable, I learned. The earth rising up from within, hot and molten, firing crystals into endless multiplication – color, texture, hardness, smell, taste – I loved determining what gem or mineral I held in my hand. On a larger level I loved that the earth could be so ever-changing, passionate, brutal, beautiful, impervious – coastline splitting off from the mainland, sending homes that ought not to have been built crashing into the ocean; hills, mountains, turning to mud in an earthquake; sinkholes gobbling up land. Nature had a way of winning, asserting itself, fighting back, although it was never fighting, of course. It just was.

Kiri was impossible to get hold of once she returned to

Eureka. It became an obsession, trying to call her. I tried morning, noon, night, at three in the morning once. I wrote her letters. 'I'll be there in three weeks. I'll probably drive if I can borrow a car. Call me. Where are you? You couldn't have gone far (In search of large pregnant woman trying to escape destiny. Blonde hair. Answers to "mother").' I waited to hear back, something about my exquisitely bad taste. No word. Finally I reached her. She picked up the phone halfway through the first ring.

'Kiri, where have you been?' I said.

'I went back to school.'

'In your condition?'

'Spare me, will you?' she said. '*Condition*? I'm taking eighteen credits this quarter.'

'What are you going to do when the baby's born?'

'Incompletes,' she said. 'It's all arranged.'

'Did you move?' I asked. 'I've called—'

'And written, I know.'

'You sound so depressed.'

'I'm tired,' she said. 'My back hurts, my feet hurt, my hips hurt. I can't sleep.'

'Have you seen a doctor?'

'All the time, dummy. I'm having a baby, remember? My parents send money for that at least.'

'I'm coming up soon,' I said.

'Why?'

'You know why. I'm coming for the birth,' I said.

'I don't want anyone there. Not even you. Just the doctor.'

'But we agreed,' I said.

'And now I'm backing out of the agreement.' Her voice sounded flippant and I pictured her as she'd been in high school talking on the phone, chewing on a match stick. 'I want to be alone,' she said.

'I don't think you do, Kiri. You need someone there for you.'

'No, *you* think I need someone there.'

The conversation went on this way for a while, until finally we reached another agreement: I would come for the birth but remain at her apartment. Spend all visiting hours with her until she was ready to come home from the hospital – with the baby, I still hoped, useless as that hope was. In any case, I'd be there for her, and when it was all over, with the baby or without, she would return with me to Stockton.

Nick contracted the flu before I could go, after an elaborate cooperative Easter celebration in which everybody in the household prepared three dishes. Nick and I roasted a turkey, mashed enough potatoes for forty-odd guests, made a batch of banana ice cream. There were curries and casseroles and salads and fresh-baked bread; Nick's band performed; Thompson screened his film of women's breasts. I read Tarot cards and identified rocks and minerals. T.J. got into a fight with his current lover's boyfriend, a lazy marijuana fight in which they slung epithets from across the room, then rolled around on the lawn outside and fell asleep.

I cheated on Nick. One of his musician friends had been following me around all day, a guy with brown ringlets and snaky blue eyes. Jasper. I didn't even like him, and what a stupid name. I kept telling him it wasn't his real name, he'd made it up; his name was probably Norman or Morris. He insisted I go on a motorcycle ride with him and everyone agreed, egging me on, knowing my fear of motorcycles. Nick said nothing, didn't seem to care, which angered me. I'd had too much to smoke and drink. Finally I hopped on back of Jasper's motorcycle and we roared off, but only down to the park where we made out. He told me he'd see me next week, I should drop by his place; I told him maybe. His body was so bony I felt bruised and nastied by the experience, but now obligated to him, chained to him. After all, I'd risked what I had with Nick to mess around with him – I must like Jasper at least a little. Maybe I was madly in love with him and didn't know it. Love might cause one to do outrageous things.

The next day Nick fell ill. Maybe he'd guessed and this was the result – the knowledge made him sick. He gazed at me with dim, faraway eyes; yes, he must know. Guilt informed my every thought and movement. 'Do you want some tea?' I'd ask. 'I'm making myself some.' My hands shook and appeared so pale, no longer a part of me. For God's sake, another voice inside me lectured, you didn't do anything, you made out, so what?

'No tea,' Nick said.

'You don't feel up to it?' I said. Everything seemed so laden with meaning. Up to what, is it over between us . . . ?

'I feel too sick,' he said.

Sickened by me, my ridiculous betrayal with somebody I didn't even like but feared loving. Nick soon succumbed to vomiting and I had to leave the apartment since I couldn't hold his head or wait by the bathroom door, or anything. Vomiting panicked me, always had. Nick would run to the bathroom and I lurched downstairs hugging my chest, laughing hysterically. I'd creep back upstairs, hear the retching, flee outside again, laughing and trying not to gag. I fantasized running into Jasper in his stupid black leather jacket and ripped up jeans, what a self-conscious jerk . . . he'd grab me and I'd let him. I held my hand over my mouth to keep from laughing, my lips still bruised from Jasper's teeth. The guy didn't even know how to kiss.

That night I slept on the living-room floor, preferring it to the couch, which gnawed into my back like lumps of little dead animals. I was terrified of catching the flu from Nick. I woke up screaming, Nick shaking me. 'You're having a nightmare,' he said, then stopped off at the bathroom to puke again. I waited in the hallway outside our apartment, hands clapped over my ears, humming and singing hymns from childhood and giggling miserably.

Within days Nick was better and eager to make love. I let him kiss me, repelled by his dirty hair and stubbly beard. 'What's the matter, Susan?'

'Maybe when you're better . . .' I breathed through my mouth to guard against any lingering smell of vomit.

'I am better,' he said.

'After you take a shower, then.'

'All right.' He released me and rose from the bed. The moment he turned on the shower I ran out the front door, stood at the bottom of the stairs that led outside, breathing in fresh air.

Nick's flu and my indiscretion made me forget temporarily about Kiri's baby, which wasn't due yet anyway. Then she showed up at our door – alone except for Yoshi, and no longer pregnant.

'What are you doing here?' I said.

'I had the baby.'

Yoshi whimpered, and licked my hand.

'When? You weren't due for another—' I calculated quickly '—another three weeks.'

'I had the baby four days ago.'

'But why didn't you call? Where is the baby?'

'Where do you think? Can I come in or are we going to stand here?'

I opened the door more, turned back inside and let her follow me. I sat on the couch, Yoshi instantly by my feet, our old alliance reformed. 'But Kiri—' I said.

'Do you want to see his picture?'

She didn't look as a woman should after giving birth. She looked normal, a bit bulky, but as though this had never happened. 'How could you just have the baby and leave?' I said. 'Who's the baby with?'

'His new parents. They got him two days after. I had to sign this form, that was the worst part. I kept expecting them to say, "Are you sure? Do you want to take another day to think about it?" I was crying all over the form, I could barely read it.'

'Sit down,' I said at last. I didn't feel sorry for her as I thought I should, just irritated. 'Can I get you anything?'

'A beer.' A wry smile. 'How about a cigarette? I haven't started up again – yet. I was waiting for you to corrupt me.' She flipped a thin strand of yellow hair off her face.

'As I always do,' I said by rote. An old joke – our parents wishing to blame our delinquency on each other's influence.

'So how about a beer?'

'All out.' A lie. We had one left but I didn't want her to have it. I wanted it, after she left; then I remembered she was staying. 'How about a nice glass of—'

'Water. Oh God.' What the minister's wife used to offer us back in high school, how we'd fantasized asking for scotch on the rocks, or a screwdriver. 'Water's fine. Do you have any milk? I don't even have to drink it anymore but now I'm hooked.'

In no time things got worse, as they often did around Kiri – without a baby there to protect us. I'd sneak out to see Jasper, Kiri would cover for me. Or we'd both go see Jasper, telling Nick we were going to a movie, Yoshi's white ears pricking up at the lie, as if she at least had a conscience. When Nick wasn't around we'd make jokes about all the movies we'd seen; about what Kiri had said when he asked questions about my whereabouts; or what she'd said into the phone when Jasper called. 'Why, no, Susan isn't here, Professor . . .' We imagined Jasper holding the phone out, staring at it wickedly.

All at Nick's expense, and why? I became depressed, drank too much, picked fights with him.

I blamed Kiri. I felt cheated that I'd missed the birth. If she'd treated me as though this whole thing had somehow involved me, was happening to me too, I bought it. I believed. My arms felt empty, I felt angry. A baby would save us.

I kept thinking about the baby. How it must feel to be the couple adopting that baby: getting the call the night before, standing in the nursery that's been waiting all year.

I lacked the courage to break up with Nick. Instead I let him find me at Jasper's, me with Jasper, Kiri with some scumbag friend of his. Nick followed us over there one day – finally, after swallowing all the lies we'd tossed his way. He called me a slut and hurled a book at Kiri, and kicked that scrawny Jasper down the stairs, who merely checked his leather jacket for rips and slithered away. His scumbag friend just sat there smoking a joint, and I was numbed and weirdly gratified by the sleaziness of it all.

When Kiri and I got back to the apartment, Yoshi was on the lawn waiting for us, leash attached, all our stuff scattered everywhere, thrown out the windows. The curtains were drawn, the door locked, some hopeless rhythm and blues record blaring, and T.J., expert on affairs and jilted lovers, suggested it might be best for us just to leave.

We loaded Yoshi, our clothes, sheaves of papers, books, and a table of mine – one leg broken off – into Kiri's car without bothering to sort any of it. We had no place to go and all I felt was resentment at being stuck with Kiri, ex-unwed mother and no good bitch, or whatever it was about her that brought out the bad in me; why me, I'd grown up in a nice family – nice – my father's favorite word. I would drop out of college; what else was there to do, I deserved it, I deserved to slut around and have guys hit on me, I couldn't fight them off. In twenty years I'd be dead maybe, like my mother, a victim of DNA. Or of booze. Drugs. Boredom. Who knew why she killed herself. At least she'd been pretty, 'attractive' as people of that generation say; she got her hair done, wrote lovely thank you notes, polished the silver and did volunteer work. Nice. I could see why my father had married her.

I was not nice, I decided, only I didn't know why.

Something to do with my mother, the past I couldn't recall. But I remembered so much. My room, my dolls, my stuffed animals, my books, the way the sun shone in the mornings; how in the evenings sprinklers gurgled in their beds of loam, every leaf and every flower in our backyard.

I remembered so much. I remembered nothing. The past was something closed up, left behind, forgotten; an old handbag fallen to the ground, its contents locked to me. As Kiri and I drove around Stockton wondering what to do, chain-smoking Larks and stopping finally for greasy hamburgers, I felt the unwanted chromosomal link snaking around inside me, connecting me to my dead mother like a poisoned umbilical cord.

'Stop the car,' I told Kiri at the edge of town.

She did and I got out, for just a moment, certain I'd stood in this same spot as a very small child. We were on a trip to the Sierra Nevadas, on our way to pan gold, my mother still alive then. She picked up a rock by the side of the road and showed it to me – granite with feldspar and quartz, a few shiny flakes of mica. Plain and speckled as a quail's dull egg, the rock caught the light, glittered, and I thought we were saved.

eleanor knight

....

rosa

The music student from Canada, on the recommendation of his professor, arrived in Budapest by train. During the clattering journey from the border he had accepted a biscuit from the basket of a red-cheeked old woman in the seat opposite and had smiled and nodded as she pointed through the dusty window at a pig farm that reached down from a half-derelict hut almost to the railway track twenty kilometres or so before they reached the city. Gazing out at the wide flat fields he felt a hard thud of excitement. In the low pull of the train he heard the rhythmic heavy draw of a bow on a double bass – the sound that had brought him here, the land of the Magyars, the czardas, the gypsy airs he was here to record and analyse. A people prone to suicidal depression who wrote anarchic flamboyant music that made your spine shiver for the loss of a land you had never known.

The train arrived at the station and immediately he had observed, assimilated, interpreted. A man wiped tears from his eyes as he picked up a woman's (his wife's?) suitcase. A little girl jumped and danced on the platform, spinning so that her skirt made a coloured disc around her waist. The tannoy blared instructions in what the student recognised as typical Magyar cadences, the impenetrable language having its own subtle musicality. The old woman with the basket had disappeared into the crowds beyond the booking office. Men with long moustaches and dirty felt jackets pushed towards him, offering him taxis, hotels, private rooms. He handed one of them a piece of paper with an address and followed him out to where a small brown Fiat was choking the snowy air, its engine still running.

Glancing up at faded art nouveau splendour from the cramped black vinyl seat, the car bouncing on the cobbles and tramlines, the music student spotted a man in a long winter coat playing the violin on a street corner. As they drew up to some traffic lights, he hurriedly wound down the window and fumbled in his rucksack for his tape recorder, signalling the driver to wait. They pulled up alongside the violinist and for a few seconds the car was filled with a sweet Transylvanian lament. He recognised the pattern of the phrases. The driver, however, hadn't understood him and they moved off.

And now the music student was standing at the door of an apartment block in the south of the city where the buildings were cheaper imitations of the central municipal grandeur; layers of dusty-coloured plaster, faded pink and dirty yellow, showed from the gaps in the brown. A small dog barked at him from a balcony above. A man shouted somewhere in the building and then the sound of a folksong wound down from a radio by an open window. He pressed the intercom.

'Szervusz?'

The student spoke no Hungarian.

'Rosa Mehti?'

'Ser.'

'I—I'm from Canada. I arranged a room . . .'

'Fourth floor, please. No lift.'

The intercom buzzed loudly and the door clicked open. He climbed the narrow tiled stairs, his bulky rucksack growing heavier and knocking the loose plaster from the walls as he reached the top.

The last step brought him so close to the door that as he stepped on to it and the door opened it was as if the room behind the startled woman in the pink dressing gown sucked him straight in. He fell against her, she still standing slightly back from the door, and his face came level with hers. Grasping both his arms she steadied him and kissed him hard on both cheeks.

'I am Rosa,' she shouted. 'Welcome. You can call me ROSA.'

Whether from excitement at having a visitor or just habit, he couldn't tell, but her voice was far too loud for such a small space and he felt it ring in his ears.

'Sit, sit! Please sit, I make you drink.'

The student watched his new landlady moving about her house. She was a huge and clumsy woman, and heavy. She moved as if she was resigned now only ever to move in that tiny space. The cramped carpeted kitchen, which served as the entrance to the apartment, was no more than walking space around a card table in the middle of which was a square of greying lace under a plastic cruet set. In front of him a glass door leading to what he supposed must be Rosa's room and another door which opened on to his – a clean towel and small bar of pink soap lay on the end of the single bed – and a bathroom. Rosa sighed heavily as she bent to open the fridge, from which came the smell of cheap garlic sausage; the music student now recognised the smell that seemed to seep from the walls and which he had smelled briefly on Rosa's skin as he came in. Visible below the

hem of her dressing gown, Rosa's bare feet were splayed
and yellowing under thick veined ankles.

'I stay only in my house now.' She heaved herself up
from the fridge and came to sit down at the table with a
plate of sausage and red pepper. 'My legs are bad and I
am too old. And I don't want to go in the outside.' She
resumed the shouting: 'Please, drink this apple juice!
Very good! And eat *eat*!'

With Rosa sitting at the table for a moment, he noticed
a single tattered postcard stuck to the fridge door. A
dark-haired woman in capri pants and blouse tied under
a familiar, plunging bosom pouted crimson lips from the
middle of an ersatz haystack. Rosa looked up from
cutting the pepper and followed his eye.

'Yes, *this* one is my *favourite*. She is *beautiful*! Jane
Russell. A big movie star and lovely girl!'

'You were a fan of Jane Russell? But how did you . . . I
mean, what was she doing here? You went to the movies?'

The student's mind was running grey flickering news-
reels of gaunt-faced housewives in long freezing bread
queues, crumbling buildings, demonstrations. The news-
reels hadn't shown any cinemas.

'I am always loving this girl. In my heart I am just like
her. A true gypsy!'

He smiled to himself. This would be an entertaining
idea for his research. He could perhaps suggest a paper
on 'Perceptions of gypsies in popular culture'. Rosa was
gazing at the postcard, smiling.

The student finished his meal and excused himself to
take a shower after his long trip. Tomorrow he would go
to the Institute and make contact with the professor of
Musicology and get his research set up. In his room,
Rosa's record collection spread across one wall: the
creased paper record sleeves featured mostly drawings of

women in net skirts, long black hair Carmen-style over one shoulder, and had titles that he was amused to recognise from his studies. 'Cziganydalok' or 'Gypsy Songs', 'Czardas.' The professor would be sending him out to some villages where he would hear the real gypsy music; the bagpipes, the hurdy gurdy, the flutes and the hard warm songs of the peasants.

He had fallen asleep on the bed when Rosa knocked on his door.

'I watch television,' she shouted, not waiting for an answer. 'You too!'

Still barefoot from the shower, the student left the records in a pile on the floor and opened the door to a flickering light across the kitchen. Canned laughter poured out from behind Rosa's door. He could hear her moving about, fixing up a chair for him. He knocked on the glass once and went in.

The television set was far too big for the tiny bedsitting room. Offensively big; you could travel so far around the world and there was still television. In this vibrant, teeming city of music and art, emotional extremes, the mighty bridges and the historic Danube, and here was still television. The light from the set was like a belching, numbing blue fog that filled the room. He noticed that Rosa, who had been moving frantically, fussing with the room since he came in had now, on a signal from something on the television, stopped quite still at the end of her bed. He remained standing a little in front of the glass door, feeling the carpet rising up between his toes. On television a bright blue and green globe spun helter skelter towards the centre of the screen as bright white impressionistic lightning flashes jabbed at it from each corner. There was a cheap and clumsy fanfare before the screen cleared to show a man with silver hair and brown eyes half-smiling into the camera. He read the headlines in business-like Hungarian. Rosa began to cry; first sniffing and shaking slightly, and then with the fat warm tears running into the cracks and creases of this morning's thick makeup. It was the first time the student had noticed she was wearing it.

'What's happened? Something terrible? Is it someone you know?'

The student was appalled. The tragedy must be immense to affect a woman in a cheap dressing gown living alone in a tenement.

'It is my husband!' Rosa choked.

Shocked, he felt rising panic.

'My husband . . . he is . . . a *bastard*!' Rosa screamed and threw wet balled-up tissues at the television.

'He is a very bad man . . .' She shot a fat wet finger at the head and shoulders on the screen, '. . . *a very bad man*!'

The music student began to understand that this was perhaps not headline news.

Rosa, her tears now giving her skin a wet rubbery sheen and seeping under the collar of her dressing gown where the skin was beginning to turn red and blotchy, still shouting above the noise of the television, reached over to the record player and dropped the needle noisily on to a well-worn disc already in position. A full-throated lament rasped from the inadequate speakers and Rosa brought her own voice up to volume to add her thoughts.

'My husband very like this man in the song!' she wailed, still aiming her soggy missiles at the screen where bits of wet tissue now clung to the newsreader's hair and chin.

'He has betrayed her and she still loves him . . .' Rosa

collapsed into mighty sobbing, singing loudly in her own language. The growing cacophany was joined by a broomstick banging angrily on the floor from the flat below. The dog he had heard on his way in barked deliriously.

'He fucks children! . . . *That one!*'

A young woman reporter in a rabbit-fur hat spoke earnestly into the camera outside the parliament buildings. The song gave way to an instrumental arrangement and Rosa was able to give her attention to explaining, between sobs, that she and her husband, a journalist, had lived happily together for many years until he had started working in television. His hours had seemingly got longer and longer, until one night Rosa found that he had been regularly booking into a hotel with a reporter half his age, with whom he now shared a much bigger house in a very fashionable district.

Rosa was crying less now, although the television and the record player continued simultaneously. Stepping grandmother's footsteps towards her, the music student arrived at last at her side and put a tentative hand on her shoulder. He felt the weight of her body give way beneath his hand, as her breathing became steadier. He hesitated to switch off the television – she was still looking at it, fixated – but turned the sound down. The orchestra played a last long chord and the arm of the record player lifted and clicked back to the side.

'Why don't you lie down?' he suggested, and moved over to arrange the pillows at the other end of the fake fur bed. Rosa suddenly fell back on to the bed and, looking the music student in the eye, flung her dressing gown apart and shook out her hair. 'Take one picture,' she commanded, throwing an Instamatic across from her bedside table. She thrust herself towards the camera's lens, her head thrown back, her thick red legs pulled underneath her, in her underwear, in what was clearly not meant as a grotesque parody of the picture on her fridge. 'I am beautiful gypsy. Take one picture!' He held her in the viewfinder: a sixty-year-old woman, her skin sagging and folding over cheap, tatty lingerie, nylon, thick, and greying. Her face streaked and patchy from crying, with red channels on her neck reaching out across her chest and heavy, drooping breasts. A fat hand still wearing a wedding ring modestly covered a small area of pitted flesh at the top of one thigh.

He pressed the shutter and lit Rosa for a split second in cold white flashlight.

'You take one more picture, no, two more pictures,' she insisted, 'then you take them in photograph shop and I will have pictures to send my husband like Jane Russell. A beautiful gypsy girl!'

The music student sat down next to Rosa and held her hand. She had stopped crying by now, but her eyes were still wet and swollen. And then he saw that they were astonishingly blue. He leant over and kissed her forehead.

'Goodnight Rosa. We'll see about the pictures in the morning.'

He got up slowly from the bed and walked barefoot across the carpet to the door. When he looked back, Rosa had curled up under the rug and closed her eyes.

He had hoped to set off for the Institute without waking her in the morning, but he overslept and she was making coffee in the kitchen when he emerged from his room, already wearing his coat and scarf. She pressed a small hot cup into his hand and tucked the camera into his pocket. He drank the thick black coffee quickly and raised his hand for goodbye.

Out on the street he found himself crossing a cobbled square where a group of old men were standing talking and smoking, shuffling in the ankle-deep grey slush. One of the men came over carrying a black violin case and held it out to him, smiling.

'You like gypsy music? Here is real gypsy violin.' The man opened the case and held out a brightly varnished violin with gleaming metal strings. The label inside clearly bore two lines of Chinese characters. The student shook his head and contined across the square. The man simply shrugged his shoulders and returned to smoking with the men.

Reaching a gap in the tall tenements, the student felt for the camera in his pocket. He lifted it out, flicked open the back and pulled the film out into the bright grey light.

lucy corin

....

at the estate auction

At the estate auction the audience, a collection of strangers, neighbors, and business acquaintances, waved their numbers and caught the eyes of the callers and watched the furniture parade. They sat in rows of metal folding chairs on the lawn of the great, white farmhouse, or wandered off to the concession stand which was a long, metal folding table covered with a white sheet, covered with baggies of chips, sweets wrapped in plastic wrap, and a hot-pot of hot dogs. A few people stood under the giant trees behind the rows of folding chairs holding danishes and paper napkins, sodas balanced on the grass at their feet. Even though it was not very sun-shiny out, and there were only a couple of the big trees, no one stood where they weren't under a tree. Even the concession stand was under one, as if docked there. People sat in their chairs or stood under trees as if they'd float into the fields without them.

Men and their teenage sons lifted each item for sale onto the porch, near the podium that had been set up there. Behind the podium, the auctioneer sat on a tall stool and rattled numbers into a microphone. Behind the auctioneer stood the wide double doors of the old house. Behind the doors the house was newly empty. A new coat of polyurethane stretched over its floors. New paint dried on the walls.

The men and boys held each item in the air: side-chairs with needle-point seats, crystal pitchers, marble-top dressing tables, ceramic icons of Aunt Jemima and her relatives, boxes of linen or kitchen utensils. The auctioneer named each item, referred to the number it had been assigned, pointed out nicks or missing hardware in a show of honesty that no one more than half-believed. The auctioneer's sister sat on a chair next to the podium writing on a clipboard. 'That was number eighty-one at twenty-seven-and-a-half?' she asked. 'That was ninety-two to one-oh-four?' The men and boys turned the items over in the air and called, 'This one's old!' or 'Small chip!' or 'It's rare, rare!' The auctioneer said 'Seb'n' meaning 'Seven,' and started bidding at four hundred dollars regardless of what he might expect a piece to go for, counting backwards in chunks until someone yelled 'Fifty!' or 'Five!' and the men and boys yelled 'I got fifty!' or 'Five, here!' The audience knew what the garbled sounds from the microphone meant. They knew by the rhythm, and responded as they'd decided they would, or else found themselves caught in the moment, bidding away, thinking it must be better than I thought if that guy wants it so much, surprising themselves because they knew better.

If it were not for the noise, the audience might have been able to hear the house creak. It creaked because it was spring, and the house always creaked in the spring. But this time, it was also adjusting to being empty, to dust having been sucked from between its floorboards, to its new coats of paint and polyurethane. If it weren't for the noise, the audience might have heard, if it listened carefully, the little show going on back there.

In fact, there are several movie genres devoted to this precise phenomenon. The haunted house that requires you prove your worth, or the more figurative, sentimental haunting of grandmother's keepsake chest in the attic, a situation that still requires proving yourself to inanimate objects that are repositories for human memories. It's a hard thing to take, the notion that this thing built by and for people would become so disgusted and degraded by its makers as to turn against, or expect respect. The house can start acting like a deranged dog, lashing out at anyone, because it knows that anyone is potentially dangerous. People walk around their houses and think, if it doesn't spit me out like a chunk of phlegm, I must be doing something right.

notes on contributors

....

Bidisha Bandyopadhyay was born in London in 1978. She started writing in 1993 at the age of fifteen, for *Dazed+Confused*, *NME* and *i-D*, and has since had her own columns in the *Independent* and *The Big Issue*. Her first novel, *Seahorses*, came out in 1997; her second novel, *Too Fast to Live*, was published in spring 2000. Bidisha's short fiction has been widely anthologised. She has recently completed a degree in English Literature at St Edmund Hall, Oxford.

Brett Ellen Block, born in New Jersey in 1973, received Master's degrees in Creative Writing from the Iowa Writers Workshop (where she was awarded the prestigious Teaching–Writing Fellowship) and the University of East Anglia. Her work has appeared in various US literary journals. She has recently completed a collection of short stories and has just been awarded a grant for a screenplay.

Lucy Corin's fiction recently appeared in the US literary journals *Ploughshares* and *The Southern Review*. Other stories, published under the name Lucy Hochman, have been published in *The Iowa Review*, *The North American Review*, and the anthologies *Under 25: Fiction* and *On the Edge: New Women's Fiction Anthology (Chick-Lit 2)*. 'At the Estate Auction' is included in her story manuscript *Who Buried the Baby?*

Susan Corrigan was born in Minneapolis in 1968 and has lived in London since 1990. She edits *i-D*'s book pages and is a long-term contributing editor. She is a feature writer and pop-culture commentator for newspapers and magazines worldwide. She is editor of the anthology *Typical Girls* and is currently combining work on a novel and short fiction collection with related art, curatorial, film and television projects.

Matthew De Abaitua's short stories and articles have appeared in *The Idler*, the philosophical journal *Hermenaut* and the bestselling anthology *Disco Biscuits*. His anthology *The Idler's Companion* was picked up and sold by Past Times, the high-street purveyors of nostalgia. He was born in Liverpool in 1971 and is working on a novel.

Emily Hammond is the author of *Breathe Something Nice*, a short story collection selected by Barnes & Noble for its Discover Great New Writers Series. A novel, *The Milk*, will be published in 2001. Emily Hammond has published fiction in *Ploughshares*, *New England Review*, *Puerto Del Sol*, *Colorado Review*, *Crazyhorse* and other magazines, and her stories have been anthologised in *Henfield Prize Stories* and *American Fiction*. She is at work on a new novel.

Tobias Hill, born in London in 1970, has published three award-winning collections of poetry. In 1998 he was inaugural poet-in-residence for the London Zoo. His first collection of short stories, *Skin*, won the PEN/Macmillan Award For Fiction. His first novel, *Underground*, was published in 1999, to wide critical acclaim. His second novel, *The Love of Stones*, will be published in 2001.

Pagan Kennedy leads a double life as a fiction writer and pop culture critic. She wrote the acclaimed novels, *Spinsters*, which was shortlisted for the Orange Prize for Fiction, and *The Exes*, as well as the collection *Stripping and Other Stories*. Her journalism has appeared in a range of magazines, including *Village Voice*, *Interview* and *Mademoiselle* and she is author of *Platforms: A Micro-waved Cultural Chronicle of the 1970s*. Pagan is now writing a biography of a black American missionary who went to the Congo at the turn of the century to discover 'a forbidden city.' She lives in Boston, Massachusetts.

Christopher Kenworthy's short story collection *Will You Hold Me?* was published in 1996 and his first novel, *The Winter Inside*, is published by Serpent's Tail. Born in Preston in 1968, he now lives by the Swan River in Western Australia.

Eleanor Knight lives in London. She has published journalism on diverse subjects including underwear, nuclear attack and linoleum. This is her first published fiction and she is currently at work on a first novel.

Cris Mazza is co-editor of *Post-Feminist Fiction (Chick-Lit)* and *On the Edge: New Women's Fiction Anthology (Chick-Lit 2)*. She is the author of several story collections; her most recent novel is *Dog People*. She teaches in the Program for Writers at the University of Illinois in Chicago.

Joyce Carol Oates has just completed *Blonde*, a novel starring Marilyn Monroe. She is author of numerous short story collections and novels, most recently, *Broke Heart Blues* and *Man Crazy*. She lives in New Jersey, where she is Professor of Humanities at Princeton University.

Emily Perkins was born in New Zealand and lives in London. She is the author of a prize-winning collection of short stories, *Not Her Real Name*, and a first novel, *Leave Before You Go*. Other stories have been widely anthologised and she is at work on her second novel.

Amy Prior is editor of *Retro Retro*. Her short stories have been published in several anthologies, including *IOS*. She runs fiction writing workshops in London and is working on her own short story collection. She has worked as a charity shop clothes model and is currently furnishing her new flat with a variety of yesteryear's souvenirs.

Nicholas Royle is the author of three novels – *Counterparts*, *Saxophone Dreams*, and *The Matter of the Heart*, as well as over 100 short stories. He has also edited ten anthologies, including *The Time Out Book of New York Short Stories* and *The Tiger Garden: A*

Book of Writers' Dreams (Serpent's Tail). 'Empty Boxes' was first read at a seminar organised by Nicholas Royle, Professor of English at the University of Sussex; Royle and Royle are now working on a book together, *Royle We*. Some of the ideas and settings in 'Empty Boxes' will reappear in his new novel, *The Director's Cut*, due to be published in 2000.

Tony White is the editor of the *britpulp!* anthology and the author of three novels: *Road Rage!*, *Charlieunclenorfolktango* and *Satan! Satan! Satan!* He would like to point out that Jerry Cornelius, Una Pearson, and the Bazalgette brothers (Bishop B and Shakey Mo) are based on characters from Michael Moorcock's Jerry Cornelius novels. They are entirely fictional creations, and bear no relation to persons either living or dead. Tony White would also like to take this opportunity to extend his thanks to Michael Moorcock for generously allowing him to contribute to the Jerry Cornelius mythos, and granting permission for 'The Jet-Set Girls' to be published in this form.

Readers wishing to find out more about Jerry Cornelius *et al*, are directed to *The New Nature of the Catastrophe*, a multi-author Cornelius collection edited by Langdon Jones and Michael Moorcock which contains a complete bibliography, 'Jerry Cornelius: A Reader's Guide', by John Davey.

Tony White is currently working on his latest novel, *The Bukowski Shift*, and lives in the East End of London.